I0691659

By NESSA L. WARIN

Published by DREAMSPINNER PRESS
http://www.dreamspinnerpress.com

STORM SEASON

NESSA L. WARIN

Dreamspinner Press

Published by
Dreamspinner Press
5032 Capital Circle SW
Ste 2, PMB# 279
Tallahassee, FL 32305-7886
USA
http://www.dreamspinnerpress.com/

This is a work of fiction. Names, characters, places, and incidents either are the product of the author's imagination or are used fictitiously, and any resemblance to actual persons, living or dead, business establishments, events, or locales is entirely coincidental.

Storm Season
Copyright © 2013 by Nessa L. Warin

Cover Art by Catt Ford

Map by Ashley Weber, ashley.weber.88@gmail.com

All rights reserved. No part of this book may be reproduced or transmitted in any form or by any means, electronic or mechanical, including photocopying, recording, or by any information storage and retrieval system without the written permission of the Publisher, except where permitted by law. To request permission and all other inquiries, contact Dreamspinner Press, 5032 Capital Circle SW, Ste 2, PMB# 279, Tallahassee, FL 32305-7886, USA.
http://www.dreamspinnerpress.com/

ISBN: 978-1-62380-324-7
Digital ISBN: 978-1-62380-325-4

Printed in the United States of America
First Edition
February 2013

To Martha, without whom this story would not have been finished. Thank you for never giving up on it—even when I let it hang for months—for word-warring and brainstorming with me when I struggled to write, and for encouraging me through every step of the process.

To Nancy, who also refused to give up on seeing this story published. Thank you for the invaluable editing help and gentle encouragement whenever I needed it.

To Daphné, for all her support. Thank you for poking me when I need it and for always being there to cheer me up or cheer me on.

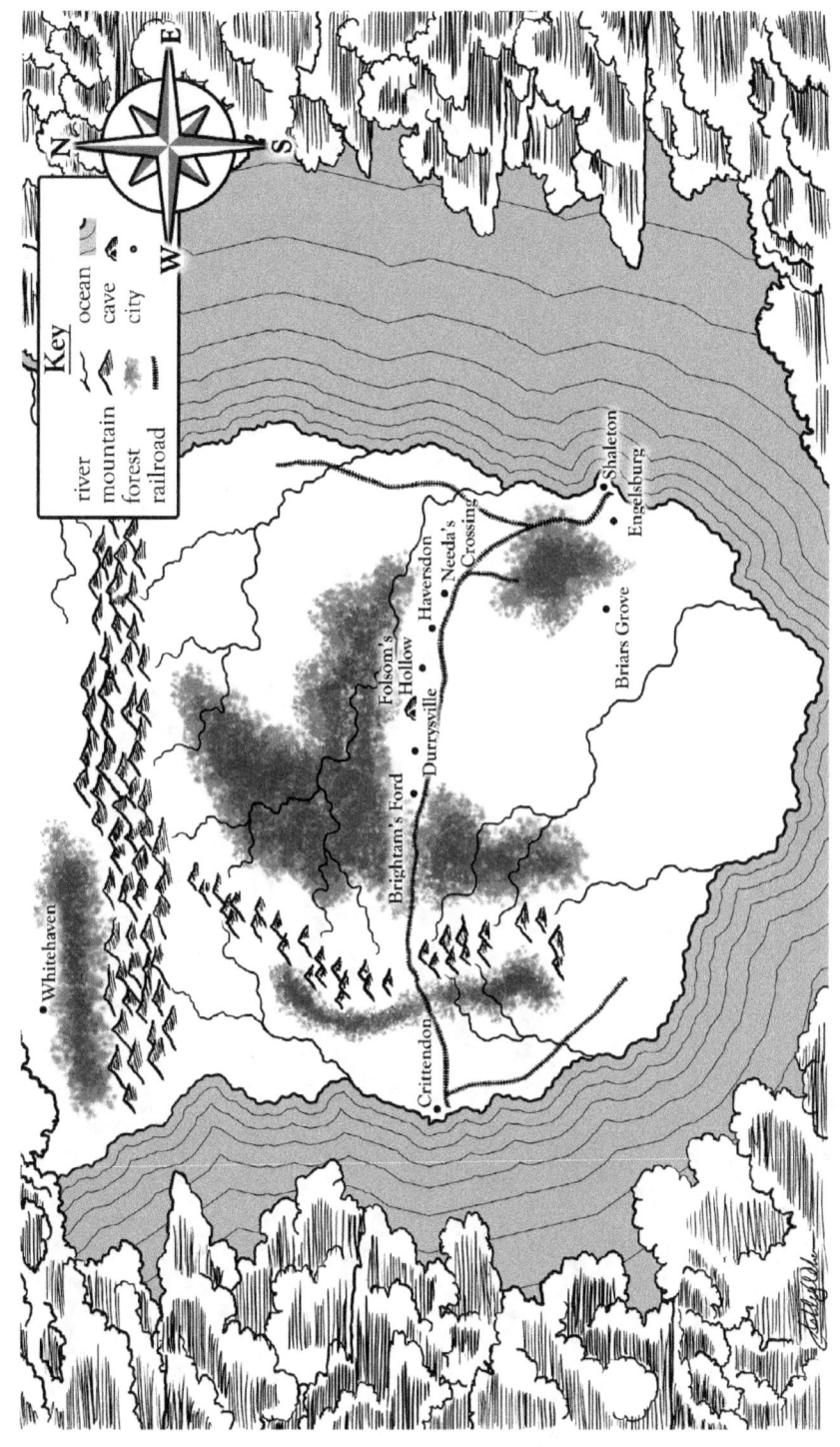

CHAPTER ONE

HE WAS a man, not a child, but there was a wide-eyed innocence about him that made him seem little more than a boy at times. Jasper first saw him while riding TJ away from the usual trails, trying with one extra-long ride to make up for all the days and weeks he'd recently missed and to fortify both himself and the horse against the days and weeks he was sure to miss in the near future. Jasper had sensed the boy's gaze before he'd seen it, but when he called out a greeting, the face in the trees vanished so quickly Jasper wondered if he had imagined the whole thing. Occasionally, he ran into some of the people who lived in and around Brightam's Ford on the trails, but he'd never before seen someone lurking in the woods, watching. It struck him as odd, and it crossed his mind that it might be one of the forest spirits he'd heard lived in these woods, but he'd almost forgotten about it by the time he'd returned TJ to the stables.

The incident would have completely faded from his mind if not for the stormy night two days later when he saw the boy again, this time huddled against the outside of the barn, using the building to keep the worst of the wind and rain off his barely clothed body. This time, when Jasper called out a greeting, the boy didn't disappear, though he did scoot backward, his eyes wide with fear as Jasper approached.

"Are you all right?"

The boy didn't answer, but when he moved, it was toward Jasper, his gaze fixated on Jasper's mouth and filled with wonder instead of fear. He touched Jasper's lips with gentle fingers and cocked his head to the side as if he were asking a question, though he didn't say anything.

"What's wrong?"

The boy gasped and jerked his fingers back as though he'd been bitten.

Jasper caught the hand, wanting to look for injury, but as soon as he touched the boy's skin, his fingers began to tingle and his mind was filled with a sound that soon resolved into a soft voice.

How did you do that? It's like the noise came out of your mouth and it sounded different and I felt it, but how is it possible? Why aren't you answering me? Can't you hear me? Do you not know—?

Jasper jerked his hand back, releasing the boy, and cursed when both the tingling feeling and the noise stopped. "Hailstones."

IT WAS easier than Jasper had thought it would be to get the boy inside, and that was where Jasper discovered he wasn't really a boy. He was tall and thin, with youthful features and an innocent look to his face, but he was definitely an adult. With a smile of thanks, he accepted the clean, dry clothes Jasper offered, and disappeared into the indicated bathroom without saying a word. He emerged a few minutes later dressed correctly, and he handed his own wet clothes to Jasper with another smile.

Jasper handed him a cup of tea, which the not-boy took with a nod as he sat at the table, making himself comfortable. They sipped their tea as the easiness faded and awkwardness crept in with each moment of silence. What was there to say when one person apparently didn't even know what speaking was?

THE clock read 2:00 a.m. and the house was silent. Jasper wasn't sure what had woken him, a sound he could no longer remember, perhaps, or maybe just the sense of someone else in the room. He was no longer alone.

He couldn't see anyone with his head on the pillow, so he sat up, and stood when sitting didn't reveal anyone lurking in the shadows. He found the boy curled up on the rug at the foot of the bed. At some point before he'd come into Jasper's room, the boy had discarded the shirt he'd been wearing, leaving only the loose cotton pants Jasper had given him to sleep in.

A flash of lightning briefly illuminated the room. Another storm, mere hours after the first one had ended. The wet season, as predicted, had come early. The animals were secure, and the house was safe enough from flooding, but it changed Jasper's plans regarding the boy. It wasn't safe to travel in the wet. Too many things could go wrong.

Thunder crashed and the boy awoke with a start, gasping and scrambling away from the noise. He sat in the corner by the closet, pulled his knees to his chest, and stared at the outside wall and curtain-covered window with wide eyes. Lightning flashed again, followed almost immediately by another crash of thunder and then the rough pattering of rain on the roof.

The boy whimpered and started rocking back and forth, his eyes never leaving the window.

Jasper approached him slowly, the way he did TJ when the horse was injured, and knelt in front of him. "We're safe here. This house was built to withstand the storms." He put a hand on the boy's arm, bracing himself for the mental assault that never came. His skin tingled and he thought if he concentrated he might be able to hear something, but there were no words streaming into his mind this time, just a feeling of absolute and overwhelming terror.

He pulled the boy to his feet and led him through the closet to the room hidden behind it.

The room wasn't fully stocked yet as Jasper hadn't anticipated needing to use it so early in the year, but there were some essentials left from the last wet season, and it would be enough to get them through the night. This wasn't a dangerous storm and if he needed something that wasn't in the room, he could leave and get it without any danger. Only the boy's fear had made him think of the room.

The boy didn't stop trembling until the door was latched shut, drowning out the sounds of the storm. In the worst of the season, they would be able to hear the storm even in here, but this was just a little storm, a warning that would be gone in a few hours. It would be weeks yet before the almost constant storms would begin and the booms of thunder would penetrate the thick walls of the safe room.

Jasper pulled two bottles of water out of the ice box and handed one to the boy. He would have to buy more supplies this year if there were going to be two of them huddled in here, especially if the boy's fear sent them away from the windows every time the sky darkened. Jasper typically used this room only during the worst of the storms, when there was true danger. He hated it, hated being enclosed in the confined space, but it was a small price to pay for the luxury of having windows in the dry seasons. Every wet season, he thought about moving to someplace without any windows, where he wouldn't have to hide, and every dry season, when he looked out the windows at the blooming fields or at the crisp, white snow covering the ground, he would wonder why he ever had such a foolish thought. One month spent mostly in this room was a small price to pay for the ability to look out the window at unending beauty the other eleven.

The boy downed the water in one go and handed the empty bottle back to Jasper. He was calmer now, though he kept his distance from the door as he started exploring the room. He touched everything, brushing his long fingers over every surface and pausing occasionally to examine something more closely. Once, he nodded, a satisfied smile on his face.

The last thing he inspected was the door, and on this, he looked at every minute detail, pushed against the heavy wood, tightened the locks, and peered closely at the hinges. Ten minutes passed before he abruptly turned away and climbed into the bed, apparently satisfied. He curled up on his side, his back to the door, and stared at the wall.

"You've been caught in a storm before." Jasper didn't need to see the nod to know it was true. It was the only thing that explained the boy's fear of the relatively mild storm they were being treated to at the moment.

Jasper had seen one of the big storms once, when the outer walls of the community shelter he'd taken refuge in had proven unable to withstand the force of the wind. He'd been one of the last to leave the big upper room for the safer underground chambers, and as he'd left, he'd looked over his shoulder and seen part of the wall ripped away. The night had been spent huddling in terror, and he'd left the coast the following dry season, moving inland where the storms lost a little of their strength and the truly dangerous season was shorter. If the boy had actually been caught in one of the violent storms, even this far inland, Jasper could very well understand his fear.

He joined the boy on the bed, putting himself between his guest and the door. "I wish you could tell me about it."

The boy rolled over and grabbed Jasper's arm and suddenly Jasper's mind was filled with images of astounding clarity.

A small cave, little more than a nook in the hillside, filling slowly with water from a nearby stream that had long since overflowed its banks. Tree branches and dead animals clogging the entrance and then being savagely ripped away, taking some of the rock with them. Huge, painful drops of water blowing all the way to the back of the cave and lashing unprotected skin until it bled. A lightning strike nearby destroying the illusion of safety.

The images kept flashing, one after another, each worse than the one before. Jasper struggled, trying to break free, but the boy didn't let go until he'd shown Jasper everything. Then, just as suddenly as they'd begun, the images stopped, leaving Jasper trembling and fighting for breath.

"Is that...?" He couldn't finish the sentence, but the boy knew what he was trying to say and nodded. "No wonder you're afraid."

The boy curled up tighter and hugged the pillow to his chest. Jasper pushed past his own fear and laid a hand on his shoulder. No images flooded his mind, and he let out a sigh of relief. "We're safe here. The room is secure and this is a mild storm. We could be out in the bedroom for this." There would be worse to come, though, and they both knew it.

WHILE the boy still slept, Jasper slipped out of the room so he could check the animals and assure the boy the storms were indeed over, at least until late afternoon when the rains were sure to start again. There were, of course, ways to tell from inside the safe room, but Jasper doubted the boy would believe them, not until their accuracy had been proven.

The horses were as happy to get outside as Jasper, though he noticed they didn't stray quite as far from the barn as they usually did. The unexpectedly early storm had unnerved them, and even the bright sunshine couldn't drive away all their uneasiness.

Nor did it drive away all of Jasper's, though for quite different reasons.

He hadn't even known the boy—no, the young man—for a full day and already he'd begun thinking and planning for a future that included him. It was ridiculous, really. Jasper didn't even know the other man's name and he was planning on buying double supplies to make it through the wet season. It had made sense in the dark when the wind and rain had been lashing at the house, but now in the bright sunshine and with stout walls between Jasper and the boy, it seemed off.

Not wrong, just weird. He wasn't considering discarding the idea, but it struck him how naturally it had come to him, how comfortable he'd been with it.

WHEN Jasper went back inside, he was surprised to see his guest had ventured out of the safe room. He sat on the windowsill of Jasper's bedroom, his hands and nose pressed against the thick glass. His eyes darted everywhere, from the water slowly trickling off the house to the horses in the field to the woods lying beyond and finally to the western sky. It was there he paused, his eyes narrowed and focused instead of wide with wonder.

Jasper didn't need words to know what he was thinking. "It won't storm again until evening. It's too early in the season for the daytime storms." It was too early in the season for even a relatively mild storm like they'd had the previous night as well, but he wasn't going to point that out.

The boy jumped, looked at Jasper for a long moment, and nodded, but his gaze returned to the west, his eyes alert for every nuance of color and wisp of cloud.

The sky was blue in all directions and wouldn't darken for several hours yet, but that was something the boy would learn on his own given time. When he'd first moved here, Jasper had spent days with his face pressed against the same window, watching the sky darken and the clouds thicken until it was no longer safe to stay close to the thick glass. Now he could tell at a glance how likely and close a storm was, but those hours had given him the knowledge.

The boy had the right idea, though his efforts would not be worthwhile until afternoon.

Jasper's stomach growled and the boy looked over again, his eyes widening as though surprised Jasper was still present. He probably was; the look on his face had shown an intensity that blocked awareness of everything but what he focused on. It was definitely time to pull him away or he'd be there all day.

"Would you like breakfast?"

The boy's stomach growled, echoing Jasper's own, and he nodded, though his eyes flickered back to the window.

Jasper held out his hand. "Come on. After we eat, we can go into town and buy some supplies. I haven't stocked for winter yet, and I wasn't planning on having a visitor, so there's not much left."

It was uncertain how much the boy—no, the *man*, Jasper had to keep reminding himself—understood, but he took Jasper's hand and let himself be led to the kitchen. He ate with such enthusiasm that Jasper wondered when he'd last eaten... and if he had enough in his account to cover all the food he was certain to need.

HALFWAY to town, Jasper risked a glance at his companion. "What's your name? Can you tell me? I need to call you something. People are going to wonder who you are and why I'm buying so much more than usual." He shook his head both at the sentiment and the way he was rambling to fill the silence. "I may not go into town very often, but it's not a big place, and they all know me."

The boy peeled his gaze from the truck window and peered at Jasper over the knee he'd drawn up to his chest. He was obviously uncomfortable in the moving vehicle, but since the storms had started, Jasper hadn't dared take the horses. Brightam's Ford was a half-day's journey on horseback and Jasper didn't trust they would make it back before the rain began to fall.

Slowly, the boy—man—reached out and placed his hand on Jasper's arm. Jasper felt the almost familiar tingle under his skin and then—

Tobias.

"Is that your name? Tobias?"

The young man—*Tobias*—nodded and when Jasper next risked a glance he saw a quizzical, expectant expression on Tobias's face. It took him a moment and Tobias's fingers twitched toward his arm again, but then Jasper realized what his companion wanted to know. He felt like a complete idiot for not realizing it earlier.

"I'm Jasper."

A grateful smile blossomed on Tobias's face and Jasper almost drove off the road looking at it.

BRIGHTAM'S FORD was a small town by the coastal standards Jasper had grown up with, but it was a typical size for the inland areas. Despite the relative safety of the continent's interior, people still flocked to the coast with its bustling metropolises and access to shipping lanes. The sea was an additional danger in the wet season, but when the storms ended, it would be covered with boats shipping goods and people from one town to the next. There were trains to take goods and people inland, and a car could potentially make the journey, but neither was as easy or as accessible as the large boats that trawled up and down the coastlines nine to ten months of the year.

The coast was the place to be if you wanted money or power.

When he moved inland after the incident at the shelter, Jasper found a peace he hadn't realized he was missing. Here he had space and land. The inhabitants of Brightam's Ford provided all the social contact and worldly goods he needed and the solitude was ideal for creating his art and writing, which he shipped back to a friend on the coast to be sold. He'd taken odd jobs to get by back when he'd lived in Crittendon, but out here the money that came back from John was more than enough to support him and the animals.

At least, it had been until he'd found Tobias huddled by his barn. What that would do to his accounts remained to be seen.

Jasper parked the car in the lot in the town center. Tobias was out before the engine was off, but he froze, wide-eyed as he stared at the buildings. Here it was mostly shops, but there was one inn to service the occasional traveler and the railway station could be seen just over the hill. To Jasper, it was small, but Tobias was looking at it as though he'd never seen so many buildings clustered in one place.

"Come on." Jasper gently tugged on Tobias's sleeve, steering him toward the grocer's. "Let's get what we need and then if there's time, I'll show you around."

Tobias's eyes grew even wider, but he followed Jasper into the shop and gamely pushed the cart as Jasper filled it. They got bottled water, canned goods, and dried meat to tide them over during the lean storm season, and they even picked up some fresh fruit for a treat. Tobias added a few things to the cart as well, a few raw vegetables and—to Jasper's immense surprise—a few sugary treats.

When they went to check out, Jasper realized he had not come up with a story to explain Tobias's presence... or his silence.

Braden, the store's proprietor, greeted Jasper with a warm smile as he tallied up the items. "Who's your friend?"

"Someone I used to know back on the coast. The son of an old colleague. He wanted to come inland, and I said he could stay with me for a bit to see how he liked it."

"Ah." Braden paused in his calculating and looked critically at Tobias. "He seems a bit...."

"Astounded?" Jasper carried on with his spur of the moment tale. "He's never been away from the coast before. It's a lot emptier out here. He doesn't know what to think of all this open space."

"They never do." Braden chuckled and shook his head. "I remember when you came out here, you thought it was so far from your ranch to town. Now I bet ya don't think anything of the trip, or wouldn't if he weren't with ya."

"It's not quite driving down the road yet, but it's not as exhilarating as it used to be either."

"Didn't think so. You're becomin' a regular 'round here, Mr. Borland." He finished putting the food in to Jasper's canvas sacks and swiped the card that accessed his accounts. "Yer friend gonna come over and say hello?"

"Doubtful. He's shy, painfully so."

Braden handed over the slip for Jasper to sign. "He'll fit in 'round here, then, but he'll have t' say a couple things to people. Not much, you know, but he can't spend the rest of his life staring out that window there."

"He'll come around."

"Good." The slip of paper with Jasper's signature disappeared into the cash register. "You stay safe this wet, ya hear?"

"You too."

Jasper took the bags from the counter. Tobias stepped forward, grabbed half with a smile at Braden, and then stepped outside without waiting for Jasper. He was leaning against the car, the bags at his feet, when Jasper found him.

"Do you want to look around some or just get lunch and head home?" They theoretically had time to sightsee and still get home before the storms hit, but Jasper was relieved when Tobias shook his head and climbed into the car. The meaning was clear enough.

Jasper opened the driver's side door and peered in. "We should at least eat. It will take us a couple of hours to drive back. There's a nice café up the street, and the inn serves decent food, or—" He paused when the terrified expression on Tobias's face registered. Eating anywhere was clearly out of the question.

They had to eat, though. "How about I go get sandwiches and we eat in the car?"

Tobias slowly nodded and Jasper set off toward the café, wondering if he'd ever learn the secrets hidden by Tobias's silence.

CHAPTER TWO

THE first raindrops hit the windshield when they were still three miles from Jasper's house. The large, heavy drops fell quickly, reducing visibility to almost nothing and coating the road with a thin layer of water. The car skidded and slid as Jasper pulled to the side.

This would be a fast afternoon storm, one that would go as quickly as it had come, and Jasper had no intention of driving any farther until it had passed. They were safe enough in the car as the truly intense storms wouldn't come until evening, but the pavement was too wet and visibility too low to drive even the familiar roads around the ranch.

There was no sense in risking their lives to save half an hour.

Tobias grabbed Jasper's arm as soon as the car stopped.

No! Go! Danger! Go!

The words repeated again and again and Jasper could feel Tobias's terror. Before Jasper realized what he was doing, his fingers were fumbling for the keys so he could start the car and drive it as quickly as it would go. Rationally, Jasper knew they were safer stopped, but at the moment, it didn't matter. He felt an unbearable urge to drive, to get home where they could hide inside from the storm.

He reached up to adjust the mirror and Tobias's fingers slipped from his arm. The feelings ceased as suddenly as they'd begun and he turned the car off again. It was foolish to drive.

Tobias's eyes widened as the key turned, and he made the first sound Jasper had heard from him—a soft whimper that tore into Jasper's heart. He looked at Tobias, who huddled as close to the center of the car as possible, his knees pulled up to his chest and his chin tucked.

"It's all right. This is just a little one." Jasper's hand hovered over Tobias's shoulder. He wanted to comfort him but was afraid to touch.

Dark curls bounced as Tobias shook his head. The set of his jaw told Jasper he wouldn't be believed until... until now.

The rain stopped as suddenly as it had begun and within moments the clouds had cleared and the sun started drying the pavement. Tobias uncurled and pressed his face to the window to watch the dark clouds in the west, and Jasper turned the key to start the car. He flicked the lever, let the windshield wipers fling the remaining water droplets off the glass, and pulled out.

"WHAT was that?" Jasper had waited until they'd brought the food inside and packed it away in the safe room, but when Tobias brushed against him and he was reminded of the strange feeling from the car, he couldn't wait any longer.

Tobias blinked and reached out, but Jasper had stepped back, reluctant to let Tobias touch him. The words popping into his head were disconcerting enough, but when he started feeling things and, worse, started *responding* to those feelings, he needed answers... and he needed to get them without anything else strange happening.

A puzzled expression flickered across Tobias's face, and then he stepped forward and tried to touch Jasper again. Jasper dodged, leaving Tobias looking bewildered and a little frustrated.

I'm sorry. I didn't mean to do that. I won't do it again, I promise.

Jasper's head started to throb as he strained to listen. This was not the soft, gentle intrusion Jasper had almost grown used to. He could hear Tobias despite the distance between them, but it felt as though it was being thrust straight through his skull rather than slipped in gently. The more Jasper strained to hear it, the more his head hurt, and when

Tobias stopped, a blinding headache pierced Jasper's skull. Hoping darkness would relieve some of the pain, he squeezed his eyes shut.

When he opened his eyes again, Tobias was sitting on the floor, looking pale and ill. His earlier fears forgotten, Jasper rushed forward and knelt with one hand on Tobias's shoulder. "Are you all right?"

It's harder with you. The sensation was once again gentle.

Jasper's brow furrowed as he tried to understand what Tobias meant. "What's harder?" he finally asked, keeping his voice soft so it didn't aggravate the pain in his skull.

This. Tobias managed a weak smile as he grabbed Jasper's hand and held on so tightly Jasper felt as though his fingers were going to break under the pressure. *It's so hard to make you hear me if I'm not touching you. Why can't you hear me if I don't touch you?*

"I... I don't know." Jasper sat down. The floor was too hard for him to kneel long. "I don't even know how you do that, or what it is, really." He couldn't provide answers. He had more questions than the man-child sitting in front of him.

But—

"I don't know, Tobias." He placed the index finger of his free hand over Tobias's lips, shushing him despite the lack of sound. It was a habit deeply ingrained from years past when he'd spent more time around people and he'd often had to quiet talkative children.

Tobias responded the same way most of the children Jasper had once quieted used to. The question stopped immediately and he looked at Jasper with a confused but apologetic gaze.

He didn't know what he'd done wrong.

"I've never met anyone like you, Tobias. I don't know how this works." Jasper lifted their joined hands. The tips of his fingers were so red they were almost purple. He looked away, focusing on Tobias's face as he tried to ignore the pain in his hand. "It's probably harder to talk to me without touching for the same reason I can't talk to you that way, but I don't know what it is. I don't know why I don't talk like you... or why you don't talk like me."

Tobias's fingers loosened and then slid from Jasper's. He climbed shakily to his feet, wrapped his arms around his chest, and staggered from the room.

THEY didn't bother attempting to sleep in the bedrooms that night. After they'd eaten dinner and taken care of the animals, Tobias grabbed Jasper's arm, tugged him past the worn flannel and denim, and fumbled with the latch at the back of the closet. His fingers trembled and he jumped every time there was a rumble of thunder from the approaching storm, so Jasper took over, smoothly lifting the latch and pushing the thick door inward.

Tobias scrambled inside, pulling Jasper after him, and pushed the door shut with a frantic effort Jasper had never mustered, not even when the worst of the storms had taken him by surprise. When the door was firmly shut and locked against the relatively mild wind and rain, Tobias relaxed, sinking to the ground with his back against the thick wood.

A crash of thunder made him jump again, and the jerky movement startled Jasper. He dropped the book he'd chosen to read before settling in for the night. Mentally scolding himself, Jasper placed the book back on the table and opened the small cabinet that housed the weather monitoring equipment. The screen glowed when he flicked the switch, brightening the dimly lit room and bringing tears of irritation to Jasper's eyes. When his vision cleared, Jasper frowned, twisted a knob back and forth, and bit his lower lip.

The screen showed a dark cluster over the house—heavy storm activity that wouldn't have fazed him a month from now or back on the coast but was far too strong for the here and now. Even more troubling was the dark mass on the edge of the screen: there would be a break after this storm, but the one coming looked to be as bad as any in the height of the season.

The coming weeks would be busy if they were going to get through the wet season unscathed this year.

THE ground squelched under Jasper's feet and the moisture-rich air left him gasping as he dashed across the lawn to the open barn door. Scraps of wood littered the ground near the entrance, making the last few feet treacherous, but Jasper didn't stop until his bare feet hit dry ground inside the building and his hand closed over the light switch. Nothing happened when he flicked it, and he frantically fumbled for the flashlight, knocking cans and tools to the floor as he blindly searched. He yelped and leaped back, breathing heavily, but calmed when the barn burst into life.

The flashlight showed the horses safely ensconced in their stalls. The barn cat and her kittens peered out from behind a straw bale, and the goat was unconcernedly chewing on a work shirt that had been blown off its peg. Jasper let out a relieved breath and patted TJ's neck as the horse whuffed at his hair and whinnied with an air of impatience.

"I know. The door needs fixing." It had needed fixing for weeks, but the storms had come early, Jasper's mysterious guest had distracted him from mundane chores, and now it was too late.

The electricity would have to wait until morning, when—if luck held—there would be sunlight and enough dry hours to find and repair the damage. The door couldn't wait, though there wasn't time for a proper fix. The animals had been fortunate, but Jasper had seen the monitor and knew what kind of storm was coming.

Lightning was flashing in the west by the time Jasper had patched the holes with plywood and was struggling to nail a two-by-four over the barn doors. He wedged one shoulder under the wood, positioned a nail awkwardly with his left hand, and hefted the hammer in his right. As he swung, the board slipped, brushing his ear as it tumbled over his back and clattered to the ground.

"Dammit!" He wedged himself under the board again, closer to the middle this time, and struggled to line up hammer and nail again.

Let me.

The hammer hit Jasper's thumb as he jerked. "Fuck!"

Sorry. I didn't mean... are you...? Slender fingers danced over the injury. *Do you need help?*

"Hold the board." There wasn't time to nurse his thumb or figure out what had convinced Tobias to leave the safety of the house. He'd barely been willing to let Jasper leave the tiny room, and now he was outside, braving rising winds and distant flashes of lightning.

When the first drops of rain fell, they'd nailed four boards across the doors. It wasn't pretty and would be a pain to break into in the morning, but it would probably hold through the night.

TOBIAS proved remarkably capable of helping repair the barn, and when a rusted truck pulled up just before lunchtime, they were about finished. With a grin, Jasper hammered in the last two nails and tucked the hammer into his belt. "Darius! It's good to see you."

The sandy-haired man grabbed Jasper's arm and pulled him into a hug. "You too. I brought your order, and some extra too, if you're interested. Carla loaded extras on the train this time, and a good thing too. Nothing else is getting out from the coast until spring."

"That bad?"

"Yeah. The rails flooded two days after our train got through. Lucky Carla."

"And us." Without the business Darius and Carla shared, bringing goods from the coast to the town, Brightam's Ford would be hard pressed to get through the winter. "Carla always did have a sixth sense about that kind of thing."

"That she has. Serves her well."

"It serves you *both* well. Where is she?" Jasper's eyes flicked to the empty truck cab. "She's not being lazy, is she?"

"Sleet, no." Darius laughed. "She's looking into buying a train, actually. We heard there was one for sale and it seemed like a good idea. We almost couldn't convince our usual guy to bring us out here. She'll be out when she's done."

Jasper nodded, and pulled the tarp off the truck. "Just when we finish, I bet. Too late to help unload, but early enough to eat my food and drink my beer."

"That's Carla. You know she—" Darius stopped suddenly and then his voice dropped to a whisper. "Jasper... there's someone in your barn."

"Someone…?" Jasper peered over Darius's shoulder to see Tobias on his back on a hay bale, three kittens sprawled on his chest. "Oh. That's Tobias. He's staying with me this wet season."

"Who exactly is he? A name doesn't give me much, Jas."

"I don't know." Jasper shrugged, grinned at his friend's dumbfounded expression, and led the way into the barn. "I found him last week—or maybe he found me—but I can't turn him out now, not when he doesn't have anywhere to go." He pushed the box onto the shelf and placed the one Darius had been carrying next to it. "Come on, I'll introduce you."

"I guess he *looks* harmless enough."

Tobias was completely absorbed with the cats and hadn't appeared to hear Darius's muttered words. When Jasper stopped over him, he grinned, gently removed the animals from his chest, and sat up.

"Darius, this is Tobias. Tobias, this is my friend Darius."

Tobias's eyes flickered uncertainly to Jasper, but Darius stepped forward and held out his hand. "It's nice to meet you."

"It's okay." Jasper nodded at Darius's hand and with his lower lip caught between his teeth and his brow furrowed, Tobias slowly gripped the outstretched fingers.

"Hailstones!" Darius staggered backward, his eyes never leaving Tobias's fingers. "What in the world was that?"

I'm sorry! I didn't mean to! The panicked words entered Jasper's mind with a force that nearly drove him to his knees. This was no barely audible call, but a full-fledged scream that left him feeling as though his brain would ooze out his ears and his eyeballs would pop if it continued any longer. He grabbed Tobias's hand, but the pain only grew worse as Tobias's mental voice intensified. *Darius, Jasper, please! Don't! I'm sorry!*

"Come on!" Somehow, Darius had crossed the distance between them and was pulling Jasper up and away from Tobias. "Let's go!"

No! Tobias tightened his grip on Jasper's hand. *Don't go with him!*

"I…."

Another tug from Darius slid Jasper's fingers almost free. "Jasper!"

No!

"Stop! Both of you!" Jasper looked up, wondered how he'd gotten on the ground, and yanked both hands free. "He's not going to hurt me." He wasn't sure who he was addressing.

"Could've fooled me." Hazel eyes glared over thick fingers as Darius pinched the bridge of his nose. "He about had both of us on the floor."

"It doesn't hurt when he touches you. I should have warned you. It's how he talks."

Darius's elegantly raised eyebrow was at odds with the snort he gave as he tossed his head and winced, but he stayed still as Tobias reached out and lightly touched Jasper's shoulder. All three men flinched.

I'm sorry. Tobias's voice was quieter than a whisper. *I didn't mean to scare him... or hurt either of you.* Dark brows furrowed and Tobias's lip was again caught in his teeth. *I don't know why it hurts you when I broadcast. It's...*

"Inconvenient?" Jasper finished, his own voice sounding loud in comparison.

Yeah. Tobias glanced at Darius and then looked into Jasper's eyes. *I can, um, fix that if you want.*

"Fix...?" The touch in Jasper's mind changed before he could finish asking the question, the light buzzing changing to a gentle pressure that relaxed tense muscles and pushed the ache from his head. His head fell forward and he let out a deep breath as even tension he hadn't been aware of released.

The pressure eased, again replaced by the light buzzing. *Better?*

Slowly, Jasper lifted his head. The room was no longer spinning, the sounds of the barn no longer driving stakes into his skull. "Much." He rubbed the back of his neck, half convinced he could feel a difference in the muscles. "Thank you."

I'd, um... I'd help him too, but I, uh, don't think he'll let me touch him.

Jasper followed Tobias's gaze. Darius had dropped to sit on the floor, one hand pinching the bridge of his nose, the other rubbing the back of his neck. He dropped his hands as he looked up at Jasper. "You all right?"

"Yeah." His eyes flicked back to Tobias. "He says he's sorry."

"Lot of good that does, doesn't it? My head's going to hurt for three thunderin' days."

"He can fix it, if you let him."

Darius looked skeptical. "And what does it involve? If he's going into my brain again, tell him no thanks."

"He can hear you, you know. He just… doesn't talk."

"Right. He just reaches in and scrambles your brain without bothering to take it out of your head first. Delightful lad, he is."

He was, but not in the way Darius meant. Since Tobias had arrived, Jasper had discovered the mysterious not-boy had an engaging sense of humor and a smile that left Jasper defending an almost stranger to his closest friend. "He said he was sorry."

"Not so I could hear."

"You don't want him to touch you!"

"So?" Even with a pounding headache, Darius was a master at exasperating his friend. Given the chance, he'd push every one of Jasper's buttons.

"Oh for the love of sun!" Jasper threw his hands up in the air. "Stop being such a child! Suffer, if you want. I don't care."

The corners of Darius's mouth twitched. "Don't you?"

"No." It wasn't a very believable lie, but he kept a straight face until he'd climbed to his feet and started out of the barn. "If you want to unload the truck with a migraine, I won't stop you."

Jasper brought the next load in by himself while Tobias worked his magic on Darius's head.

CHAPTER
THREE

A SCRATCHING at the kitchen door made Jasper look up from the dishes, but it was gone before he had rinsed his hands, and he pushed it out of mind. No one would be out this late, not with the howling wind, rumbling thunder, and rain only moments away. Likely it was just a branch blown free from a tree. Nothing to worry about, not when he wanted to finish cleaning up and join his guest in the safe room.

It came again as he was drying the last plate, and he frowned. The animals were secure in the barn. Tobias was upstairs, where he'd retreated immediately after dinner, leaving Jasper alone with Darius and Carla. Both of his friends had overcome their initial wariness of Jasper's guest, but there was no easy, pain-free way for Tobias to talk to three of them at once, and dinner conversation had been awkward. But Darius and Carla had left over an hour ago, heading out early to beat the storms, and would by now be safe in their own home.

There was no reason to go to the door, to open it to the elements, but the scratching continued, audible now over the wailing wind between rolls of thunder. The door was open before Jasper had truly thought about what he was doing.

A large black dog bounded through the door, barking and jumping, nails clicking on the tiled floor, and his muddy paws leaving wet smears on Jasper's shirt.

"Down!" Jasper struggled through an armful of dog to push the door shut before the wind did any damage to the kitchen. It clicked and he snapped the lock as the dog, whimpering, pushed at his hand with a wet nose. Jasper took the animal's head in his hands and fumbled for a collar. "What do you want, hmm? Where did you come from?"

The dog didn't answer. Instead it licked Jasper's arm with a sloppy tongue and bounded farther into the house, yapping excitedly. The dog darted around the table, sniffing under every chair and barking at Jasper every time he looked up.

Jasper scrambled after him. "Down!" he shouted as the dog climbed onto the table. At least the animal knew that one, though he stayed as far from Jasper as he could as he climbed off and headed to explore the next room. "Stop!"

The dog didn't know that one, or didn't choose to acknowledge it, which Jasper personally thought was more likely. It was hard to stop the animal without knowing its name or anything else about it, including where it came from, how it got to Jasper's house, and if anyone was looking for it.

"Stop!" he tried again, futilely attempting to prevent a wagging tail from knocking knickknacks off the coffee table. A wooden bowl and two hand-carved figurines tumbled to the floor. Jasper winced at the clatter as they struck, but no pieces shot off and, in the brief second he could spare to look at them, they appeared unbroken.

He had to catch the dog.

It was headed back to the kitchen, no doubt determined to do some destruction there, when there was a squeak on the steps that caught both their attention. Jasper tried to grab the dog while it was distracted, but as soon as Tobias entered the room it bounded into his arms, knocking him back to sit on the steps.

Kyree!

The word cut straight into Jasper's skull, sending him to his knees as a blinding light flashed behind his eyes. From the constant stream of mental praise and babble, it was obvious Tobias knew the dog, but none of the words piercing Jasper's pain-fogged brain answered any of his questions.

Good girl! Good Kyree dog! How'd you find me, girl?

"Tobias...." Jasper moaned. This had to stop. He couldn't see. He could hardly breathe. The dog's tail was thumping against the floor, accentuating the pain in Jasper's head until he was on the verge of passing out. He had to tell Tobias....

Man and dog were suddenly right in front of him, and a gentle touch eased the pain in his head and neck. *Sorry.*

"It's... thanks." He wouldn't say it was okay. It wasn't okay. "Who's the dog?"

Lithe fingers twitched against Jasper's neck. *Kyree. Her name is Kyree.* Tobias paused, rubbing the back of his own neck with his free hand. *She's, um, she's my dog. I lost her when I, um, while I, uh... before I got here.*

He pulled his hand back swiftly, leaving Jasper with too many unanswered questions. When, while, what? What had Tobias been doing before Jasper found him? Why had he come here? Why didn't he talk about it and why didn't Jasper ever think to ask? How had the dog found them?

A wet tongue lapped at Jasper's cheek, bringing him back to the present. Two sets of brown eyes peered beseechingly at him, remarkably similar expressions on the vastly different faces. There was no getting around it. "Why," he asked, not wanting or expecting an answer, "do I keep taking in strays?"

The expression on Tobias's face meant more than the light, *Thank you,* he conveyed with a brush of his fingers.

THE dog adapted remarkably quickly, seemingly just as happy as her master to cower from the storms in the relative safety of Jasper's secure room. The tiny area was getting crowded—it had been designed for one, two in a pinch, and now it housed two plus a dog with a tail that never stopped wagging.

It thumped against the bed, the wall, the floor, the closet door, anywhere Kyree sat or stood—and she moved all the time. Jasper checked the monitors and tried to settle down, but every time he'd almost drifted off, the dog would move and the tempo of the thumping would change, drawing his attention to it once more. It was too much, too loud, too crowded, too close. He couldn't stay.

He couldn't go, either. The storms were bad—the worst so far this year—and they'd reached the level where it was dangerous to stay near the thick glass windows. They'd held through the entire previous year, but they would shatter eventually, and Jasper didn't want to be in the room when it happened.

He glared at the dog, glared at the monitor, glared through the ceiling at the storm raging outside, glared at the slender form watching him through the shadows as it crouched before the dog and stroked the animal's back. Darius and Carla were right. This was crazy. He was mad to have taken in Tobias, madder still to have accepted the dog. And now the two of them would drive him insane.

Perhaps they'd have him committed, locked away in a safe place forever, and take the ranch. Clearly, it had been the plan all along. The dog was the masterful bit. Thump, thump, thump. Who would suspect her of anything but enthusiasm? Thump thump—

The noise stopped with a suddenness that jerked Jasper upright. Kyree had simply laid down, her head on her paws and her tail wrapped around her back leg. "Hailstones, dog," he muttered as he let himself fall back to the mattress. The silence was almost as disconcerting as the noise.

Warm fingers gently brushed his arm. *Sorry. She's excited. She'll stay quiet now, though.*

That was a relief, but not the point. "How...."

I asked her to. She says she'll try. She didn't know wagging her tail was bothering you.

The dog didn't know... and now she did. This was getting weirder by the minute. "You talked to her?"

Nodding, Tobias settled down on the bed and found Jasper's skin again, this time his fingers lightly touching the back of Jasper's hand. "Is that how she found you?"

I can't talk to her—to anyone—over long distances. There was an almost-familiar pressure in Jasper's head, and he forgot where his questions had been leading.

KYREE took to the barn as easily as the house, sniffing the horses, making friends with the goat, and giving the kittens "baths" that, amazingly, the mother cat tolerated. By the time they went inside, she'd marked half the yard as hers, claimed a blanket to sleep on, and eaten more food than Jasper and Tobias combined.

Dog food went at the top of the new grocery list, underlined several times. With luck, they'd make it into town once more at the end of the week, but that would be it until the wet was over. The windows rattled later in the morning and earlier in the evening every day. Within a week, clear skies would only prevail for an hour or two a day, and within two, the sun would be gone for at least a month. The last thing Jasper needed was for the dog—or Tobias—to eat all of his valuable supplies.

By the end of the day, Kyree had calmed significantly and Jasper found himself idly petting her when she walked by. The dog fit in as well as her master, blending into Jasper's life with an ease that was disconcerting if he thought about it. He'd only known Tobias for a week, and it seemed like forever.

When they settled in for the night, Jasper wasn't worried the dog would keep him awake, and Kyree found her blanket and lay right down. It was Tobias who had trouble relaxing.

He paced the room, driving Jasper mad with every footstep and restless movement. His hands twitched, then rubbed the back of his neck or fumbled with his shirt hem. His pace increased, getting faster and faster until Jasper grabbed his hand as he walked by. He jerked when he stopped, his eyes curious and his muscles tense.

"What's wrong?"

Someone's coming.

It seemed an odd thing to have Tobias so worked up. Whoever it was would hardly be arriving before morning. No one in their right mind would be outside with the storms as close as they were. "Who? When?" What was so distressing about these people?

Brown curls flopped as Tobias rapidly shook his head. *I don't know! Soon! Tonight!* He tugged his hand free and resumed pacing.

This time when Jasper caught Tobias's arm, he tugged until the other man sat on the bed next to him. "No one is coming tonight, Tobias."

Yes! Yes they are! They'll be here soon and we can't let them in!

Anyone caught out in the storms would be offered shelter if they made it to a dwelling. It was how things worked, the social code of society, and if Jasper turned anyone away, whatever happened to them would be on his head—morally and legally. "We can't—" he started, but was cut off by a violent shake of Tobias's head.

No! They're not looking for shelter! They're looking... they want....

"What do they want?" Jasper prompted after a moment of complete silence.

I don't know. Even in Jasper's head, Tobias sounded defeated. *I just know they're coming tonight and they don't want shelter. I can't tell anything else, even when I try.*

The question "Try what?" flashed across Jasper's mind, but he pushed it aside. Tobias hadn't been aware of Darius or Carla's impending arrival either time they'd visited, nor had he been aware of the dog until the mutt was in Jasper's kitchen. "How do you know they're coming?"

I don't know! I just.... Tobias slumped forward, resting his forehead in his free hand. He looked dejected and lost as he turned his gaze to Jasper. *I don't know how to explain it. I just know.*

"We're safe in here. The house is locked, this room is hidden." If they were looking for something other than shelter, they'd bust in and leave without ever finding the safe room.

I know, but—

Jasper stopped him simply by breaking the contact between them. "Stop worrying. If something happens, we'll deal with it then."

Tobias looked dubious, but he toed off his shoes and stretched out on one side of the narrow bed. Jasper lay next to him, his back to the younger man, and mentally added sleeping arrangement revisions to his to-do list. The single, narrow bed seemed smaller every time they climbed into it.

KYREE heard the sound first, perking her ears up at a noise Jasper couldn't hear and whimpering softly. Tobias was next, sitting straight up with wide eyes and finding Jasper's arm with a fumbling hand. It was only then Jasper heard a faint crash, muffled by the walls of the safe room and the howling wind.

Tobias had been right. At least one person had braved the starting storm and was in the house.

They're here.

There was something in the tense mental whisper that required reassurance. "They won't find us," he whispered, placing his hand on top of Tobias's where it touched his arm. "They'll take what they want and leave." Or perhaps they would stay and shelter from the storm, but he didn't mention the possibility. They could stay in the safe room until whoever was downstairs had left.

No. They know we're here. They're looking for us. He looked straight into Jasper's eyes, his own expression wild. *I can hear them.*

"They won't—" Jasper started, but stopped as Tobias shook his head. The other man was right. The room was hidden enough someone wasn't likely to stumble across it, but it wasn't so hidden a determined searcher couldn't locate it in short time. "We could go to the barn." Maybe they'd already looked there. It wouldn't be ideal for riding out the storm, but they'd survive. The animals did.

Tobias shook his head violently. *No. We won't get past them.* His eyes darted around the room. *We have to keep them out. Can you call for help from in here?*

Jasper nodded. There was a phone in the corner, and if the lines survived the night he'd be able to phone Darius in the morning. The radio in the corner hadn't been used in years, but it too could theoretically connect to the town. If they could last through the night, he could summon help in the morning. "I could call now," he offered hesitantly, unsure if he wanted to worry his friends when they wouldn't be able to safely act for hours.

No. They could hear.

It was a good point, and Jasper kept his voice low as he helped Tobias up. "Help me move the bed against the door." It would provide the best barrier in and out.

Tobias nodded and broke contact to start pushing things out of the way. They both grimaced several times as heavier-than-they-looked items scraped loudly on the floor, but only the bed was big enough to block the door, and they had to rearrange everything to move it.

They had just managed to move the bed itself when Kyree lunged to her feet, growling softly. Jasper froze, his eyes locking with Tobias's as his mind raced. Did they dare keep moving the bed? He could hear the men in the bedroom. The noise would draw their attention to the closet and the room behind it, but if they didn't move the bed and the men got into the closet anyway, they'd be found and vulnerable. There was nothing inside the safe room they could effectively defend themselves with.

Tobias leaned across the bed and touched Jasper's arm. *Keep going. Please.*

Jasper opened his mouth, and closed it again. He couldn't say anything, didn't dare risk even a whisper for fear it would be heard in the bedroom. A helpless expression on his face, he glanced to the door, then back to Tobias.

The buzzing in his head changed slightly. *Just think, I'll hear you.*

His mouth opened and closed again. "But," he whispered. "How?"

Just think! I'll explain later, or try anyway, but please! If you need to say something, think it, okay? They'll hear otherwise.

It was a weird and worrying idea, but Jasper nodded. *Okay.* They'd sort it out later.

Thank you. Tobias nodded at the bed. *Let's move this, yeah?*

They'll hear us, Jasper thought, his eyes widening as Tobias shrugged. This was too weird.

If we don't move it, we won't be able to keep them out.

It was so exactly what Jasper had been thinking moments earlier, he wondered if anything he'd thought since Tobias had arrived had been private. If it hadn't, if Tobias had just told him now because of the situation… no, he wouldn't think that. Not now. There were more pressing matters.

Nodding, Jasper bent his knees and grabbed the bed again. *If we move fast,* he thought, unsure if Tobias could hear him when they weren't touching, *we might be in time.*

Tobias nodded and positioned himself on the other side of the bed.

Ready? Jasper thought, and Tobias nodded again. *Go!*

The bed scraped loudly across the floor, the distance closing rapidly. Five feet, four feet, three—and then the door burst open, revealing two burly men wearing emerald green dusters and thick black boots. Their faces and hands were tattooed in a strange pattern of swirling green and black, and one had what appeared to be an amethyst set into the back of each hand. They swaggered inside, lowering their guns as they entered.

Kyree growled, teeth barred and legs spread in a defensive stance. "Good doggy." The first man sneered. "Led us right where we wanted to be."

They'd followed the dog. It made sense in a weird way, though it didn't answer the questions of who they were or why they were in Jasper's house. "What do you want?" he asked, concentrating on straightening and hoping his voice didn't break. He'd never been held at gunpoint before, not even back in the big city with its ever-changing population and high crime rate.

"Him." The gun flicked briefly from Jasper to Tobias, but it was back before Jasper had a chance to act. "Let us take him, and we won't hurt you."

No! I won't go!

The panicked words pierced Jasper's skull and he turned to see Tobias backing into a corner, fumbling behind himself, picking up and discarding every loose object he touched. Jasper could guess what he was looking for, but there was nothing large, heavy, or solid enough to be used as a weapon, even in defense.

"That's it." The man with the stones smiled and stepped closer to Jasper while the other kept his gun trained on Tobias. "Just don't interfere and you'll be fine. The world will be a better place when we're done."

"No," Jasper whispered, shaking his head in denial. This couldn't be happening. People didn't break into houses and hold the owners at gunpoint to abduct their guests. They didn't.

"Yes." The man stepped right up to Jasper so their toes were touching and Jasper's eyes were locked on the tattoo covering the man's nose. He was taller up close than he'd looked from the door, and he'd looked huge there. "I'm going to take him, and you're not going to stop me."

Jasper tried to step back, but his legs wouldn't respond. He wanted to do something, say something, anything, but there was nothing he could do, no weapon close at hand, no brilliant plan springing to mind.

The second, slightly smaller man circled around the bed and stalked toward Tobias, a vile gleam in his eyes. "Come quietly and it will be easier on your friend."

No! Tobias moved with surprising swiftness, skidding around his attacker and tumbling over the bed before anyone could react. He was out the door before Jasper could blink, the smaller man on his heels and the larger man not far behind. Kyree lunged, snapping at their legs, barking and growling as she skidded across the slick floor. She caught the hem of a duster in her teeth and pulled, then flew back into the room with a yelp as a lashing leg caught her in the side.

The dog's whimpers broke Jasper's paralysis and he ran after them, wracking his brain trying to plan the best course—one that would get him to the kitchen or the study where he could grab a weapon. The wind howled outside and crashes of nearby thunder obscured the noise of the pursuit. Footsteps reached the bottom of the stairs as Jasper arrived at the bedroom door, and he waited to hear which way they turned before barreling after them.

No! It was stronger and louder than Jasper had ever heard before. He was on his knees before he knew he'd moved, unable to stop the moaning that accentuated the pain and pounding in his head. The room swam as he tried to move, but he had to get up, had to keep going. This wouldn't end without a fight.

He'd barely stumbled to his feet when an even stronger blast knocked him down again. *Jasper! Help!* His vision narrowed to black-lined tunnels as he tried to move against the pain, but the words tore at him. He wouldn't let this happen, not in his house, not to his guest. He had to move, had to get downstairs, had to stop them.

The dog came running around the corner, almost tripping Jasper as she bounded down the stairs, again barking ferociously. If Kyree could attack injured, Jasper had to be able to help through the mental assault of Tobias's terror. He stumbled to his feet, took one halting step, then another.

NOOOOOOOOOOOOOOOOOOOOOOOOOOOOOO! The word degenerated into a voiceless yell that drove spikes into Jasper's brain. The room swam, then blackened, and he was hardly aware of hitting the floor before blessed oblivion claimed him.

CHAPTER
FOUR

JASPER woke slowly. The dog was lapping at his face and his left leg was twisted back at an uncomfortable angle, but the idea of moving was more unpleasant than a twisted knee and dog breath. His head was pounding, his neck and shoulder muscles tense to the point that moving his arm elicited an unconscious hiss of pain, and he couldn't remember why he was on the floor. They had been in the safe room and Tobias had....

Hailstones!

He jerked upright, moaned at the throbbing in his head, and fell backward, twisting his knee further beneath him. Storms! Carefully he rolled to his side, exposing more face to Kyree's tongue, but freeing his knee. It was a fair compromise.

As Jasper lay in the hall, listening for the storm and trying to convince his muscles to move, time passed slowly. He needed to go after Tobias, needed to secure his house and rescue his friend, and he needed to do it immediately, before the storms got too bad to venture outside. His muscles had other ideas, and he lay in the hall, limbs limp despite his thoughts on the matter. The tick-tock of the hall clock sounded almost as loud as the rattling branches and rumbling thunder. With every click of the hand, it reminded him that precious time was slipping by.

The clock chimed once before the burning urgency in the pit of Jasper's stomach overrode the listlessness of his muscles. Slowly, so as

not to further aggravate his aching head, he sat up. The room spun and
he clutched at his forehead, willing the sensation to stop. He had to get
to his feet, had to get downstairs, had to find Tobias. Time was running
out.

Tick-tock.

The world spun again as Jasper climbed to his feet, but this time
he ignored it, stumbling down the stairs with only his tenuous grip on
the handrail keeping him upright. At the bottom, momentum carried
him forward into the wall across from the steps, and the room spun
once more as his head thwacked against plywood and sent him
stumbling backward to sit on the bottom step.

It was harder to get up this time. The blow to his forehead drew
his attention back to his headache, and his pulse pounded in his skull in
rhythm with the clock.

Thump-thump.

Tick-tock.

The front door was still locked. They'd come in through the
kitchen then, same as the dog. As he stumbled toward the back of the
house, a detached part of him took note of the scattered and broken
belongings. He assigned the clatter he'd heard to the tumbling of the
fireplace pokers, and the crash that had preceded it to the dishes
scattered on the kitchen floor.

It began to rain, and Jasper hurried across the kitchen, crunching
ceramic and glass beneath his feet, desperate to discern the direction
they'd taken by looking for footprints before the rain erased all
evidence of their passing. He limped and hopped, cursing as though the
words could halt the pitter-patter of the rain. Each drop that hit the
ground turned dirt to mud and mud to soup, washing away footprints,
making it difficult to move, and destroying Jasper's chances of finding
his guest in the wet and dark.

Pitter-patter

Tick-tock.

A haze rose from the ground as Jasper squinted into the night, his
blurring vision further impaired by the darkness and the rain. He leaned
out, his hands braced on the empty doorway, and identified what

looked like the door in the mud beside the house. There were footprints near it, though coming or going he couldn't tell without a closer look.

His need to know outweighed his fear of the storm. Taking a deep breath and bracing himself against the increased onslaught of the storm, Jasper stepped outside. One foot inched into the rain, then another. A third step brought his whole body clear of the building and a fourth took him to the edge of the tiny back stoop.

The wind howled as Jasper touched the first step with bloody toes, shifted his weight, and slid to sprawl in the mud. His elbow hit the bottom step as he landed and he cursed as he floundered in the mud, splattering the stoop and the dog that had come out to stand on it.

He was just gaining his feet when lightning crashed, hitting the pole on top of the house and making Jasper's hair stand on end. The storm had arrived. Jasper only had time to glance at the footprints before another crash sent him scrambling inside, sliding backward as blood and mud-coated feet slipped on wet wood. He reached the doorway on hands and knees, Kyree running in front of him, barking loudly as she scampered through the mess on the kitchen floor.

Hail hit the tile as Jasper crossed into the living room, pushed the interior door shut behind him and sank to the floor. With the kitchen exposed, he needed to take the dog upstairs and wait out the storm in the safe room, but he lacked the energy to move. If the winds didn't change direction, the kitchen should be relatively safe and the thin door at his back would protect them.

He wouldn't think about what would happen if the wind shifted, blowing rain, sleet, and hail deep into the house and lashing against the thin wood separating the two rooms. He wouldn't think about the possibility his guest was out in the cold and wet. He wouldn't think about how long it would be until he could look for him or why he felt this frantic urge to find a man he was only just getting to know and barely understood. He wouldn't think at all.

"JASPER!"

The door behind Jasper's back rattled, jerking him awake. He knew that voice.

"Jasper! Can you hear me?" The door shook harder as the accompanying pounding increased in volume. "*Jasper!*"

His fuzzy brain registered he should say something to alert the person—Darius—he was there and could hear him. "Wha... mmm." His mouth wasn't quite on board with the plan.

"Jasper!" The pounding ceased but the door started to push against his back, slowly inching him forward. "Are you okay? Answer me!"

Answering didn't seem like a good idea at the moment. If Jasper just stayed still and quiet, his eyes could drift closed and.... the door swung forward and pushed him several feet into the room. "Sleet!" His arms flailed, futilely attempting to maintain his balance as the door was pulled away from his body.

Rough hands caught him and yanked him upright. "Careful."

"Carla?" He'd heard Darius before, but it was Carla who helped him gain his balance and then sat cross-legged on the floor in front of him. "I thought—"

A bottle was pushed into his hands and the voice he'd been expecting said, "Drink."

"Never mind." Jasper's brain was obviously not where it needed to be.

"Drink," Darius repeated, gesturing at the bottle in Jasper's hand. "Then tell us what in the clear sky happened here."

"That's—" he started, but stopped when both his friends directed pointed looks at the bottle in his hands. Slowly, so as to not aggravate his aching muscles, he twisted the cap off and raised the bottle to his lips. It was cool, refreshing, and gone before he realized it.

Carla took the bottle from Jasper's fingers and set it on the floor next to his knee. "Now talk."

THE door still lay in the yard, covered in mud and still wet from the rain. The door itself was unbroken, but the hinges had been cut with some tool Jasper couldn't identify. The metal was warped to the point it looked almost melted, though it was cold to touch after hours out in the cold night air.

Two of the footprints Jasper had thought he'd seen the night before were gone, washed away by the storm, but Darius found one by the side of the stoop, protected from the worst of the storm by the house. It pointed in the direction Jasper had expected, and confirmed that his quick glance as he ran from the storm had been correct. There was no more time to waste.

"Jasper, wait."

Darius's hand on his arm stopped Jasper, not his words. He glanced down at it, shook it off, and proceeded in the direction he'd been heading. There were places in the woods where shelter could be found. It was possible the people who had broken in—and Tobias—had survived the night. He hoped so. That way he could hurt them himself.

"Jasper." This time both arms were grabbed, one by Darius, the other by Carla.

Jasper jerked, but his friends had a firm grip and he only succeeded in irritating his tender muscles. "Let me go."

"No." Darius tugged slightly, turning them back toward the house. "You can't just run off after them."

"Why not?" He'd told them exactly what happened. They had to understand why he needed to go, why time was of the essence. The people he was after already had a head start. The advantage granted by Jasper's knowledge of the area was fading quickly. "The longer I wait, the harder it will be to find them."

"Because," Carla released her grip and slung an arm over Jasper's shoulders, "you need to prepare first. You won't get far in bare feet and pajama bottoms."

She had a point. "I'll change. Then I'm going."

"You change, we'll pack some supplies. Then we'll *all* go."

"Supplies?" Jasper was clearly failing at his attempts to think around the pounding in his skull, and failing even more at hiding it. "For what?"

Darius stopped just in front of the steps and put one hand on each of Jasper's shoulders. "Jasper," he said, speaking slowly and carefully as though Jasper were an idiot or a child, "you haven't eaten. We don't know how long we'll be out there. We don't know who we're following or what they want. I'm not running into the woods without some way to mark the path and something to defend myself if we stumble onto an animal."

"Or a crazy person," Carla added with a grin that made her look like one of the referenced crazy people.

The joke made Jasper feel worse rather than better, but Carla's expression was so maniacal he couldn't help but chuckle. "All right," he acquiesced, rubbing the back of his neck in a futile attempt to loosen the tense muscles. "I'll change; you pack. Then we're leaving." There wasn't time for any additional delays.

By MIDAFTERNOON, Jasper was glad they'd taken the time to pack some supplies, and even gladder he'd dressed in warm clothes and left the pajama bottoms where they fell to the floor of the bedroom. The sky, when they could see it through the trees, was clear, but the wind was blowing strong and the air was crisp. They'd been out for hours, with Kyree leading most of the time, and Jasper, even with his knowledge of the woods around his house, was lost. They'd gone farther than he had explored, and they still hadn't found the people who had invaded his house or the guest they'd taken from it.

He hitched his jacket up on his shoulders and wrapped his arms around his torso in a futile attempt to better protect himself from the chill wind. In the trees, they at least had some protection, but Kyree had led them to a clearing where there was nothing to stop the icy gusts. Shivering, he stepped back into the shelter of the trees.

Darius stopped next to Jasper while Carla followed Kyree across the open ground. "We're going to have to turn back soon. We need daylight to find the markers I left."

"We could find someplace to shelter for the night." Even as he said it, Jasper knew it wasn't a good idea. They had only prepared to be gone for the afternoon, none of them willing to brave the storms when there were other options, and if they did stay out, they might never find their way back. Darius had marked the trail cleverly, but the wind and rain were likely to destroy his work.

Darius squeezed Jasper's shoulder. "You know we can't."

"Yeah." Jasper looked at the sky, calculating the time and how early the storms were likely to start. "Another half-hour, okay? Then we'll turn back." He shrugged apologetically, feeling like mud for asking. His friends had already given up their day to help him search for someone none of them really knew. "I just keep thinking we'll find something the next time the dog barks."

"She seems to think she's following something, but I don't know what. I don't think she's a tracker."

"I guess we'll see when we find it." Or not, as the chances of finding anything were diminishing rapidly. Jasper had to at least pretend to be optimistic though, so he focused on positive thoughts to counteract the aching muscles and pounding head that had only gotten worse as the day progressed.

Darius was kind enough to simply agree, nodding as he shoved his hands into his jacket pockets. "Yeah."

They waited in silence, Darius staring across the clearing at Carla, and Jasper rolling his head, attempting to loosen tight shoulder and neck muscles. He'd almost gotten a troublesome spot when Carla turned, waving frantically.

"Darius! Jasper!" She could barely be heard over the wind and distance. "Come over here! I think we found something!"

Jasper didn't hesitate—he ignored the aches of his body as he ran full-tilt across the open ground, Darius at his heels. "What is it?" he asked as he skidded to a stop in front of Carla. He leaned forward and rested his hands on his knees as he attempted to catch his breath.

Carla held out a torn, black bandanna. "The dog found this. It hasn't been here for long."

She was right. It was ripped down the middle, but as Jasper examined it, he couldn't find any other sign of prolonged exposure to the elements. The cloth was wet and dirty, but the fibers were tight, the unbroken edges still perfectly squared, and the stitching around the edges completely intact. It had clearly been purchased recently, and

Jasper would have been surprised if it had been worn more than once or twice.

His stomach twisted as he fingered the edges of the cloth. They were on the right track, he could feel it. "Where was this?" He scanned the trees nearby as though he'd be able to pick out the rag's former location by simply looking at the landscape.

"About six or seven yards in. It was snagged on a tree branch." Carla started into the trees, but stopped after a few steps to look back over her shoulder. "Do you think it belonged to one of the men you saw last night?"

It was hard to remember. "Could be." He shrugged. "I wasn't really focused on what they were wearing. Green coats, I remember that, but not much else other than the tattoos." The more he thought about it, the less likely it seemed this did belong to the people they were searching for. Black bandannas seemed amateurish, and the men who had broken in were definitely professionals.

"It was on this branch here." Carla touched a fingertip to a branch just below eye level. "The dog was jumping up trying to get it."

"Where's the dog now?" Darius turned in a slow circle. "I don't see her."

"As soon as I touched the bandanna, she ran off. I tried to follow, but she lost me, and I thought Jasper should see this."

"Sleet and snow!"

Jasper nodded his agreement to Darius's curse, but privately, he was glad Kyree had disappeared. It had been at least ten minutes since he'd promised Darius they would turn back in a half-hour, and he had a feeling they'd need more than twenty minutes to complete their search of the area. They wouldn't turn back without the dog.

At least, he amended as he watched Darius stalking deeper into the trees and calling Kyree's name, he didn't *think* they'd leave without the dog. They'd at least search for a little bit longer than twenty minutes. He hoped.

Jasper was about to start calling as well when Kyree came bounding through the trees, barking excitedly. She dashed right past Darius, who tried to snag a non-existent collar, and stopped at Jasper's feet, her tail wagging and her ears perked up. She barked once, ran a few feet in the direction from which she'd come, stopped to look behind her, and ran back to sit at Jasper's feet again.

"What is it, girl?" Jasper asked, crouching to scratch behind the dog's ears. He was allowed to for only a moment before she barked again and repeated her earlier antics.

Carla sauntered up, her hands stuffed into her jacket. "I think she wants you to follow her."

It was a brilliant idea. Jasper scratched Kyree's ears one more time and then stood, ignoring the creaking of his knees. "Go on!" He pointed in the direction the dog seemed to want to go.

Kyree barked again and ran off. This time Jasper was right behind her, and after looking back to make sure he was following, she kept moving.

Darius and Carla joined them, and the four made their way over a tiny hillock to a creek bed swollen with the recent rains. It would get deeper before the wet season was over, but it was deep enough they wouldn't be able to ford without getting wet—something they needed to avoid if possible. None of them wanted to make the long trek back to Jasper's place in sopping clothes and biting wind.

Just as it looked as though Kyree was going to jump into the creek, she turned and headed alongside the narrow gorge to the base of another hill. Here she stopped and sat down, staring at a tree.

It took a moment to see it, but once Jasper had, the scrap of emerald cloth was glaringly obvious, a patch of bright green amongst dull browns and occasional oranges. His hand trembled as he pulled it from the branch. The purple stitching along one side left no room for doubt. "This is theirs. We're on the right track."

"We're out of time."

"No." Jasper shook his head. They weren't. They couldn't be. It didn't seem possible, but a glance at the tiny patch of sky above the creek confirmed Darius's quiet announcement accurate. They had to head back if they had any hope of reaching the house before the storms started.

"We can start here tomorrow. We'll find it faster without stopping to look around all the time."

Carla meant well, but they all knew the markers they'd left would most likely be gone in the morning, and it would only be sheer luck that would let them find this place again. It would take even more luck to get close, as by going home, they were giving the advantage of time to the people they sought.

It was a lose-lose situation. If they left now, they'd give up any advantage they might have gained. If they kept going, they'd have to face the storms without the protection of a building. This early in the season, they would probably survive, but they would not be undamaged.

Jasper couldn't decide which he'd prefer. He stood, frozen, unable to come up with the best solution. He didn't want to abandon Tobias—he had a responsibility there—but he couldn't ask Carla and Darius to brave the storm either. It wasn't their responsibility, nor was it Kyree's, and they'd all be in danger if Jasper didn't agree to leave. Reluctantly, he turned around and started back down the creek. "Let's go, then."

He had only managed four heavy steps when Kyree started barking, yapping louder than she had all day. Jasper turned to quiet her but stopped, unable to believe his eyes when he saw the source of the commotion. Stumbling over the top of the hill was a dark-haired, half-naked man, his arms crossed over his chest and his frame shivering so violently Jasper could see it even fifty yards away.

Jasper's feet carried him forward without conscious thought. He scrambled up the hill, only marginally aware of Darius and Carla following, and calling out as he approached, "Tobias!"

CHAPTER FIVE

THE rain started when they were still a mile from the house, big fat drops falling from the sky slowly at first, but with rapidly increasing intensity. The forest canopy kept the worst of it off, but they were soaked by the time they reached the edge of the trees to peer out at the open ground that stretched between the woods and Jasper's house. It was only about five hundred yards, but with lightning flashing and rain turning to sleet and hail, it would be an arduous trek across muddy, uneven ground.

Jasper glanced back, checking one last time for the men Tobias had somehow gotten away from. He saw no one, just as he had every time he'd looked since he'd found Tobias, and he forced himself not to wonder where they'd gone. After turning back, he scanned the field, trying to calculate the safest route between their present position and the back door, but the flashes of lightning didn't illuminate the ground for long and only served to add to his worry. They would be the tallest things for a good distance as they dashed across the field.

It will only get worse. The hand on Jasper's shoulder trembled as Tobias shivered. He was wearing Jasper's coat, Darius's hat, and Carla's scarf over the thin pajama bottoms that had been his only covering when they found him, but he'd spent close to twenty-four hours exposed to the elements, and the little bit they'd been able to provide wasn't enough to keep him warm.

"I know. Let's go." Jasper took the hand from his shoulder and held it in his own, both so Tobias would be able to talk to him without making his headache worse and so he could help the shivering man if he stumbled. Tobias's normally olive skin was a pale white and his breath came in ragged gasps through blue-tinged lips. Jasper wasn't sure he would make it all the way to the house.

They ran quickly, Tobias wincing with each step as his bare feet hit frozen ground or slick mud. They slipped and slid together, Darius, Carla, and the dog close behind. Muttered curses and pain-filled yelps filled the air as they picked their way across the uneven ground, the full force of the sleet and hail hitting their skin, wind burning as it whipped water into their eyes, and the ever-present threat of a lightning strike urging them to move faster though they could hardly lift their legs.

They were almost to the house when Tobias went down, his feet sliding in opposite directions and his mental cry slicing into Jasper's brain despite the contact of their skin. Jasper tugged up on the hand, trying to help, but Tobias slipped again, his feet hit Jasper's, and they both ended up on the ground.

The lashing wind, biting precipitation, and slick mud made it nearly impossible to get up. Even after he let go of Tobias's hand, Jasper still slid in the mud as he tried to convince cold-stiffened limbs to cooperate.

"Here." Carla held out a hand, and Jasper cautiously took it, mindful of how Tobias had pulled him down. As he braced himself, Darius's hands slid under his arms from behind, and between the three of them, he got to his feet.

Tobias was still shivering in the mud when Jasper turned and grabbed his hands. He was prepared to help Tobias up by himself, but to his surprise, Darius and Carla both grabbed one of Tobias's arms at his shoulder, and the three of them hauled the near-frozen man to his feet.

Thanks. It was a soft whisper Jasper barely heard when he slipped Tobias's arm over his shoulder.

Darius's mouth twitched into a small smile as he helped hold Tobias steady until Jasper could fully support him. "You're welcome," he yelled over the howling wind, flinching as a particularly close bolt of lightning flashed, followed immediately by a loud crack of thunder. "Now let's get inside before this gets worse!"

It wasn't until they reached the back door Jasper remembered what he'd forgotten in the panic of the day. As he groped for the handle in the blinding rain, he cursed, his fingers scraping against rough plywood instead of painted metal. They'd boarded up the back doorway before setting out, propping the actual door against the kitchen wall to protect it from further damage. "We have to go around front!" he yelled as he guided Tobias back down the steps and started around the building.

Jasper kept Tobias as close to the house as possible. The silent young man had gotten even paler since they'd fallen, and he was stumbling with almost every step. Twice, either Darius or Carla had to help catch Tobias before he pulled Jasper down as well, and Kyree danced just off to the side, whimpering every time her master slipped.

The front door was blessedly easy to open and they stumbled inside, heedless of the water dripping onto the wood floor. Jasper wanted nothing more than to collapse into a chair and rest, but he forced himself to push the door shut and lead the way to the stairs.

JASPER convinced Tobias to take a hot shower to drive the chill from his bones. By the time he stumbled down the stairs sporting wet curls and wearing Jasper's warmest clothes, Jasper, Darius, and Carla had cleaned up the worst of the mess in the kitchen and had soup on the stove and bread warming in the oven. Jasper had half-expected Tobias would go straight to bed, and said as much as he placed two steaming bowls of soup on the table.

It smelled good, Tobias replied with a smile and a quick brush against Jasper's arm before Jasper went to cut the bread.

They ate in silence, the dull, rapid click of spoons against plastic bowls—all that had survived the destruction of the kitchen—a testament to their hunger. The soup and bread were devoured in minutes. Their warmth spread through Jasper's body as he sat back with a satisfied smile on his face.

Carla cleared the table, and while she was rinsing the dishes, Darius leaned forward and looked pointedly at Tobias. "An explanation would be nice."

"What is there to explain?" Jasper asked, indignant on Tobias's behalf. The urge to protect his guest was rising again, this time directed at Darius.

No, he's right. Tobias gently pushed Jasper back in the chair. *I should explain. Just,* his eyes flickered to the plywood covered doorway and the window over the sink, *not here. Upstairs, okay?*

Jasper conveyed the request to Darius with one word. "Upstairs."

Lightning flashed just outside and they all promptly agreed.

THE safe room had been built to hold one adult, two if they were close. Four plus a dog was downright claustrophobic, but with careful rearrangement of the furniture left haphazardly around the room, they were able to make it bearable.

Tobias took over quickly, touching first Darius's shoulder and then Carla's. Both moved to sit on the blankets they'd spread on the floor to serve as their bed as Tobias crossed the room to where Jasper was hovering by the door. *Come on,* he said, wrapping his hand around Jasper's.

Jasper followed and allowed Tobias to sit him on the bed. His mind was occupied with the strange feeling he'd gotten in the pit of his stomach when Tobias had taken his hand rather than touched his shoulder like he'd done for Carla and Darius. It meant nothing, he was sure—Tobias was just used to taking his hand, or maybe he'd thought Darius and Carla would be more comfortable with being touched on the shoulder. It was a silly thing to worry about.

And yet, his stomach fluttered when Tobias didn't let go and he wanted to stare holes into Darius and Carla as they touched Tobias's legs. It was just so Tobias could talk to them all, so they could have a conversation without his repeating everything Tobias said, he knew that. It was to make all their lives easier, including Jasper's, and yet there was a part of him that wanted to pull Tobias away, to keep him for himself, to—

No. He was not thinking that. Tobias was his guest, a young man he'd taken in to help, not a potential love interest. That was all it was. Jasper hadn't had anyone since he'd moved out from the coast and Tobias was attractive, tactile, and intriguing. It was only lust, and he wasn't going to think about it. He was going to ignore the twisting feeling in his stomach and the way Darius and Carla were casually touching Tobias's legs and—

"Jasper!"

The smack Darius gave his knee snapped Jasper out of his reverie and he blinked. "What?" Darius simply raised an eyebrow, and Jasper's cheeks burned. "Right. Sorry." He was *not* going to keep thinking those thoughts. "Go on."

Tobias shifted uncomfortably next to him. *What do you want to know?*

"Why we had to spend all day trying to find you for a start," Darius muttered loud enough for Jasper to hear. He looked uncomfortable sitting on the floor and kept glancing at his hand where it rested on Tobias's leg.

They wanted me so I could do something for them. I don't know what. Something to do with my... abilities. Tobias shrugged. *They said something about... Sheldin? Sheltin?*

"Shaleton," Jasper supplied. "It's a city on the south-east coast. The people there are a little... odd." That was the most diplomatic way to put it. Shaletonites tended to be particularly fanatical about the storms that ravaged the continent each wet season, and they stupidly braved the storms in attempts to worship or defy them. Back in Crittendon, there had been heavy betting each year as to how many Shaletonites would commit suicide by storm. Jasper had never bet, but he'd known someone who won big one year.

Yes! Tobias agreed. *That's it. They wanted to take me to Shaleton so I could... do whatever it is they wanted me to do.*

"Hailstones!" Carla exclaimed, and Jasper nodded his agreement to the sentiment. If the men wanted Tobias for his psychic abilities and they wanted him to use them in Shaleton, the outcome could only be bad.

"How'd they find you, though?"

Hostility dripped from Darius's voice, but Tobias didn't seem to notice. *Kyree. They followed Kyree. They were looking....* His expression grew pained and desperate. *I think they're the people who took Sam.*

"Sam?" Jasper's stomach did that burning, clenching, flipping thing again and he viciously pushed the feeling aside. It didn't matter how much this Sam person meant to Tobias. "Who's Sam?"

Samantha. My sister. The knot in Jasper's stomach vanished. *Something hurt her last year while she was... out, and she never came back. The men, they mentioned a girl, and I think it was her, and whatever it is they want me to do, Sam couldn't—or wouldn't—do it and I think they hurt her and they'll hurt her more when they get back and I don't know what they want her to do or what they want me to do or where this Shaleton place is and I need to help her, I was trying to find her!*

"Whoa! Calm down." Jasper put his free hand on Tobias's shoulder and waited for his breathing to resume a normal cadence. The mental speech could go on and on without pausing for breath, but Tobias's breathing was too ragged for Jasper to be comfortable.

Large brown eyes met Jasper's. *I have to find her. I have to help her.*

The desperation in Tobias's voice tore at Jasper's heart, and he squeezed the shoulder he was touching. "We'll figure something out." He didn't know what, or how, or even if they could, but he had to reassure Tobias if he wanted any more information.

Okay. Tobias looked down, bit his lip, and picked at the hem of his shirt with his free hand.

Jasper reached across him and stilled it. "Now slow down and try again. Where was your sister out from? Why do you think these people took her?"

Tobias took a deep breath and let it out slowly. *She was out from home, taking part in a ritual to appease the forest spirits, and something went wrong. She and Aaron—the other person doing the ritual—didn't come back and we couldn't find them. I felt something, though, just before they disappeared. The whole town did. I felt something just like it before I came here, too, and a little of it today. I think the men who came for me were the same people who took Samantha.* His fear was evident in his tone.

"Felt? What do you mean felt?" Darius asked, the earlier hostility gone from his voice.

I, um, I'll show you.

The sensation Jasper felt as Tobias was talking changed slightly, in a way he couldn't identify, and then the world changed with it.

THE *air was cool, but not yet so cold as to be worrying, and Tobias smiled as he walked down the street, waving and sending greetings to his friends as he passed. He wanted to get to the general store early; Sam could be back as early as that afternoon, and he wanted to have her favorite foods ready to cook for dinner when she arrived. She'd been excited to be the one chosen to go into the forest this year to ask the forest spirits for protection from the storms and for a bountiful harvest. She'd been determined to do well, and even, she'd confided to Tobias alone, secretly hoping to be one of the rare, lucky women who were blessed with a babe from the nights spent in the forest.*

The past two days and nights had been filled with pleasurable thoughts sent from both Samantha and Aaron, the young man chosen to go to the forest. The whole town was happy, confident they would survive another wet season unscathed. Everyone Tobias passed knew his sister was one of the two pleasing the spirits this year, and the greetings he received were especially enthusiastic.

He was filling a basket with fresh fruit when the feelings of pleasure changed to terror and pain so intense Tobias fell to his knees, which sent apples and berries rolling over the store's floor. Samantha! *Searching for his sister, he stretched his mind out, and hoped the bond they shared would let him reach farther than normal.* Samantha!

Around him, his neighbors were on the floor as well, clutching at their foreheads and sending waves of distress throughout the store, but Tobias had thoughts only for his sister and her distress. He stretched his mind farther, desperately seeking something he could do and needing to somehow help, but he couldn't reach her, only the fear and pain she was sending. He focused on it, stretching his senses to find the source, and encountered something so dark he instinctively recoiled, drawing his mind back as quickly as he could.

The darkness followed, overwhelming his senses, delving into the deepest corners of his mind. He understood Samantha's terror, and clung to his worry about her as he strove to push the darkness away. It pushed back, harder, more powerful, and Tobias's limbs shook. His heart thumped rapidly in his chest as he struggled to drive it off, struggled to break free, struggled to make his mind his own again. He couldn't breathe, couldn't think, couldn't see.

The darkness pushed harder and deeper, causing physical pain that left Tobias curled up on the floor, gasping for breath and whimpering with the little power he had left to send. He couldn't hold out much longer, couldn't fight any more, and then it was gone. Wondering what he'd just felt, he tried to catch his breath.

"S LEET, rain, and hail." Carla looked as though she was going to be ill, her hand clutching her stomach, her face pale. Jasper had to agree, and was certain he didn't look much better.

"*That* was what you felt?" All the hostility was gone from Darius's voice.

When Sam disappeared... and... before I left the mountains. Today, it wasn't as close. It wasn't as powerful, I guess.

"Still…." Jasper shook his head. Even a less-powerful version of what he'd just experienced through Tobias's memory could be enough to incapacitate someone. He should have done more to keep the men away from his house, away from Tobias.

I got away. It was difficult to tell who Tobias was reminding.

"How? The way Jasper told the story, I thought we'd have to charge in swinging sticks or something and rescue you." Darius's grin faded into a serious expression. "The last thing we expected was to see you at the top of that hill."

I'm glad you did. I don't think I would have made it back all by myself.

Jasper didn't like the direction his brain went with that comment. "What if's" were pointless, but he kept thinking them all the same. What if Kyree hadn't barked? What if they'd turned back the first time Darius had mentioned it? What if they'd taken the time to really clean up the mess before they'd started searching? What if Darius and Carla hadn't had supplies from town to deliver that day? They were dangerous thoughts and he couldn't stop thinking them.

"How did you get as far as you did?" Jasper asked, trying to focus on the facts. Kyree had barked. They hadn't turned back right away. They hadn't thoroughly cleaned the mess left by the break in. Darius and Carla had come out with deliveries. They had found Tobias.

Um, Tobias hesitated, his gaze flickering from one person to the other, until Jasper realized what he wanted.

He squeezed Tobias's hand reassuringly. "Go on and show us."

TOBIAS *was colder than he'd been in a long time, and he hurt everywhere. He would have bruises later—one on his arm where a particularly large hailstone had hit him, one encircling his wrist where he'd been grabbed and dragged, and countless small ones from branches, rocks, and rain. He'd woken halfway through the night, tied up in the back of a make-shift shelter that did little to keep the elements out, and had panicked, which only gained him a whack to the side of the head and a rough threat to drug him again if he wouldn't cooperate.*

Sunrise meant being forced to walk on bleeding feet over rough ground, his left wrist continuously gripped by one of the men in a hold that left no hope of escape. The pain and the residual effects of the drugs they'd given him the night before left him stumbling, earning jerks on his arm and curses when he fell. They didn't stop all day, not even to eat, but kept moving along an erratic route that made no sense to Tobias. They twisted and turned seemingly without thought, often going against the lay of the land, following a path only his captors could discern.

In the afternoon they were joined by a third man, also dressed in an emerald coat and covered in swirling tattoos. Several times Tobias stopped suddenly, yanking hard as he attempted to free his arm from the hand gripping it, but the grip on his wrist proved impossible to break and he ended up being dragged on his knees.

They didn't stop until Tobias could hear thunder rumbling in the distance. He was again bound—his hands tied behind him and his feet bound together—and thrust to the ground near the base of a tree as packs were unloaded and the makeshift shelter went up once more. Gruff words were exchanged, too low for Tobias to hear, but his two original captors drew weapons and stalked out of the camp, leaving Tobias alone with the newcomer who squatted in front of the shelter and arranged sticks to build a fire.

Barely able to believe his luck, Tobias steeled himself, and hoped the men didn't know too much about his abilities. He hadn't been able to do this when there were multiple people to worry about, but with only the newcomer present, Tobias was able to cautiously reach out toward his mind. He slipped in without resistance, carefully crafted a thought he hoped would seem natural, and planted the suggestion. As he withdrew, he held his breath, hoping he'd been successful. Nothing happened for a minute, and another, and another. Then, just as Tobias was about to give up hope, the man moved from the pile of kindling and, without saying a word, untied Tobias's bonds.

Tobias didn't waste any time. As soon as he was free, he dashed away, heedless of the danger presented by the man standing over him and the other two men in the woods around the camp. He ran, as fast as he could on frozen, bleeding feet, in the direction he thought they'd come from. Branches whipped his torso as he ran past, stumbling over tree roots and loose rocks. He was desperate to get as far away as he could before the man realized what he'd done, before the others returned to find him missing.

The small hill was almost his undoing. The direction felt right, but the leaves that coated the slope slid under his feet. He heard familiar voices and doubled his efforts. He fell twice as he scrambled up the hill, and crested it just in time to see the people he'd been hoping to find turning away.

CHAPTER SIX

JASPER rolled over and stretched without opening his eyes, not entirely convinced he wanted to be awake. The smells wafting through the vents were tempting, but his limbs were heavy with exhaustion and his muscles ached. His stomach grumbled, asking to be filled, but the bed was soft and comfortable.

Something about the situation nagged at the back of Jasper's mind, a little worry that kept him from relaxing completely. He was snug in bed, the body next to him was warm, the food smelled delicious, and...

He opened his eyes and blinked in the light as he looked around. There were no blankets on the floor—no dog either—but Tobias was still sleeping, lying flat on his back in the bed, his face turned toward the wall. Darius and Carla must have taken it upon themselves to fix breakfast.

Jasper stretched again and winced as the effects of the previous day made themselves known. There was a gash on his right foot that throbbed when he flexed his toes, and bruises and scrapes too numerous to count. His shoulders were still tight, though thankfully his headache had vanished while he slept.

Gingerly, he stood, braced for additional pain as he moved, but none came, and he breathed a sigh of relief, the knowledge he could move freely making him feel marginally better. At least he wouldn't have to take extra care every time he moved, though he would when he walked, a fact that became clear as he shifted his weight onto his damaged foot.

As he put on a shirt, Jasper considered waking Tobias, but stopped before he touched the sleeping man's shoulder. Tobias looked terrible. The feet that stuck out from under the blanket were covered with multiple lacerations, and red marks on his ankles disappeared up under the cover. His torso was dotted with smaller, shallower cuts, and deep purple bruises had appeared around his wrists and right elbow. Small oval-shaped bruises dotted his torso, likely from exposure to the storms. His face was drawn, worried even in sleep, and a thin line of dried blood crossed his forehead above his left eye.

Tobias slept the deep sleep of the ill or injured, and looked as though he wouldn't wake for several more hours. It was best to just leave him be.

After tugging the blanket to better cover Tobias, Jasper slipped out of the safe room, quietly shutting the door behind him, and headed down to see what Darius and Carla had managed to salvage from the wreck of his kitchen. Food, company, and distraction made up the perfect recipe to keep his mind off the man he'd left sleeping in his bed.

TWO hours later, the debris was completely swept up, the cabinets fixed, and the door almost reattached. All that remained was to go into town and obtain replacement dishes, and that could wait until they'd taken care of Tobias's injuries. Jasper, Darius, and Carla were sitting at the table, debating if they should wake him when Kyree's ears perked up and Jasper heard the tell-tale groan of the ninth stair, the one he'd been intending to fix while trapped inside this wet season. "Tobias?" he called out, though there was little question as to who was on the steps. "We're back in the kitchen."

The tread on the stairs was easier to hear when it started again, a slow gait Jasper was certain had to reflect the agony Tobias's feet must be in. It was amazing Tobias was walking at all, as cut up as they were, and Jasper didn't expect to see him in the kitchen for several minutes.

He most definitely did not expect to hear the squeak of the front door being opened.

"Is he...?"

Jasper didn't wait to hear if Darius finished the question. He dropped the screws he'd been holding on the table as he hurried by. The front door was swinging shut as he crossed the front room.

He caught up with Tobias on the porch, loosely grabbing his fingers to stop him. "What are you doing?"

Tobias flinched when Jasper touched him, but didn't move away. *I'm going to Shaleton. I have to find Sam.*

Jasper looked him up and down, not believing his eyes. Tobias was dressed in the clothes he'd been wearing when Jasper first found him—pants that had holes at nearly every seam, a too-thin torn shirt, and shoes held together with more hope than stitches or glue. He would be lucky to last a night dressed like that, particularly not after the experience he'd just had, and he would never make it all the way to Shaleton. "You can't."

I have to.

"Why now? You seemed happy to have shelter before those men came."

Because they came! Tobias moved forward, pulling his fingers free of Jasper's hand.

"Do you even know where Shaleton is?"

Tobias shook his head, but didn't stop inching along the porch, though each step clearly caused him great agony. Both his hands were clenched into fists, with his fingernails digging into his palms, and Jasper had the feeling that if he could speak, Tobias would be screaming. He couldn't let Tobias continue, no matter how determined—or delusional—he was.

"You can't walk there. You wouldn't make it, even if you knew the way, not with the storms just starting and those men looking for you."

That got Tobias's attention. He stopped, his spine straight and his expression pained, and held a hand out toward Jasper. Desperation and pain flooded Jasper's mind as he took it.

I have to find her! They'll be mad I got away and if she can't do what they want her to do this year they'll hurt her, I know they will! I have to find her and figure out how to stop them or she'll never come home! Tobias sank to the ground, still babbling, and wrapped his free arm around his knees, but made no effort to free himself from Jasper.

It was impossible to know what to say. Jasper sat as well, rubbing Tobias's back until the sense of desperation slowly receded from his mind. "Better?"

Tobias nodded again, but kept rocking. *I have to find her.*

"I know." And he did. He'd felt Tobias's frantic need and knew it would not be assuaged by platitudes or logic. It was a burning need Jasper knew he would feel the ghostly echoes of until it was filled. "But not like this, okay?"

How, then? He turned wide brown eyes toward Jasper and at that moment Jasper remembered why he'd originally thought Tobias was just a boy. He looked so lost and innocent, Jasper wanted to gather him in his arms and protect him from the world.

"There are trains that will run to Shaleton in the dry season." Even as he said it, Jasper knew it wouldn't be acceptable.

No. Tobias shook his head violently, sending his curls bouncing and making Jasper wonder if his head was going to stay attached. *We have to go now.*

"We'll figure something out, then, but we can't walk. It's too far, and your feet—" He broke off as he really looked at Tobias's shoes and noticed the red tinge slowly spreading up Tobias's socks. "Sleet! You're bleeding!"

I am? Tobias's gaze followed Jasper's and with trembling fingers, he touched the bloody fabric. *Oh. I am.*

"Let's go inside and take care of that."

But—

"We'll figure something out," Jasper promised as he helped Tobias to his feet and put an arm around his waist to help him limp inside. He just wasn't sure what.

DARIUS was a true country driver, speeding along single lane roads, swinging the car over the middle line every time they rounded a curve. Jasper had never ridden with Darius before, and would have been quite happy to keep it that way, except Tobias was slumped against him, his breathing shallow and his expression oscillating between terror and confusion.

Where are we going?

"Into town." Jasper kept his voice low and his answer vague. The idea of meeting new people had already sent Tobias into a panic once, and Jasper didn't want it to happen again while they were in the car. They all still had headaches from the backlash of his first outburst.

Tobias blinked and shook his head. *Why?*

"To take care of your feet, remember?"

When Jasper had gotten Tobias inside, they discovered that it wasn't just one cut that had re-opened, but all of them. Tobias's feet were a bloody mess, and the cuts were too numerous and deep to be handled using the first aid kit. Tobias had cooperated as they'd slowed the bleeding with towels, but the moment Darius had mentioned taking him to the doctor, Tobias had flipped, emitting a wordless scream that had driven the others to their knees.

When he'd recovered enough to stand again, Jasper had chased after Tobias, only to find him sitting on the back stoop. He'd looked at Jasper with a puzzled expression, complained that his feet hurt, and let Jasper lead him inside. They had been careful not to mention the doctor again, though that was where they were going.

No. But my feet do hurt.

Jasper was starting to wonder if Tobias had hit his head or lost a lot more blood than they'd originally thought. His short term memory seemed shot. "We're going to take care of that."

Okay. Tobias looked so vulnerable that Jasper had to fight the urge to wrap him in his arms and promise he would make everything okay. It would be a lie, and he had no right to think those thoughts.

The car swerved suddenly, and Jasper found himself holding Tobias despite his resolve not to. He quickly let go, but as the car swerved again, Tobias doubled over, clutching at his stomach, and Jasper had him back in his arms without making a conscious effort to do so. *Hurts*, came the thought, but requests for elaboration were met with silent moans of pain. Jasper didn't know if he should ask Darius to speed up so they'd get there faster or slow down so the bumpy road and quick turns didn't hurt Tobias further.

THE doctor was a good friend of Darius's, and agreed to come out to Darius's house on the edge of town rather than have them bring Tobias into his office and risk attracting the attention of half the townsfolk. It was a small favor for which Jasper was grateful. The doctor alone was bad enough. Tobias didn't need to meet Mrs. Bidwell, Mrs. Haverds, or any of their numerous daughters and daughters-in-law. The two families existed simply to outdo each other with small town gossip, and in a slow time even Jasper's semi-regular trips to the town store became a major event. A new person—a new *injured* person—would set off a week's worth of rumors even before they discovered that he didn't talk.

Whoever ferreted out that knowledge would have the juiciest bit of gossip for the whole wet season and would spend the next three or four months in a position of particular honor among her family. It was far better to take Tobias straight to Darius's. Doctor Parks' trip out would generate enough gossip on its own.

Tobias sat still and silent as he was treated, only moving when Dr. Parks asked it of him, and not sending anything, not even to Jasper when the doctor wasn't touching him. His eyes widened and his muscles tensed when the doctor brought out needles, but he accepted the shots of antibiotic and sedative with the same pliability he'd exhibited while the doctor examined his cuts and bruises. Jasper helped him lie back, and he was asleep before the doctor had removed the suture kit from his bag.

Forty five minutes later, the doctor tied the bandage around Tobias's left foot and began cleaning up. "He needs to stay off his feet as much as possible for at least a week or those cuts will break open again. I put twelve stitches in the biggest ones, but more of them will need stitches if they open again."

"But he'll be okay?" Jasper asked, glancing from the white bandages to the doctor's face. "He was disoriented earlier."

"His pupils dilated evenly." The doctor picked up a penlight, lifted Tobias's eyelids one at a time, and checked again, nodding when he got the same result. "He just needs rest and food. I could hear his stomach growling while I worked on his feet."

"He hasn't eaten much," Jasper acknowledged.

"Feed him when he wakes up, and have him take one of these." The doctor handed Jasper a packet of small, red pills. "If he won't sleep," the doctor continued, pressing another packet into Jasper's hand, "there are sedatives in here. He should take one of the red pills every eight hours until they're gone. Only give him the other if he needs them."

"Thanks." It wasn't much, considering how helpful the doctor had been and how few questions he'd asked, but Jasper didn't know what else to say. His mind had already jumped ahead to how he was going to break it to Tobias that they wouldn't be able to go anywhere for a week. He stayed by the bed, watching Tobias sleep and contemplating the conversation they would have when he woke, while Darius saw the doctor out, thanking him much more adequately than Jasper had been able to manage.

DARIUS'S maps were old—he and Carla operated primarily between the west coast and Brightam's Ford—but they were adequate for Jasper's needs at the moment. Even if some of the roads indicated had been washed out in the years since the map had been made, it would still be possible to drive to Shaleton in the wet season. Brightam's Ford was only one in a string of towns that crossed the continent, and based on the map it looked possible to travel from one to another between storms.

"They look like rows of ants." Carla peered over Jasper's shoulder. "I never noticed before how evenly spaced the towns are."

"Probably so people *can* travel in the wet season," Darius ventured with a sour expression. "Though why anyone would want to, I have no idea."

Jasper ignored the last part. "When people first came here, they landed on both sides of the continent and planned to settle there. The inland was rough, hard to travel, and full of unknown creatures like the forest spirits. But they landed in the dry season, and when the wet season came, they discovered it was safer inland where the wet season was shorter. So they moved inland, fleeing the storms, but they could only go so far before they had to stop and shelter. Even in the dry season, it made sense to stop in already established camps, and gradually the towns grew up around them. Most of the inland towns are named for the first people who stayed when their companions moved on."

"How do you know that?"

"There's not much else to do but read in the wet season, particularly once the storms start during the day." Jasper shrugged. "I had a friend back in Crittendon who was a history buff, and he passed on all his books to me when he finished them. I found the chronicles of how the colony was populated to be especially interesting."

"Hmm." Darius looked at Jasper appraisingly. "The things you don't know about your friends."

Jasper would have responded, but there was a noise from the other room and then he felt a pressure that made him wince. *Jasper?* It was so soft, Jasper thought he'd imagined it, but the start of a headache and another crashing sound convinced him otherwise.

"Tobias's awake."

Darius looked skeptical, but both he and Carla followed Jasper into the other room, where they found Tobias on the floor a few feet from the bed. The stool Doctor Parks had used to hold his tools as he worked was on its side, and a few video discs were scattered over the floor as well, scattered around Tobias.

"Sleet!" Jasper crossed the room in three long strides, crouched down, and put his hand on Tobias's forearm. "What happened?"

I fell. He looked at his bandage-wrapped feet, frowning. *It hurt, a lot, when I tried to get up.*

"You're not supposed to get up."

I have to.

"Not yet, you don't. It's late; we're not going anywhere right now." The storms would soon be raging outside and Jasper wasn't ready to face them again.

In the morning, then.

He sounded so determined and looked so pathetic that Jasper had to bite his lip to keep from laughing. "Let's get you back in bed," he said instead, slipping his hands under Tobias's arms and helping Tobias to his feet.

A wail of pain invaded Jasper's mind as soon as Tobias's weight was on his feet. Jasper gritted his teeth against the onslaught as he guided Tobias closer to the bed, but it got worse with every shuffling step, and he was ready to fall himself when Darius slid under Tobias's other shoulder. "Lift him up before you both fall."

Tobias didn't let go of either of them when they got him to the bed. *We have to go tomorrow.* His grip tightened. *I have to get to Samantha.*

Jasper was ready to give in, to promise that they'd leave first thing in the morning no matter what, but Darius gave Tobias a stern look. "You need to rest and heal. You won't do your sister any good if you kill yourself getting to her."

I won't! I'm fine! I have to go!

"No." Darius took Tobias by the shoulders and pushed him down onto the bed, breaking the grip Tobias had on Jasper's shoulder.

Tobias rolled onto his side and took Jasper's hand. *I don't want to wait.*

"I know." Jasper squeezed Tobias's trembling fingers, trying to convey a certainty he did not feel. "We'll leave as soon as we can." It was the closest he could come to defying his friend or saying no to Tobias's pleading look. He would do what he could to delay and let Tobias heal, but he knew he was going. He simply had to figure out when and how.

CHAPTER SEVEN

THE road got bad about ten miles outside of Brightam's Ford. It wasn't unexpected—motor traffic between towns was sparse, as most people and goods traveled via train, not car or truck—but Jasper slowed anyway, unwilling to risk damage to their vehicle so early in the journey.

Tobias stretched his hand across the cab and rested it lightly on Jasper's shoulder. *Why are we stopping?* The words were indistinct, as though he wasn't quite awake—also unsurprising, as Tobias was still exhausted from the injuries that Doctor Parks had treated four days earlier. He hadn't had the energy to argue when Jasper had insisted Kyree had to stay with Darius and Carla.

"We're not." Jasper risked a glance, smiling at the sleepy way Tobias blinked his eyes. "The road is getting bad. I don't want to risk blowing a tire."

Oh. Frowning, Tobias leaned forward to peer at the road. It was early still, and though it had been clear in town, patchy fog still lay over the road ahead of them, making it difficult to see all the cracks and potholes that were jarring the truck even at their slow pace. *Will it get better?*

"It might." Jasper shrugged. "This far away from the towns, the roads don't get much use, or care. I doubt this stretch sees more than twenty vehicles a year."

Tobias continued to frown, staring intently into the fog as Jasper carefully maneuvered around large cracks and potholes. *Will we get there on time?*

"Get where on time?" Jasper jerked the truck to the right, narrowly missing a large tree limb that blocked half the road. "It's at least two weeks to Shaleton this time of year, longer if some of the roads are washed out. We should make Durrysville before the storms start tonight, though."

Tobias bit his bottom lip. *Two weeks? That's*—he broke off, pointing with his right hand as his fingers clenched tightly around Jasper's shoulder. *Look out!*

Out of the corner of his eye, Jasper saw a tree slowly toppling toward the road, picking up speed as it fell. He stomped on the gas, jerking the wheel rapidly from right to left to avoid the pothole in front of him, relying on luck as much as speed to get them past the tree before it blocked the road in front of them or, worse, fell on them.

Branches scraped the truck bed cover, but the tree fell behind them, hitting the road with a loud thud. The ground shook. Both Jasper and Tobias looked back with wide eyes as Jasper brought the truck to a stop.

"Wait here." Jasper climbed out of the cab and circled the truck, looking carefully for any damage. The back was scraped and would need to be repainted during the dry season, but the cover lock was intact and the bumper was still sound. He was staring at the tree, wondering why it had chosen that moment to fall, when Tobias limped up next to him. "You shouldn't be on your feet."

Tobias shrugged, but eased himself onto the bumper of the truck before holding his hand out to Jasper. *It's big.*

"Too big." Jasper agreed, releasing Tobias's hand and walking to the edge of the road near the base of the fallen log. As he ran his hand over too-smooth wood on one side of the break, a chill ran down his spine. "Get back in the truck." He turned to see Tobias still sitting on the bumper. "Now."

Jasper moved faster than Tobias could hope to in his current condition, and had the truck started before Tobias climbed inside. He hit the gas as soon as the passenger side door closed, and the truck shot forward with a sudden burst of speed. Only quick reflexes saved Jasper from hitting the worst of the rough asphalt as they careened forward, leaving the fallen tree behind in a spray of gravel and dust.

It was only after they'd rounded the next two bends in the road that Jasper let off the gas pedal and allowed the vehicle to slow to a more reasonable speed, though he still kept it going faster than they'd been moving before the tree fell. The tight knot in his stomach that grew every time he thought about the fallen tree wouldn't let him slow any further.

As they rounded another bend, Tobias slid over on the bench seat so his shoulder was pressed against Jasper's. *What did you see?*

"The tree didn't fall across the road on its own. It was cut to fall that way. Someone cut the tree enough it would fall across the road when the storms knocked it down." Jasper resisted the urge to hit the gas pedal again. They were safe, so long as they kept moving.

Cut? Tobias turned around in the seat, climbing to his knees as he peered out the back window. *Do you think...?* He didn't have to finish the sentence for Jasper to know what he was asking.

"I don't know." He carefully maneuvered the vehicle around another obstacle in the road and then motioned for Tobias to sit back down. "It's... likely, though. Most people don't travel this far from town, especially in the wet season. We passed the last of the outlying farms a few miles back and we won't reach the next town for hours."

So they found us—me—again. Tobias lightly touched the fading bruise around his wrist.

"Probably." Jasper seized Tobias's fidgeting hand and gently squeezed his fingers. "They can't do anything while we're moving."

And when we stop?

"We'll figure something out."

It was a hollow reassurance.

THEY drove straight on until early afternoon, but hunger and the need to stretch his legs eventually forced Jasper to start looking for a good spot to pull over. The trees were thinner along this stretch of road, and about twenty minutes after he started looking, Jasper found a clearing wide enough he felt comfortable stopping in it. He turned the truck around so it was facing the road, ready for a quick getaway, before climbing out and stretching his aching back.

Tobias slid across the seat and sat with his feet hanging out of the truck, one arm braced on the steering wheel and the other resting on Jasper's shoulder. *Why did we stop?* He made no move to get out.

"We need to eat." Jasper turned, careful to keep Tobias's hand on his shoulder. "This is a good spot to stop."

Brown eyes darted around the clearing, peered down the road. *But—*

"We're only halfway to Durrysville, Tobias." Jasper kept his voice calm, trying to project a certainty that he did not feel. "If I don't eat and move a little now, we'll have to stop later when we might not be able to pull off the road so easily."

But—

Someone had put Tobias on repeat. Jasper squeezed the denim-clad knee and smiled in what he hoped was a reassuring manner. "This *is* a safe place to stop. The truck is parked so we can leave quickly. The space is open enough that if anyone comes, we'll be able to see them before they get to us."

Tobias still looked doubtful, but the longer they waited to eat, the longer it would be before they were on the road again, and Jasper wasn't any more anxious than Tobias to stay in one spot for long. He'd seen no further evidence that anyone else was on the road with them, but that meant little since he'd concentrated solely on putting as much distance between them and the downed tree as possible. "Do you want to get out while we eat, or would you like me to bring you some food?"

I'll, um, I'll get out. He slid to the ground, wincing as his feet took his weight. *Can we hurry, though?*

There was something in Tobias's tone that made stopping seem like a very bad idea, and Jasper found himself staying close to the truck and peering down the road as he relieved himself and stretched his legs, working kinks out of under-used muscles. Tobias stayed even closer, leaning on the vehicle as he grabbed food from the cooler in the truck bed and limping back toward the cab with his uneaten sandwich clenched tightly in one hand.

It fell from his hand as he froze, halfway into the truck. *We have to go!*

The words—and the panic behind them—slammed into Jasper's head, and he dropped his own food, just barely catching it before it hit the ground. "What?"

Please.

Jasper would never be sure if it was Tobias's pleading tone or the way he seemed ready to slide back out of the car that convinced him Tobias was earnest, but he nodded and quickly secured the cover over the truck bed. He could hear the distant roar of a motor by the time he reached the door.

Tobias slid across the seat and yanked Jasper into the cab. *Please hurry.*

The keys were in his pocket, caught on a fold. "I'm trying," he protested as he tugged. Both the rising sound of the motor and Tobias's anxiety were making it difficult to focus. The keys popped free and slipped from his fingers, tumbling to the mat with a musical clink. Jasper groped blindly for them, holding his sandwich up as his fingers fumbled over slips of paper and bottle caps before hitting the body heat-warmed metal of the keys.

They scratched against the ignition as Jasper tried once, twice, three times to slide the key into the narrow slot. It slipped in finally, and Jasper turned it with trembling fingers, fighting irrational fears of stalled engines and dead batteries. He held his breath as the key clicked, then the engine caught and roared to life with a rumble that ruled out a stealthy escape.

"Take this." Jasper thrust the sandwich at Tobias and then jerked the truck into gear and slammed his foot on the gas pedal. The vehicle shot forward, tires squealing as he turned sharply onto the road.

They're here! Tobias twisted in the seat, the sandwich forgotten beside him as he wrung his hands and peered out the back window. *Faster!* He clutched at Jasper's shoulder with a surprisingly strong grip that wrenched the wheel and almost sent them careening into a tree.

"Stop!" Jasper twisted his shoulder free as he jerked the wheel, narrowly avoiding a collision. "Sit so I can drive."

Tobias turned, pressing his body against Jasper's in a way that sent Jasper's thoughts places they shouldn't go, particularly in the middle of a car chase. *They're gaining on us.*

"I know." The cargo van behind them was the same distinctive emerald green as the coats of the men who had attacked them and featured writing and designs in the same dark purple as their tattoos. It was closer every time Jasper glanced in the rearview mirror, but the fog had returned and the dangerous road made it impossible to go faster.

The writing on the van remained elusive despite the increasing proximity of the other vehicle. The fancy script and mirror view made it impossible to read in the brief seconds Jasper could spare to look in the mirror. He peered harder, attempting to discern words in the jumble of backward script, then jerked his eyes back to the road as the truck hit a bump that set its passengers bouncing.

Jasper spared only a second to glance and determine if Tobias was okay. "What does the van say?"

Tobias twisted in the seat again, climbing to his knees to peer out the back window. *Um, something Industries. ClearSky Industries. There's something else written below it, but it's too small.* He stretched out, leaning over the seat to press his face against the back window. *Something about storms and... Sleet!*

The truck jumped forward as the van slammed into the back, jerked to the right, and only narrowly missed a fallen log as Jasper wrenched the wheel back, fighting for control. Tobias tumbled against the console, grabbing at Jasper's arm in an attempt to halt his fall and projecting a storm of curses that left Jasper's head spinning. It was hard to see, hard to focus, and—bam! The truck was hit again, jumping forward with a sickening lurch that left them half off the pavement.

Don't stop! Tobias scrambled back into the seat, bracing himself next to Jasper and watching the mirrors with wide eyes.

"I wasn't planning on it." If he could just... there. The truck rounded a curve and Jasper floored it, kicking the truck's powerful engine into high gear and sending it surging forward along the relatively straight stretch of road. The van picked up speed as well, but didn't surge as quickly as the truck with its more powerful engine. Slowly, the distance between them increased, and then leveled out, closer than Jasper would have liked, but far enough away that they were safe from further ramming.

For the moment, anyway. Jasper had no illusions about the tenacity of the people behind them or his ability to maintain his speed all the way to Durrysville. The road would worsen again or the men would become foolishly desperate and Jasper would find himself forced from the road... or worse.

He slowed slightly to take a curve and his stomach churned as he saw the van did not take the same precaution. It tilted slightly as it rounded the corner, but when all four wheels were on the ground again, it was significantly closer. "Sleet!" He risked a quick glance at Tobias. "Get the map. We need to lose them."

The map crinkled as Tobias draped it over his lap onto the seat. *Where are we?*

"About...." Jasper glanced at the odometer and quickly did the math in his head. "About fifty miles east of Brightam's Ford, heading toward Durrysville."

A long finger traced the line on the map as Jasper navigated around potholes and fallen limbs. *There's a turn off in a mile or two, I think. I don't remember passing it. If we take that, I, think that will take us to another road that goes to Durrysville.* He glanced up, and their eyes met in the rearview mirror. *If I'm reading this right, anyway.*

They would have to trust that he was. "Is it on the right or the left?"

Tobias traced the route again. *Right. Just after a big curve. I think.*

Jasper ignored the uncertainty in Tobias's mental voice, focusing instead on the road ahead and the van behind them. Ahead, the road vanished around a curve, and if Tobias was right.... They might be able to get away, if luck was on their side.

The curve drew closer, and Jasper watched the rearview mirror with apprehension. He'd have to time this just right, to avoid accelerating until they were out of sight, and to get fully off the road before the van rounded the curve. If it wasn't timed perfectly...

"Hold on. And tell me when they're out of sight," Jasper said, sparing a quick glance to be sure Tobias wouldn't be flung around the cab as they took the sharp turns. He lightly hit the brakes, slowing the truck as he approached the curve, watching the road carefully for the turn off, and hoping they wouldn't get to it before they momentarily lost sight of the van.

The big curve they were currently rounding straightened up ahead, only to turn back in the opposite direction a few hundred feet down the road, forming a giant "S." Just before the second turn, there was a gap in the trees, and what looked to be a dirt road heading through it. It was perfect, if they timed it right.

Now!

The word jolted into Jasper's head with an intensity he'd never felt before and he hit the gas without conscious thought. The truck engine roared. Jasper tightened his hands on the wheel, fighting to hold it to the road. The truck careened around the curve, barely keeping all four wheels on the ground, and covered the distance between the curve and the turn-off in just a few seconds. Jasper didn't look in the mirror as he turned the wheel, taking the turn at a speed far too dangerous for the angle of the curve and the dirt road they now found themselves on. He didn't want to know if the van had caught up, if the men in it had seen them turning off the main road. If he didn't know, he could pretend it had worked the way he'd planned.

He kept the pedal pushed all the way to the floor and the truck sped down the dirt path, only easing up when the bouncing from the uneven road threatened to tear the truck apart. It was only then that he dared ask. "Did we lose them?"

Tobias twisted around, peered out the back for a long moment. *I think so.* He turned back around and settled next to Jasper with their shoulders pressed together. *I can't see them. Or the road.*

Jasper eased off the gas a little more, slowing the truck to a speed more appropriate for the rough dirt path. It was barely wide enough for the truck, with branches occasionally scraping both windows, and the ground cracked behind them, the dry top layer of dirt giving way under the weight of the truck to the water-saturated mud underneath. If anyone thought to look, it would be obvious that they had passed that way.

He drove on in silence, focusing on the road so he could ignore the way Tobias's shoulder was pressed against his, the way Tobias's hand kept bumping against his thigh with every jolt of the truck. It was only so they could talk, nothing more.

A LARGE drop of rain hit the windshield, and then another. Jasper cursed and leaned forward, peering through the slanted glass and tree limbs at the rapidly gathering clouds above. He could feel Tobias's panic rising, and his own wasn't far behind—they were still more than a mile from Durrysville if he was reading the odometer and map correctly, and at least half of that was on the dirt path, which would be impassible once the rain truly started.

Tobias scooted closer, pressing his shoulder tightly against Jasper's, and twisted his fingers together in his lap. *Hurry, please.* The words were soft, barely a whisper in Jasper's mind, but the desperation behind them was clear.

"I'm trying." Jasper gently pushed forward on the gas pedal, easing the truck to a higher speed. The road ahead looked clear, but the dirt hid obstacles more easily than pavement, and the sparsely falling rain was increasing the danger.

They were in sight of the paved road that would take them into town when the rain started falling in earnest; a sudden torrent of large drops drenched the windshield and blinded Jasper. The truck skidded forward as he hit the brakes, slipping in the new mud, and he fumbled desperately for the wipers as he struggled to keep the vehicle straight.

The back end slid as they crept forward, barely staying on the path. Jasper's eyes were riveted on the road ahead, but he could feel Tobias next to him, frozen in his seat, more still than Jasper had seen him since they'd met. Jasper wanted to offer comfort, to pat a knee or squeeze a hand, but he couldn't release the steering wheel, even for a second.

Lightning flashed in the sky as Jasper carefully navigated the turn onto the paved road. The lightning was still distant, close enough to be seen, but far enough away that there was a pause before the thunder rumbled lightly. The drops hitting the windshield were large and coming fast, but they were still water, not ice.

As soon as the truck had fully turned, Jasper hit the gas hard, shooting the truck forward over the rain-slicked pavement. A spray of water arced in their wake as the truck hit puddle after puddle, but this close to town the road was smooth, and he could again give into the urgency that had been driving him all day.

Durrysville was boarded up, shut tight against the evening's storms, but Jasper had been there once before, not long after he'd moved inland, and was able to find the local inn even in the dark and rain. It didn't take long to secure a room—the owner did not want to be out in the storm any more than Jasper did, and there was no question of turning someone away once the storms had started—and they were able to slip inside, bags in hand, before the wind picked up and the true lashing rain began.

The room was warm and secure, with thick walls and no windows, and for once, Jasper found the enclosure comforting. He sighed, slipped off his shoes, and collapsed onto one of the twin beds, vaguely noting Tobias doing the same on the other. He could barely keep his eyes open.

A warm hand stretched across the gap, brushing against Jasper's arm. *Good night.*

"Night," he mumbled in return, as he rolled closer to the warmth of Tobias's hand and let sleep claim him.

CHAPTER EIGHT

DESPITE the excitement, Jasper didn't sleep well, tossing and turning fitfully through the night and waking several times to rumbling thunder and pounding rain and sleet. The last time he woke, the air was quiet, heavy with moisture that stuck in his throat even in the secure walls of the rented room. Sleep was elusive, his muscles itching to move as he rolled and stretched beneath the sheets.

When Jasper gave in to the inevitable and opened his eyes, Tobias was still asleep, sprawled out across the other bed, the covers tangled around his legs and one arm hanging into the gap between the beds. Jasper rolled onto his side to watch the other man sleep; he wondered at the twisting in his stomach as his eyes followed the tanned arm up to the slender figure resting on the bed.

The feeling deep in his gut grew as his eyes slid over the figure to the mess of sheets and blanket. The distance between them stretched, the three foot gap seeming wider than it really was. Somehow, over the past few weeks, without Jasper realizing it, sharing a bed with Tobias had evolved from an act of necessity into a luxury.

Smiling softly, he crossed the distance between them and gently untangled the sheet from around Tobias's legs, arranging it over his shoulders. There was no reason for them both to be up this early; Jasper planned to grab some fresh food as well as a few additional things he'd thought of in route from Brightam's Ford. He needed to send a message to Darius and Carla as well, in the hopes that they'd know more about the men now that they had a name to associate with them.

As Jasper picked up Tobias's hand to tuck it back in the bed, the younger man stirred, rolled slightly, and tugged Jasper toward him. One brown eye opened and peered out from under a mop of tangled curls. *Is it time to get up already?* The urgency from the previous day was missing from the sleep-muddled words.

"I was going to send a message to Darius, do some shopping. You can sleep if you want." Jasper sat down on the edge of the bed, smiled down into Tobias's sleepy eyes. "It will take two days to get to the next town, so we can leave a little later if we want."

Two days? Tobias's eyes widened as his hand tightened around Jasper's.

Jasper could feel the way Tobias's clenched fingers quivered and didn't need to be told what was causing his sudden panic. "There's a spot about halfway that will work for a night, but nothing was ever built there," he soothed, smiling and squeezing a sheet-covered shoulder. "We'll be safe from the storms there."

Are you sure? Tobias clenched his fingers tighter. *If it's safe, why didn't they build? Why isn't there a town or something there?*

"The area isn't suitable." Jasper shifted, turning to look straight into Tobias's worried eyes. "There's a large cave, it's supposed to be fitted with a wall, or something, to keep the weather out."

It's just a cave? There's no way we can make the next town? No other place to shelter?

"It's too far. The land between here and Folsom's Hollow isn't suitable for building. The cave is safe enough. We won't be the first to shelter there. We'll be safe, I promise."

Tobias stared back for a long moment, nodded. *Good.* His eyes slipped shut as his body relaxed again, his fingers loosening on Jasper's hand. *Don't want to get caught in a storm again. I don't like them.*

"No one does." Though Tobias had more experience with them than most, and was able to say so with far more authority than Jasper.

Yeah, well.... Tobias grinned, his eyes opening just enough to sparkle mischievously at Jasper before he rolled over and pulled Jasper fully onto the small bed.

Jasper yelped, too surprised to protest more, and blinked when Tobias let his eyes drift fully shut again. "Tobias?" He did *not* need to spend the morning lying next to Tobias, not when there were things to be done.

What? came the all too innocent sounding response, the sleepiness in it belied by the strength with which Tobias clutched Jasper's hand. *You have to still be tired.*

Jasper wanted to protest that he wasn't still recovering from injuries, that he didn't need much sleep, that there were things he needed to do before they could leave, any number of excuses he could come up with, but his limbs were heavy, the bed soft, and Tobias's body warm next to him. A few minutes couldn't hurt. He would lay there, rest a bit, let Tobias fall back asleep, and then go do what needed to be done.

He wasn't giving in, just humoring his... companion. Friend. Whatever he was.

THE post office had drastically cut down their hours due to the storms, but they sold envelopes and stamps and were still making deliveries as far as Brightam's Ford, which was all Jasper really needed. The inn had provided a pen and paper enough for him to scribble a note to Darius, telling him of their encounter on the road and what they'd seen on the truck.

He didn't start the note until he got to the post office, afraid that if he did, they'd have already cut the route back to Brightam's Ford. When the clerk cheerfully informed him that they were still delivering—though she would make no promises about for how much longer—he had started scratching away at the hotel stationery.

He was almost done when a commotion arose across the street at the store where Tobias had gone to browse. Jasper scrawled the last line and signed quickly, stuffing the paper into the envelope and tossing it to the clerk with a shout of thanks as he ran out the door.

Just as Jasper reached the street, Tobias stumbled out of the shop, shoved by a pair of hands and followed by angry shouts. He staggered a few steps, almost falling before he regained his balance and limped to Jasper.

"What happened?" The mob pouring out of the shop did not look happy, and people from neighboring businesses, including the post office Jasper had just left, were joining them, scowling and casting threatening looks toward Tobias even before the low murmur that circled the crowd told the newcomers what had transpired inside the store.

I, uh, Tobias looked around with wide eyes, pressed himself closer to Jasper's side. *I sent to one of them. The woman in the purple.* He glanced over at a woman in the center of the crowd with a bright purple dress and a canvas bag over her arm.

"Tobias...." Jasper kept his voice soft and out of the ears of the nearest bystanders.

It was an accident! Tobias pressed close to Jasper. The crowd grumbled in agitation, with several people stepping closer, steely gazes directed at Tobias.

"How?" Jasper turned shocked eyes toward Tobias. "Can't you control it?" If Tobias was losing control....

Yes! I just.... He scanned the crowd, pulling Jasper with him as he backed away from the main group. *She bumped into me and I just told her to go ahead. I wasn't thinking. I didn't want to send anything to anyone; just to look and pick something out, I swear! I didn't even realize that she would hear me until I'd already sent it, and then it was too late and she was all mad and screaming about devils and spirits and—*

The stream cut off as strong hands yanked Jasper backward. People surged around him and cut off his view of Tobias. "Wait! Stop!" He struggled to get free, twisting his shoulders, but the tight grip on his forearms didn't loosen as he was dragged backward through the crowd.

"Just calm down and we'll take care of it."

Jasper turned his head to see the tall, heavy-set man who had been behind him at the post office now restrained his left arm with thick fingers. "Take care of what?" He tried to jerk his arm free again, but the man's fingers only tightened, squeezing with enough force to leave a bruise.

"The boy," the man growled. "He's got you under some sort of spell, or somethin'. It's not natural talkin' like that."

It took a moment to register that the man was referring to Tobias. Jasper had long since stopped thinking of him as a boy, though he remembered his initial impression as his mind made the connection. "There's nothing to take care of! He didn't do anything!"

"He's got you out traveling in the storms." The man looked Jasper straight in the eye, his expression steely. "We've seen this before. Only thing to do is run them out of town. We'll put you up for a few days and see if someone can't help you get back home."

"I don't *need* to get back home. I need to keep going. I brought him with me, not the other way around."

"He's got you under a strong spell, if you believe that."

"There's no spell!" Jasper twisted again, ignoring the pain as the man's fingers dug deep into his flesh. He *needed* to get free, needed to see what the mob was doing to Tobias. He could hear them, yelling and taunting, making threats he was afraid they'd carry out. "He's just a friend!" Desperate to do something, he grabbed the man's shirt with his free hand and pulled him close, ready to start making threats of his own if something didn't change... immediately.

"People like that ain't friends to nobody."

Let him go!

The words slammed into Jasper, snapping his mouth shut and sending him staggering back a step before he was jerked up short by the other man's tight hold on his arm. Jasper let go of the man's shirt, his fingers involuntarily relaxing, at the same moment the man let go. Jasper's arm tingled as blood rushed back to the area. "Tobias?"

Come on!

The crowd parted in front of Tobias, sweeping Jasper with it in the people's haste to keep away from the strange young man. He tore his shirt as he fought his way free of well-meaning, but misguided townsfolk, and struggled forward against the flow of people.

He was almost to Tobias when the man from the post office stepped into his path, his legs spread wide and hands balled in fists on his hips.

"I ain't gonna let you go."

"It's not your decision." Jasper dodged and shouldered his way through the crowd, trying to find the path of least resistance, but it opposed him even as it parted around the burly man, and Jasper once again found himself blocked by a flannel covered shoulder and a stern look. "Let me through."

"No." The man crossed massive arms crossed over a barrel thick chest as he widened his stance. "He's just gonna hurt you."

"No. He won't." Jasper craned his neck, peering over the man's wide shoulder in an attempt to find Tobias in the crowd. "And it's not your concern if he does."

"It is if he does it in my town."

I'm not *going to hurt him!* The crowd stepped back, an angry murmur coursing through it as Tobias, his hands clenched into fists and his expression venomous, appeared at the man's left elbow. *Let. Him. Go.*

There was a tense moment, the air thick with anticipation, then the man stepped back, a dazed look on his face, and Tobias immediately grabbed Jasper's arm and yanked him forward. Jasper stumbled as he tried to keep up with Tobias's rapid pace, and to process what had just happened through his growing headache. "What...?" he started, only to be cut off as Tobias steered him around a corner.

Come on! We can't... they're not going to... we have to leave.

That was obvious, even through the haze in Jasper's head, though how wasn't quite as clear. They hadn't picked up any of the things they'd planned to get, hadn't even re-loaded the truck or returned the key to the innkeeper. "The truck... the inn...." He wasn't sure what he was trying to say.

I know. This way. It wasn't the way they had come—that was blocked by the crowd—but Tobias showed incredible insight in navigating through the small town, pulling Jasper down back alleys that led to the inn in a remarkably short time.

"How did you...?" Jasper broke off, wincing and staggering to a stop as the pain in his head suddenly blossomed, nearly blinding him. "Sleet." He pinched the bridge of his nose, closed his eyes, and sank down against the nearest wall. The world narrowed to the sharp staccato thud of his heartbeat echoing in his ears and to the pressure that spread from his sinus cavity and crept around his skull to the back of his neck.

I'm sorry. Tobias slowly massaged Jasper's tense muscles and the pressure in his head gradually vanished.

Carefully, Jasper looked up, ready to snap his eyes back closed if the light proved to be too much. It was bright but not unbearable, and he blinked at Tobias, trying to make sense of the last few minutes. "How... what...?" He didn't know what to ask.

Tobias stood, pulled Jasper to his feet. *Everyone was wondering which way I'd run, thinking about how to get back here, and trying to decide if they should stop me. They wanted me to leave, but not with you. I picked up how to get here from their thoughts.*

That answered one question. "Do you—" Jasper shook his head. He didn't want to know how often Tobias picked things up out of his thoughts. "How did... how did you get that man to move?" And why was he so persistent... though that wasn't a question Tobias would be able to answer.

I, um.... Tobias ducked his head as he led Jasper into their room. He tried to pull away, heading toward the bag on the chair, but Jasper tightened his fingers, refusing to let go until his question was answered.

"Tobias?"

I, uh, don't know how exactly to explain it.

"Try. Please." He needed to know, needed to understand what had happened out there.

Um, I.... Hail! Tobias whipped around, his eyes locking on the door. *They're coming here. They want... we need to leave. Now.* He grabbed the bag from the chair, stuffed the few clothes that were laying out into it, and fled.

Jasper tossed the room key onto the dresser as he followed.

THEY encountered the roadblock two streets away from the hotel. Jasper cursed and slammed on the brakes. The truck skidded and squealed to a stop just yards away from the line of people stretched across the street. Several flinched, but they all held their ground.

"Do you know another way?" They weren't taking the route Jasper knew, nor would the truck fit through the back alleys Tobias had used to get them back to the room.

Tobias stared out at the blockade of people, his mouth drawn in a thin line and his eyes focused. *Turn around, then go left.*

The turn was tricky on the narrow street, and the townsfolk pressed closer, a few brave souls grabbing at the door handles and banging on the windows with heavy objects. Tobias slid to the middle of the seat, his hand tight on Jasper's arm, his whole body shaking. *Hurry!*

"I'm trying." He just had to get… there. The engine roared as the truck shot forward, tires squealing as it careened around the corner into a narrow road with cars lined along one side.

Faster!

Two cars stopped at the far end of the lane, blocking the exit. A glance in the rearview mirror showed two more pulling in behind them, the man from the post office behind one of the wheels. They were at the mercy of the town, and none of the people looked happy.

"Sleet!" Jasper banged his hand on the wheel, let off the gas.

No! Keep going!

Pressure built inside Jasper's head. His foot twitched once, twice, he opened his mouth to argue… then he slammed on the gas, barely keeping the truck under control as it barreled down the alley. He nicked a mirror, then a bumper. The crunch of metal echoed through the cab, and yet he couldn't stop. He pushed his foot down harder as they got closer to the end of the road.

The cars weren't moving. They were going to crash, die, never make it to Shaleton, never find Tobias's sister or figure out who the men who wanted him were. It was all going to be over in just a moment and still Jasper couldn't take his foot off the gas, didn't *want* to take his foot off the gas.

As they got closer, Jasper could hear screaming, see the townsfolk losing their resolve and scattering away, fleeing into the relative safety of buildings and alleys. The cars stayed where they were, the drivers' expressions resolute as the truck got within two hundred yards, a hundred, fifty... and then the cars backed up. Metal scratched against brick and wood as they took the sharp turn at high speed, careened backward down the cross street, and knocked into mailboxes and potted plants as they pulled into gravel drives.

Jasper whirled the steering wheel, his foot never leaving the gas. As the truck turned, everything inside went flying from one side to the other. Tobias slammed into Jasper, then the window. Still, Jasper didn't let up, barreling down on people who scattered and screamed as they dove out of the truck's path.

Turn there! Tobias pulled himself up on the doorframe, pointed to the wide cross street ahead.

"Which way?" He didn't have time to wonder at Tobias's voice in his head without touch, at Tobias's presence on the other side of the truck, at how Tobias knew where they needed to go even though he'd never been to Durrysville before. They needed to go, to keep moving, or surely Jasper wouldn't be able to leave for quite some time, and not with Tobias. The thought terrified him even more than the way his foot wouldn't leave the gas pedal and the way he'd stopped caring about who or what he hurt in his haste to get out of town.

Right. Go right. Tobias grabbed the panic handle and twisted in his seat, looking with wide eyes out the windows. *Hurry. They're trying to get a solid roadblock up at the edge of town. We need to beat them.*

The truck wouldn't go any faster, not on the winding route through narrow alleys. Jasper knew it and yet his foot pressed harder, urging the truck to greater speeds, racing past the people lining the street. The whole town had turned out, even small children huddled at the edge of properties and threw rocks and sticks at the rapidly moving vehicle.

The clatter of stone on metal and glass was distracting, frightening, but Jasper didn't dare take his eyes off the road ahead as he whipped the truck around curves at speeds far too dangerous according to the voice of reason in the back of his head. Tobias's silent directions overrode reason and they careened through the town, taking six more turns to end up on the straight road out, heading toward Folsom's Hollow.

The last two buildings on the edge of town proper were houses, and it looked as though everything the people who lived in them owned had been dragged out onto the road, creating an ever-growing pile of rubble. Chairs, tables, even a bed, were piled in a haphazard pile that kept growing as people pulled out doors, furniture, even a large mirror.

Jasper didn't hesitate, aiming the truck toward what looked to be the weakest spot and letting his foot push as hard as it could. The townsfolk ran, barely getting away before the truck hit, sending wood flying into the air, scattering off the truck, and crunching beneath the tires.

Tobias peered out the back window, watching the townsfolk as they gathered in the center of the road. Jasper glimpsed it in the mirror, but didn't stop, didn't think about the property he'd just destroyed or the people he'd almost hurt. He just kept going, pushing the truck as fast as he could and leaving the angry town in the dust.

CHAPTER NINE

THE road on the east side of Durrysville was in decent condition, at least close to town, and Jasper took full advantage of the smooth pavement for as long as possible, quickly putting distance between them and the town even after the urgent need to get out had faded. Tobias stayed on his knees, peering out the back window until long after the town could no longer be seen behind them. When he finally settled, he leaned against the passenger door, his hands twisting in his lap and his eyes looking everywhere but at Jasper.

They rode in silence for several miles, Jasper concentrating on the road ahead and on keeping the truck moving as fast as possible so he wouldn't have to focus on the distance separating him from his passenger, wouldn't have to think about what had happened in the town. They couldn't talk like this, not in a way Jasper was willing to risk, not with Tobias's hands firmly in his lap and the entire bench seat between them. The length of the seat seemed to increase with each question Jasper wanted to ask, with each mile that passed without conversation.

It was past midday before he could let himself ease off the gas and pull the truck to the side of the road. He had long since slowed in deference to the worsening pavement, his foot twitching and his mouth opening with a question every time he hit the brakes, but after glancing at the silent figure on the other side of the cab, he always snapped it closed and forced himself to drive on.

Tobias looked up as the truck stopped, his deep brown eyes full of questions, but he made no move to bridge the distance between them. When Jasper turned, Tobias pressed himself closer to the door, squeezed his legs together, and wrapped his arms around his chest.

Jasper stretched out his hand, let it drop to the seat when Tobias made no move to take it. "Are you hungry?"

An almost imperceptible shake of the head was his only answer.

He waited a moment, hoping for further response. None came. "Tobias...." he started, stopping again when Tobias turned away, staring out the window into the field they were parked beside. Jasper sighed and stretched his hand across the seat again even as he wondered if he needed to "Please...."

Tobias slowly slid his hand along the leather seat and curled his warm fingers around Jasper's. *Can we please just keep going? I just want to get away from—to get to Shaleton. To Sam.*

Jasper didn't miss the odd pause, or the correction in wording. "You're going to have to talk to me eventually. I need to understand what happened."

Yeah, I know. Tobias smiled faintly. *But not now, okay? Just... drive, please?* He twisted toward the window, casting a worried glance at Jasper before returning his gaze to the field again. *I'll, um, I'll tell you when... when we stop for the night, okay?*

There was too much he needed to know, too many heavy questions pressing down on his mind, skittering at the edge of his awareness like a headache that was about to start. He shook his head, squeezed Tobias's hand tighter. "I need—"

Please. Just... just drive. Tobias folded his hand back into his lap, pressed his body more tightly against the door and rested his forehead against the glass of the window.

Jasper watched him for a minute before nodding and turning the key. "All right. We'll talk when we get there." He wasn't waiting any longer than that.

THE wind was blowing hard, bending tree branches and flattening the grass. Lightning flashed in the distance, the soft rumble of thunder coming seconds after each flash in the sky. The late afternoon sun fought to get through the gathering clouds, giving the road an eerie twilight look.

The steel doors fitted to the cave entrance were shut when Jasper stopped in front of them. He contemplated the thick bar fastened across the opening and let the truck engine idle. "Come on." He pushed the gear stick up, leaving the truck in park as he climbed out.

Staring at the bar with a distressed look on his face, Tobias slowly limped the few yards to the door.

"We'll be safe for the night here. Come on." Jasper pushed, tipping his end of the bar up and letting it slide until it hit rock. "Tobias?" He eased the bar back into its cradle. "I can't do this by myself."

Tobias focused, blinked, and brushed his hand against Jasper's shoulder. *Sorry.* Then the touch was gone and Tobias's hands were positioned under the bar, ready to push up.

It was awkward—the bar was sturdy and long, though surprisingly light for its size—but they opened the doors, dragged the bar in, and propped it against the cave wall so they could use it to secure the doors from the inside. Tobias leaned against the wall next to it and sank down, the stones of the cave catching his shirt and pulling it up behind his head.

The truck fit just about perfectly in the entrance, leaving just enough room to unload it and secure the doors and providing additional protection to the wider, sparsely furnished back area. Jasper left the keys in the ignition when he climbed out and held a hand out to Tobias. "Let's get this shut and unload for the night."

Tobias ignored the hand, slowly pushed himself to his feet, and grabbed his end of the bar. He stayed far from Jasper as they unloaded, jerking his hand away every time Jasper came close to touching him. When Jasper caught it, he tensed, tugging against Jasper's secure grip.

Please don't. Just, let's get inside, yeah? Get settled. He yanked hard, pulling free, and headed toward the back of the cave with a bag and a blanket.

Jasper followed, pausing only to secure the bed cover after grabbing his own things, and found Tobias had already spread pallets out on the floor and removed his shirt and shoes. He sat on the makeshift bedding, watching Jasper coolly, his whole body radiating a tension so strong Jasper could feel it halfway across the cave. There was something bothering him, and Jasper was starting to think it was more than what had happened in Durrysville. "Are you okay?"

Tobias nodded, drew his knees into his chest, and rested his chin on them as he watched Jasper putter around, thinking up little, stupid things that didn't really need to be done but that gave him an excuse not to sit, not to start the conversation he'd been wanting to have all day but still dreaded. It was only when Tobias stretched out his arm and looked at him with a pleading expression that Jasper came over and sat down next to Tobias. "Can we...?" he began, but was cut off by a shake of Tobias's hand as the younger man lay down.

I'm sorry. His eyes closed, his hand relaxed in Jasper's.

"For what?" But then he didn't need to ask. Tobias's whole body relaxed, his hand falling limply to the pallet and Jasper's world exploded into excruciating pain that left him unable to see, unable to move, unable to think. He fell backward, not noticing as his head hit the rock under the thin pillow, and struggled to pull the blanket up as protection against the coming cold. Consciousness fled before he'd found it.

THE lantern was burning low, but the light was too bright and sent stabbing pains through Jasper's skull. He rolled, fumbled for the switch, and plunged the cave into blessed darkness with a flick of his wrist. He groaned as he rolled back, fumbled for the blanket and arranged it over his shoulders as he let his eyes fall shut again. "Tobias?"

He got no answer, but the warm body next to him shifted, and an arm was flung across his chest, a leg hooked over his. Soft hair tickled the underside of his chin and slow, steady breath ghosted across the exposed skin of his chest as Tobias pressed close, pillowing his head on Jasper's shoulder and relaxing with the heavy, limp weight of someone who wasn't going to move for some time.

"Tobias, what...?" he started, then stopped, letting his raised hand drop back to the pallet and his muscles relax further. His head was pounding, his shoulders ached, and he was far too tired to fight what was clearly a losing battle. It wasn't uncomfortable to have Tobias draped across him, just unexpected. Nor, he realized as he drifted off to sleep again, was it unwanted.

THE darkness was overwhelming, pressing down on Jasper, leaving him cold despite the warm body draped across his chest. He rubbed his eyes with his free hand, blinked several times, but the darkness was absolute. If the sun was out, none of the rays were getting past the door in the front of the cave.

Moving slowly so as not to strain sore muscles or wake Tobias, he fumbled for the lantern. He hit it once, twice, and nearly knocked it over before he was able to grab the handle and pull it closer so he could properly flick the switch. He groaned as the light pierced his skull, turning his head away and squeezing his eyes shut against the sudden onslaught.

Jasper? Tobias's hand slid over Jasper's chest and his fingers lightly touched Jasper's temple. *What's wrong?*

"Head—" he started, stopping halfway through the word to lower his voice to a whisper. "Headache." Even that hurt a little, echoing in his skull until his ears were ringing.

Sorry. Here.

The now-familiar sensation enveloped Jasper, but stopped too soon, leaving him with tight shoulders and a slight pressure behind his eyes. He waited a minute, but the sensation didn't return and Tobias's weight grew heavy and still on his chest. He lifted his head, squinted at the still figure wrapped around him. "Tobias?"

I'll finish. He tilted his head and gave Jasper a good view of drooping eyelids and shadowy bags under his eyes. *Just give me a minute, okay?*

"No." He rolled them both over, ignoring his headache as he pinned Tobias to the pallet. It was just a normal headache now, something he'd get from too little sleep or low blood sugar—not anything to worry about. The weariness on Tobias's face and the way his limbs flopped as they rolled, however, were a different story. "What did you do?"

Tobias stared up at him, his eyelids dropping as Jasper waited patiently, his own gaze steady. It didn't take long for Tobias's expression to wilt and his eyes to slip closed. *I kept the pain away while you drove. I knew you wouldn't be able to drive if I didn't, and we couldn't stop, not close to the town. They would have....* He opened his eyes, shook his head. *I don't know, but it wouldn't have been good.*

"We could have stopped—"

No. His head rolled back and forth in an exaggerated shake. *I don't think I would have been able to take it all away by the time we stopped. It was hard enough to just keep doing what I was doing. That's why I fell asleep right away. I couldn't... I'm sorry... I didn't have the energy. I used too much earlier.*

That was the real question. "What did you do earlier?"

Tobias's eyes met Jasper's for a brief moment. *You're not going to like this.*

Flashes of an uncontrollable need to *go*, of an uncontrollable urge to get out of town without care for how or why, of driving recklessly, of people almost hurt and of property damaged played through Jasper's mind. No, he wasn't going to like it. He knew that. He still needed to know. "Tell me."

Tobias wriggled, freeing himself from Jasper's grasp, and sat up, his back to Jasper, his knees pulled up to his chest and his chin resting on them. Slowly, one hand slid back and one finger lightly touched the side of Jasper's hand. *I, um, I projected.*

Jasper watched the still figure, waiting for further elaboration, worried at Tobias's stillness and reluctance to talk. "I don't know what that means," he eventually ventured, breaking the painful silence.

Tobias visibly deflated. His shoulders slumped forward and his finger almost left Jasper's hand. *I pushed what I was thinking... feeling... onto the people in that town.* He looked back over his shoulder, chewing on his bottom lip as his eyes met Jasper's. *Onto you.* He turned his head away, burying his face in the arm wrapped around his knees.

Jasper's mouth opened and closed several times as he tried to figure out how to respond to that... if he should respond to that. If he understood correctly it explained what he'd done in town, why he'd been so panicked, so reckless, but his mind refused to wrap around the idea. "I...."

Let me show you. Tobias's hand slid back, fully enveloping Jasper's, and then the world changed.

THE *crowd in the town yelled and threw things at Tobias and told him to get out without caring that they were keeping him from the only person who could help him leave. He tried to push through, slipping around people who recoiled if he moved to touch them, taking advantage of their fear and superstition to get to Jasper.*

He stretched up, standing on his toes as he tried to see over the crowd, but there were too many people to pick out the one he wanted. Sighing, Tobias went back down onto flat feet and opened his mind to the surface thoughts of the crowd. The onslaught was painful, disorienting, and he stumbled into someone who recoiled in horror. The man's mental shriek pierced Tobias's skull as the audible one pierced his ears.

He staggered away, hands over his ears and his eyes closed, blindly heading in the direction the onslaught of thoughts indicated he could find Jasper. The pain faded as he focused on those thoughts, and he picked up speed, moving as quickly as his still-healing feet and the crowd let him. He could sense Jasper now, could almost reach him, but the crowd was tighter here, angrier. He saw a man dragging Jasper away, saw Jasper struggling to get free, and his fear and anger exploded.

Let him go! *He put all of his fear, his anger, and his desire to free his companion into the words, sending the feelings along with the thoughts, making the man want to let go. He started forward as soon as Jasper was free, but was stopped by the crowd and forced to watch as Jasper was grabbed again, broke free, and was stopped by the man who had originally held him.*

He was saying something, words Tobias couldn't hear over the angry murmur of the crowd, and he pushed forward, projecting his desire to everyone around him, and reached them just in time to hear the man suggest he would hurt Jasper. His blood rushed his ears, blocking out most of Jasper's protest and whatever the man said in response.

Let. Him. Go. *He sent, his fists clenched and his need to get that man away from Jasper sent forcefully with every word. His blood simmered as he waited, watching the man give in to feelings not his own and step back. Tobias pounced, grabbed Jasper's arm, and took advantage of the crowd's confusion to break free by following the twisting trail to freedom he'd gleaned from their minds.*

JASPER blinked, shaking his head to clear it as he reoriented his senses to the cool cave and dim lantern light. The hand over his was warm and comforting, but his stomach twisted as his mind processed what he'd just been shown and it took every ounce of willpower he possessed not to pull back, not to scramble across the cave and create an illusion of safety and resistance to his companion's strange powers.

Jasper?

He noticed Tobias's hand moving more than he heard the quiet word amidst his jumbled thoughts, and he looked up to see Tobias worrying his bottom lip. "Yeah?"

Are you… did that… should I… do you…? He raked his hair back from his forehead and sighed, his shoulders slumping as he peered into

Jasper's eyes, looking for the answer to a question Jasper didn't understand.

"I don't know." It was the only honest answer he could give. He was glad Tobias had gotten them out of Durrysville, didn't want to think about what would have happened if Tobias hadn't been able to make the burly man leave him alone, but he didn't like what he'd felt, what he'd seen, what Tobias had showed him. He didn't like the idea of Tobias making people do things, no matter the justification, *really* didn't like the idea of his own vulnerability to this particular talent Tobias possessed. He didn't want to know how much of the drive out was feelings Tobias·had projected onto him.

Or maybe he did. "What did you do to me?" he asked, immediately regretting it as his stomach tightened and his heart rate increased, but unable to take the words back.

Um. Tobias furrowed his brow, sucked his bottom lip further into his mouth. *Are you sure you want me to show you?*

"I don't want you to show me. I'd be happier not knowing about this at all. But now that I do, I need to know how much of what I did back there was from me and how much of it was from you. I don't drive like that, Tobias! I almost hit people! I know I damaged the truck, damaged things in the town!" He wanted to get up, to pace the cave and rant and scream, but the thought of the worse headache he would end up with if Tobias tried to respond stopped him, and he made himself sit still, made himself keep his hand under Tobias's.

We needed to go.

"So that makes it okay? We had to get out of Durrysville so as long as we managed that it didn't matter how we did it?"

They were going to separate us, keep you there or take you back home and force me out into the woods, into the storms! You don't know what they were thinking, what they wanted to do, what they thought I was! They wanted to drive me out of town and into the storms. I would have had to find my own shelter, find my own way to the next, try to find someone else who would help me, try to get to Shaleton—to Samantha—on my own. Tobias squeezed Jasper's hand, looked at him with a desperate expression. *I couldn't—can't—do that.*

"I know what they wanted to do. They told me." Jasper kept his voice harsh, focused on the churning in his gut and the way he'd plowed through the barrier at the edge of town rather than the pleading brown eyes that could have melted his heart. "It doesn't mean that making them—making *me*—do things is okay. There had to be another way!"

I didn't make anyone do *anything. I can't. I can only make people feel things, not do them!*

"And think things? What about that?"

Tobias's eyes closed and his shoulders fell forward, making Jasper's stomach drop. *Sometimes. My thoughts sound too much like me, not them. It's hard to match patterns and tone and if you don't get it exactly right, they just hear me in their head like you do now instead of believing that they thought something. Maybe I'd be better if I practiced, but I haven't even tried in years.*

"But you make people feel things all the time?"

No! Tobias's eyes snapped open and he shook his head violently. *I did something like it with thoughts when I escaped the men who had me, but other than that, yesterday in that town was the only time I've done it on purpose since I left home. I don't like to do it, didn't want to do it, I just couldn't think of any other way.*

"All right." Jasper nodded, started to smile, but then something about what Tobias had just said hit him hard like a punch to the gut and he grabbed Tobias's wrist to stop him from pulling away. "You said 'on purpose'."

Tobias looked at him blankly. *Yeah... so?*

"Does that mean...." He stopped, swallowed around the lump in his throat. "Does that mean you've done it accidentally?" The small nod was sufficient answer to make his heart sink and his gut twist. "Is that why I was so anxious to leave Darius's? Why I was so desperate to be off with you that I would barely listen to my best friend?"

Tobias tore his gaze away, pulled his knees back up to his chest. Jasper could practically feel the nervousness radiating off him. *I don't know. Some of it, maybe.*

Jasper jerked his hand back, unable to handle the contact for one second longer. "When were you going to tell me? After I drove you across half the continent? Or maybe after I'd gotten you and your sister home? Or never? Were you just planning on using me to accomplish your little scheme and then leave me to wonder why I felt the way I did?" He rose, stalking away so he wouldn't have to look at Tobias, wouldn't have to hear him.

If I did, it wasn't intentional! Tobias lunged forward, catching Jasper's ankle and holding on tightly. *At home, I have to try to make people feel things. We all resist it some, we all send our emotions if we can so we all know what our friends really think and feel and want. I didn't know you weren't resisting, didn't know it was making you feel anything, didn't know you were acting on my feelings. I'm sorry.*

Jasper looked down, jerked his foot free. "Yeah. I bet you are."

CHAPTER
TEN

THE cave was too small. No matter where Jasper moved, he could still see Tobias sitting on the pallet, the blanket draped around his shoulders and his eyes following Jasper as he paced. Even going to the truck didn't provide relief, and sliding back the cover over the small opening on the door only confirmed that too much of the day had been wasted sleeping and arguing for them to leave before the next morning. They were stuck here for another sixteen or so hours and then there was the drive to the next town, trapped together in the cab of the truck. Jasper was going to be crazy by the time he was able to get any real distance from Tobias.

He spun around so he could pace back to the other end of the cave, but stopped short when he saw Tobias had risen and crossed the distance between them. "What?" he snapped in a tone far harsher than any he was accustomed to using.

Tobias reached out, but Jasper jerked away, unwilling to be touched right then. He backed up a few steps, his eyes never leaving Tobias. It was only so he wouldn't be surprised again, he told himself, though his eyes were drawn to the exposed collarbone where the blanket was slipping down Tobias's shoulder. He wasn't—wouldn't— think those thoughts, especially not after what he'd been told. He couldn't trust that the feeling was his, couldn't trust that any of his feelings were his.

He forced his eyes up to Tobias's face. "I don't particularly want to talk to you right now." He received no response, but with the distance between them, he didn't want or expect one. "It's too late in the day to go anywhere. We'll leave in the morning and I'll take you to the next town." As tempting as the idea was, he wouldn't abandon Tobias out in the wilds. Once he was in civilization, however, there was no need to be concerned any longer. He'd have done far more than most would have given under the circumstances and would have no need to worry about Tobias any longer.

Long seconds passed as they stared at each other, neither moving. Seconds turned into minutes and still Jasper waited, his arms crossed across his chest, his body tense and poised to flee at the first sign of movement toward him. He wasn't backing down, wasn't moving, wasn't going to give in no matter how long Tobias waited.

Tobias reached forward, stopped when Jasper jerked back, and let his hand drop to his side as his shoulders slumped forward and the corners of his mouth drooped. He turned, surprising Jasper by limping back to the pallet and lying down, his face to the wall and the blanket that had been draped over his shoulder pulled up over his ears.

Jasper watched him, alert for any sign of subterfuge, but he just lay there, unmoving, his breathing slowly evening out until it was clear even from a distance that he had fallen asleep and wouldn't be attempting conversation or influencing anyone for some time. So why, then, was it so hard to resume his angry pacing? Why was it so hard to tear his gaze away from the sleeping figure, to stay mad instead of giving into the desire welling up inside?

JASPER'S body had mixed up day and night. The rain was pounding against the door outside, loud enough that Jasper could hear it even deep in the cave where he lay on his pallet, trying hard not to think about how much warmer it would be if he'd left it next to Tobias's, trying not to remember the way Tobias had pressed close and used his chest as a pillow the night before. He opened his eyes and stared into the dark, telling himself that he was looking toward the entrance, toward the truck, toward anything other than Tobias.

A noise against the other wall caught his attention, and he rummaged for the lantern, flicking the switch with a fast twist of his wrist, creating a small pool of light near his pallet. Tobias was still in shadow, but Jasper could see that he was sitting up, his elbows on his knees and the heels of his hands pressed against his eyes. It was a position Jasper recognized, having suffered from far too many headaches over the past few weeks, and he was halfway across the cave, lantern in hand, before he'd consciously decided to move.

Please leave the light over there.

Jasper paused, his own head bursting into pain at the soft intrusion, and set the lantern down. It was too bright for his eyes as well now, but he wasn't willing to turn it off and plunge the cave into complete darkness. Though it was empty except for the two of them and some sparse supplies, the floor was rough and uneven, and it would be far too easy to trip in the dark.

He sat on the edge of Tobias's pallet, as far from the other man as he could manage without crouching on the cold stone of the cavern floor, and bent his head so he could see Tobias's face. "What's wrong?" He didn't want to acknowledge the worry he felt, didn't want to admit that it might be real, but he was unable to leave anyone, even Tobias, in physical pain if there was any chance he could do something to fix it.

Tobias looked up, blinking blearily and keeping his eyes averted from the small pool of light in the center of the cave. He locked eyes with Jasper as he extended one hand and let it hover between them, his palm up and fingers slightly curled. He didn't need to say anything for Jasper to know that it was up to him to complete the contact.

Slowly, Jasper reached out and took Tobias's outstretched hand. He tensed as his grip was returned but resisted the sudden urge to step back. Immediately, he felt soothing pressure in his head and neck, the pain fading completely from his head and his tense muscles relaxing, despite his nervousness. The pressure faded as Tobias's hand relaxed in Jasper's, leaving the contact completely in Jasper's control.

"Thank you."

You're welcome. Tobias clenched and unclenched his fist, and his free hand came up to pinch the bridge of his nose.

Jasper repeated his earlier question. "What's wrong?"

Headache. Tobias looked up around his fingers, his eyes catching Jasper's. *I did a lot I've never done before yesterday, and I'm paying for it now.*

"Good."

Tobias wilted, his hand falling from his nose to his lap, and his gaze following it. *I'm sorry. I know you don't care, but for whatever it's worth, I'm sorry. I was panicking, and I didn't know what else to do.*

Jasper regarded him incredulously; unable to believe the words he heard echoing inside his skull. "Is that really what you think I'm upset about?" He shook his head, amazed at Tobias's naïveté. "That's not it at all."

Then what? Tobias's brow furrowed, his dark eyebrows forming a deep V-shape. *Why are you upset with me?*

The realization hit Jasper hard, sending his head spinning as he tried to process the information. "You really don't know."

No. I don't.

It would have been easy to give in to the lost look, to lose himself in those confused brown eyes, to just give in and go on as though he hadn't learned what he had the previous evening. He couldn't, though, couldn't forget it, couldn't risk the chance that it would happen again, and so he focused on the things he'd done, the things he'd felt since meeting Tobias, and reminded himself that he didn't know which of those feelings had been his own, and likely never would. His lips turned down into a frown at the thought.

"I can understand what you did in Durrysville," he began, speaking slowly and distinctly as though he were talking to an idiot or a small child. "I don't like it, and I'm sure there was another way for us to leave, but I understand your reaction."

Tobias sucked his bottom lip into his mouth, a habit that could quickly become endearing if Jasper let it. *Okay....* He sighed, ran his free hand through his hair, brushing the ear-length brown curls back from his forehead. *Then why?*

Jasper again fought down the urge to move away, to pace back and forth and wave his arms while he yelled and screamed. "Because of everything else you've made me feel." He forced himself to keep his voice calm and level despite the anger broiling in his belly.

Everything else?

Oh no. Jasper wasn't going to let Tobias off that easily, no matter how innocent and bewildered he managed to look. "You admitted earlier that you'd made me feel other things, made me want to help you and I don't even know what else." He tightened his grip on the hand he was holding, focusing the energy he would have spent pacing into making sure Tobias couldn't pull away and end the conversation before Jasper was ready. "I can't trust anything I've felt since I met you. For all I know, you've been manipulating me since we met."

No! That's not it at all! I didn't—I couldn't—do that. It's.... He paused, shifting position on the pallet so he was closer to Jasper, their knees practically touching. *What I did yesterday, in that town, then keeping you from feeling the pain from what I'd done... you saw how tired I was, yeah?*

Jasper nodded, let their joined hands drop to rest on their legs. "Yes."

If I'd been actively influencing you, I'd have been that tired from the first time I did it. It takes a lot of energy to make people feel things, to make them think that the feelings are theirs. He grinned wryly. *Plus, you would have had a lot more headaches than you have.*

The number of headaches he'd had since meeting Tobias was easily as many as he'd had in the years since moving inland prior to meeting Tobias. The idea of having more sent an involuntary shudder down his spine. "So then what did you do?" He'd done something, Jasper was sure of it, both from how he'd acted and Tobias's earlier admission.

I, um, projected. Not to make you feel anything you weren't feeling, he added quickly, *but to share what I was feeling. Back... back home, that's just how it is. I always—we always—send feelings with words. It's easier that way; there are fewer misunderstandings. I think that, maybe, since you're, um, not like me, you didn't know what I was doing, didn't know what you were receiving, and, um, thought they were your own feelings. I didn't realize.*

It made sense, sort of, but Jasper still felt betrayed. He'd acted on feelings not his own, embarked on a cross-continent journey during the wet season because of someone else's feelings. He'd viciously defended Tobias against such accusations back in Durrysville, against Darius's fears and Carla's worries, and then he'd discovered that the man from the post office had been right after all. Intentionally or not, Tobias had influenced him.

"And now that you do realize?" he asked, his tone low and faintly menacing. "Can you stop? Will you?"

Yes.

"Really?" Jasper knew how difficult years of habit were to change.

I think so. I'm going to try.

That was more like it. "And how will I know? How can I trust that you do? How will I know if you don't? How can I trust what I'm feeling?"

I don't know.

The burst of doubt and uncertainty that accompanied the words was obviously from Tobias, but it only proved Jasper's point. "Neither do I." He sighed, shaking his head as he climbed to his feet, his hand still clasped around Tobias's. "We should sleep; start early in the morning."

Yeah, okay. Tobias leaned back, stopped before breaking contact with Jasper. *Stay?*

It was far harder than it should have been to say no.

TOBIAS picked at the worn hem of his borrowed T-shirt and flipped the zipper pull on his jacket up and down, up and down. He let his left hand fall to the seat and slid it a few inches toward Jasper before bringing it back and again beginning the dance of picking and flipping. Even with his eyes on the road, his attention focused on the potholes and fallen limbs that made travel between storms so difficult, Jasper could see the fluttering fingers out of the corner of his eye and hear the creaking of the leather seats as the restless body on the other side of the cab shifted.

He steered the truck to the side of the road and parked it in a gap in the trees where it would be out of the way should someone else come along and need to get around them. That was highly improbable, but old habits died hard and years of living in the coastal cities had taught him never to stop where someone else might need to be.

"What's the matter?" He held his hand toward Tobias, palm up and fingers outstretched.

Tobias grabbed it immediately and squeezed tightly. A wave of relief rushed over Jasper, flooding his chest, but stopped just as suddenly, cut off with a ferocity that left no doubt in Jasper's mind the feeling hadn't been his. *Sorry.* Tobias clutched tighter at Jasper's hand, his fingers squeezing Jasper's together in a grip that was almost painful. *I didn't mean to, I wasn't trying...*

Jasper held up a hand to stop the mental babbling. "I know."

Thank you.

There was no need; Jasper was certain he hadn't meant what Tobias seemed to be taking from the simple comment, but it wasn't worth the argument or the worry. The feeling had stopped more quickly than it had started as Tobias had realized what he was doing, which was all Jasper could really ask at the moment, no matter how badly he wanted to demand more. "What did you want?" he asked instead, grateful for the chance to think about anything else.

Um. Tobias's gaze flashed to the windshield and the heavy, low-hanging clouds that could be seen through it. He was ridiculously easy to read even when he wasn't sending anything. The nervous flickering of his eyes and the way his free hand still picked at his shirt hem said far more than any words echoing in Jasper's skull could.

Jasper let his own gaze drift to the clouds, assessing them with a thoughtful eye. They were dark and low, heavy with moisture, but they were small still, not quite ready to burst. This storm was still several hours away. "It's just clouds."

Yeah, I know. Tobias's lips twitched up into a clearly forced half-smile as his free hand moved to the jacket zipper, flipping the pull up and down, up and down. *Clouds never used to make me this nervous, you know?* He shrugged, glanced quickly at Jasper, and resumed looking at the clouds. *But now I just... I don't want to get caught out in another storm. I had hoped... we're not going to make it to Shaleton before the daytime storms start, are we?*

"No." *They* wouldn't make it to Shaleton at all if Jasper had the courage to go through with his plan, but he couldn't say that. Not yet. "I'd say the first real daytime storm is two, maybe three days away. We're at least ten out from Shaleton."

Sleet. Tobias slumped, his free hand finally stilling in his lap. *Once it starts storming during the day, how will we travel? If we can't—*

"We'll figure it out." Or rather, Tobias would, by himself, without Jasper. Really.

THE town was small. Two gravel-covered roads branched off the main one that headed on toward the coast, looping around to join it again, and a few muddy paths headed away, presumably to outlying fields or tiny homesteads. Businesses—a post office, a general store, a cobbler, and an inn—lined the main road. The bank shared space with the post office, a tailor seemed to be situated above the cobbler, and the inn's old-fashioned taproom doubled as the local restaurant. There was a bookstore just off the main road, and a candy store around one of the corners. Small, windowless houses lined the picturesque streets, disappearing behind the larger storefronts. Perhaps there were a few side roads toward the outskirts, but other than a few houses the entire town could be seen from the creaking wooden sign that announced they had reached Folsom's Hollow.

The sun was still out, though it hung low in the sky and was partially obscured by the increasingly heavy clouds that were now threatening to let their contents loose at any moment. The wind that whipped the hanging sign back and forth was more than a gentle breeze, and the air was thick with the moisture of the impending storm.

The streets were nearly empty, though lights could be seen in a few stores, and it was difficult to tell if the quiet was due to the late hour or the low population.

Jasper's stomach rumbled as he slowly drove down the street, taking in the quaint atmosphere that made Brightam's Ford look like a bustling metropolis. "We'll stock up first, eat at the inn after." He focused on the excuses, all the other reasons he wanted to stock up immediately instead of waiting for morning. They could leave earlier. They wouldn't risk getting run out of town without things they needed. They weren't likely to encounter as many people. The list went on and on.

He could decide in the morning, after a good night's sleep and perhaps some regular conversation in the inn. At the moment, he just had to be sure he was ready to act on whatever decision he made.

Tobias's eyes were focused on the gathering clouds, but he nodded and reached across the gap between them to lightly touch Jasper's shoulder. *Okay. I'll um, never mind.*

"You'll what?"

Nothing. This time the touch was barely a brush against his elbow, gone before he was really aware of it and not likely to be repeated by hands now jammed into jacket pockets.

Shaking his head and ignoring the fondly amused feeling welling in his chest, Jasper guided the truck to the general store, turned into the gravel lot beside it, and swung around the building to park the truck under the corrugated metal roof in the back. As he climbed out, he glanced down the road toward the inn, wondering if they had a similar setup and froze, the warm amusement turning into an ice cold stab of fear.

The inn too had a covered lot, the corrugated metal currently covering one vehicle—a purple and green van with a dented bumper and broken mirror.

CHAPTER ELEVEN

TOBIAS scrambled back into the car, nearly catching his jacket in the door as he slammed it shut. *Come on!* He slid across the bench seat, leaning around the steering wheel to yank at Jasper's arm. *Let's go!*

Jasper braced himself against the door and peered more closely at the van in the other lot. It was empty, the owners likely inside the inn. "Hold on."

We need to go! Tobias tugged again, nearly throwing Jasper off balance. *They're here! They'll see us—me—and they'll....* He shuddered, shook his head. *We need to leave. Now.*

"We need to get supplies." Jasper looked Tobias straight in the eyes and tried to project a calm he didn't really feel. "Come on. They're in the inn. They won't see us."

Tobias stared back, his chest heaving with deep, shuddering breaths. *How do you know? What if they come out? What if they recognize the truck? What if they come into the store?*

Jasper could feel the panic behind the words, but it was clearly *Tobias's* panic with only a strange echo in Jasper's gut, and he briefly wondered if Tobias was responsible for the difference or if it was simply a result of his own new awareness. He pushed the thought aside as he gently removed Tobias's hand from his arm, keeping it clasped in his own. "They won't. They don't know we're here. They have no reason to leave until morning."

But what if they do?

"They won't."

But—

"If they do," Jasper said in the same calm tone he used on skittish horses, "we'll leave right away. No matter what we've gotten. But we need to try to get something, or we'll be hungry tomorrow." Somehow during the last three minutes, he'd decided to take Tobias all the way to Shaleton, and he said the plural pronoun without a twinge of guilt. "I promise," he added when Tobias stayed still, his eyes focused on the van and his hand tight around Jasper's.

Slowly, Tobias turned to look back at Jasper. *Yeah, okay.* He cast another nervous glance at the van and slid out of the truck, his hand never leaving Jasper's grasp. *Let's go.*

Tobias moved so quickly that Jasper was left trailing behind, his hand extended in front of him as Tobias practically dragged him through the shop door and down the first aisle. "Easy!" he protested, digging his heels into the wooden floorboards and halting them in front of some produce. "There's no need to run!"

We need to get stuff and get out of here. Tobias handed Jasper the basket he'd grabbed on their way inside and started loading it with fruits and vegetables.

"Nothing is going to happen while we're here." Jasper began removing items from the basket, taking out about every other item Tobias added so that none of it would go bad before they had a chance to eat it. "It will start storming soon; no one else is coming here tonight."

Exactly! His hand still on Jasper's arm, Tobias headed to the next aisle, where he grabbed boxes and bags seemingly at random and tossed them into the basket for Jasper to sort through and put back. *They knew we'd be here! They're waiting for us, and if we don't leave soon we'll be stuck and have to stay in the inn and I can't! Not with them there. I don't want to find Samantha by joining her.*

Jasper stopped cold, a box halfway back to the shelf he thought it had come from. "Sleet." He hadn't thought about where they'd go, where they'd stop when the storm made driving too dangerous. He mentally reviewed the map, trying to remember anything that would indicate a place nearby where they could wait out the storm, but drew a blank. The town had barely made the map; nothing smaller would. They would be completely chancing it if they left before morning.

"We could just not go in the main room," he suggested, though he knew it was foolish even as the words left his mouth. "If we go straight up to a room, eat something we have with us, and leave as early as possible, they may never know we're here."

May never know we're here? Tobias dropped his latest acquisition without making sure his hand was over the basket, and the box—some sugary cake mix that would do them no good on the road—tumbled to the floor as Tobias tugged at his collar, his breath suddenly coming in short, uneven gasps. *They're probably waiting for us!* He started grabbing things again, tossing them toward Jasper with obvious unconcern for their necessity or Jasper's ability to catch them.

Jasper set down the increasingly heavy basket and grabbed Tobias's arm, forcefully stopping him from tossing a bag of sugar at the basket. "Slow down. They're not waiting for us." He put the bag of sugar back on the shelf and began picking up other miscellaneous packages from the floor.

Why else would they be here? Tobias crouched down next to Jasper, picking up the boxes that had missed the basket and replacing most of them on the shelf with unneeded ferocity. *They knew we were going to be here. They're waiting for us.*

"Tobias...."

Tobias met his gaze, his brown eyes flashing. *There's no other reason for them to be here!*

"They're going the same direction. We knew they were going to Shaleton, remember?"

Yeah, but... why here? Why tonight? If they got ahead of us when we took that detour, why are they still in this town? Why didn't we see them in Durrysville? Why didn't they keep going when we stopped for an extra day? He shook his head as he shifted from his knees to sit on the worn, dusty floor. *They want us. There's no other reason for them to be here.*

Jasper could think of several, but he didn't push the point. It was clear he would never get Tobias into the inn willingly, and trying to force the issue would only draw the attention of the other patrons—something they both wanted to avoid. "All right. We won't stay there." He climbed to his feet and held out his hand for Tobias to take again. "Let's get what we need and leave."

Thanks. Tobias let Jasper help him up and took the basket without protest when Jasper handed it over. *Come on.* Flashing a smile, he set off down the next aisle, moving far more quickly than was necessary.

THE storm started suddenly, large droplets pelting the truck with a ferocity that had Jasper frantically pumping the brakes and cursing as the back tires skidded on loose stones. They'd left the main road a few miles back, following the vague directions of the shopkeeper toward an abandoned farm that Jasper hoped would offer protection for the night.

The shopkeeper had been surly at first, resenting Jasper's questions and suspicious of strangers in his small town, but he'd soon been taken in by a story Jasper weaved. He told the shopkeeper his farmhouse had been damaged by one of the early storms and he didn't have the money to repair it, but he had relatives on the coast who were willing to help... if he came to them. As Jasper had hoped, the shopkeeper commiserated, sharing stories of nearby farms that had been abandoned, some by people moving to town for the winter, others by people abandoning the quiet inland for the high life on the coast.

It was toward one of the latter that Jasper was headed. He was uneasy enough with the idea of squatting. Camping out, even for one night, in a house that was only temporarily abandoned pushed his sensibilities too far, and he'd deliberately driven past two empty but still furnished homes. The permanently abandoned one he'd settled on was supposedly less than a mile ahead, though it would be a long drive in the pounding rain with the dirt and gravel road turning to mud beneath the tires.

Tobias leaned forward, peering into the downpour. He was pressed close against Jasper's side, the rest of the seat filled with the cardboard boxes and paper bags they'd taken from the general store.

Tobias hadn't been willing to take the time to properly pack the truck, and Jasper hadn't been willing to argue about it. Someone had been standing in the doorway of the inn and though the figure had been too shadowed to see clearly, it had given Jasper the chills and he'd acquiesced to Tobias's pleading request with nary an argument.

I think I see it.

Jasper didn't dare take his eyes off the road to confirm. "Where?"

On the left, just up there. The drive is... 500 yards ahead, maybe? He shrugged, his shoulder rubbing against Jasper's. *It's hard to tell in the rain.*

Jasper eased off the gas pedal and slowed the truck until it was barely creeping along, the mud-slick gravel crunching under the tires, the rain hitting the windshield faster than the wipers could fling it off. Dark shapes loomed along the side of the road—long grass and squat bushes surrounding taller trees, all leaning dangerously with branches whipping and leaves blowing off in the wind and rain.

A squared, broken post stuck up some distance from the nearest bush, looking oddly out of place as the headlights swept over it. *There!* Tobias leaned forward, his finger pointing at the area just beyond it. *Just after that post.*

There was little to distinguish the ground beyond the post from the ground in front of it, but Jasper obediently turned, cautiously easing the truck onto the barely distinguishable path. Ahead, a dark, square shape loomed, a solid blot of black in an already dark night. The truck slid as they approached the building; the gravel of the unused drive had slowly given in to the encroaching grass and left little traction for the tires. By the time they reached the house, the rain had turned to sleet and hail had begun to pelt the windshield.

Tobias barely waited for Jasper to turn off the truck before he climbed out and grabbed two of the bags from the seat. He dashed to the covered porch and burst through the front door, barely pausing as he forced it open. Jasper took a flashlight from the glove compartment and another bag from the seat before following at a more sedate pace, though still quickly, doing his best to avoid the painful lash of rain and hail against his exposed skin.

Inside, the house was dark, the floor covered with a thick layer of dirt and dust broken only by the tracks Tobias had left. In the thin, pale beam of the flashlight, they were easy to follow, but Jasper took his time, systematically checking every room he passed, keeping his eyes peeled for any sign that someone had been there recently. Behind one door the tiny window was broken and the plywood nailed haphazardly across the opening had cracked and come loose from the wall in one corner. Wet leaves and tiny sticks were scattered across the floor and more clogged the small opening. In another room, the roof leaked, four steady drips merging into a puddle on the floor that threatened to engulf the mildew-covered rug rolled against one wall.

Tobias was in the central room which featured a solid ceiling and secure-looking interior walls that would hold against the storm. The bags he'd grabbed were in the corner and he was next to them, his chin resting on his drawn-up knees and his eyes locked on the door. He scrambled to his feet and crossed the room with swift strides as Jasper entered. *Finally.*

Jasper laughed as he set the bag next to the others. "I wanted to look around."

Arching one brown eyebrow upward, Tobias cocked his head to one side. *Why?*

"To make sure we'd be alone, mostly. I was curious and I wanted to make sure we'd be safe. This isn't the most secure building, but it will work for one night." He started toward the door, stopped when Tobias's hand tightened on his arm.

Where are you going now? There was a faint note of panic behind the sending and a wild look in Tobias's eyes.

"To get the rest of our stuff. Come on." He tugged Tobias forward. "If we bring everything inside, we can sort the things we bought."

Tobias dug his heels in. *Um, how about you bring it in, and I'll sort? Or how about we sort in the morning? It'll be easier in the daylight.*

It would, but…. "We still need to get something to sleep on. I don't particularly want to curl up on the hard floor without anything to soften it." His muscles ached when he thought about sleeping without a soft mattress beneath him for the third night in a row.

But it's already storming!

"It was storming when we came in, and the truck is right outside the door." Even in the dim light, Jasper could see the panic on Tobias's face. "It will only take a few minutes. We'll be fine." He kept his voice low and calm, his eyes locked on Tobias's. "We drove longer than I planned, and I'm tired. I'll rest better if we take care of things first."

Tobias's expression morphed, uncertainty turning to worry and finally settling on determination. *Yeah, okay.* His smile was strained, but there was no hesitation in his step as he led the way from the room.

Outside, the sleet and hail were pelting hard and lightning flashed in the sky, bright and quickly followed by loud thunder, but not so close as to be dangerous. They cleared the front seat in one trip by loading up with the remaining boxes and bags until they couldn't fit anything else in their hands and dropped them next to the others inside. On the second trip out they retrieved sleeping gear, removing blankets and bedrolls from the back of the truck and carrying them inside quickly before they were soaked by the precipitation.

Jasper shivered as he dropped the bedding, chilled to the bone by the cold, wet clothes plastered to his skin. "Come on. Let's get something to change into." Outside, the damp clothes weren't so bad, though the sleet was freezing against his hands and face and the hail was hitting hard enough to leave bruises. "We'll never get warm if we don't."

A dismayed look flashed across Tobias's face, but he nodded, wrapping his arms around himself as he stood and bumping his shoulder against Jasper's as he passed. *Quickly, yeah?*

"Yeah," he agreed, crossing his arms and rubbing his hands up and down as he followed Tobias back outside.

The contents of one duffle probably would have been enough—they were both wearing Jasper's clothes, after all—but Jasper grabbed both, handing them to Tobias as he scanned the truck bed for anything else they might need. He was locking the cap, when lightning struck, the electricity tingling on Jasper's skin as it arced up to the top of the closest tree, breaking off the upper limbs and sending them crashing to the ground in a shower of splintered wood.

Tobias jumped, grabbed Jasper's arm and steered him halfway across the porch with unexpected strength before the sudden, loud crack of thunder faded, leaving Jasper's ears ringing. The bags were shoved into Jasper's hands, and it was only as he saw Tobias fumbling with the latch on the front door that he realized the keys were still in the truck cab, a scratch on his hand a testament to how quickly and violently he'd been dragged away from them.

"I need—" he started, but was stopped by Tobias jerking him into the house.

Later!

Jasper wanted to protest, but he couldn't find the words before Tobias ran, panicked. Jasper struggled to keep up, and he was breathing heavily by the time they reached the central room. As soon as Jasper stepped through the door, Tobias slammed it shut. He sank down with his back against the door, wrapped his arms around his legs and began trembling, his breath coming in heavy, uneven gasps.

"Tobias?" Jasper crouched to look in Tobias's eyes, his hand resting on the denim-clad knee in front of him. "What's wrong?"

Nothing. Tobias managed a smile, but it was strained and tense, far from the brilliant grin that set Jasper's stomach flipping. *I just got startled, is all.*

"That was more than startled." Jasper waved his arm, indicating Tobias's drawn up knees and shaking shoulders. "This is more than startled. When you're startled, you jump, maybe yell. You don't drag someone inside at top speed, you don't stop to make sure the doors are secure, you don't end up on the floor gasping for breath and shaking like a leaf." He took a deep breath, concentrating on moderating the angry tone in his voice. "I can *feel* how terrified you are."

Sorry! The feeling flared, joined by a new fear, then cut off, leaving Jasper feeling strangely empty. *I didn't mean to. I wasn't trying—*

"That's not what I meant," Jasper said, interrupting the mental babbling. "I wasn't...." He shook his head. He couldn't explain that now, couldn't put into words the difference in the feelings he got or how this way didn't matter as much. It was too complicated, too confusing, and not the issue of the moment. "Now tell me what's wrong. Please."

The storm, all right? The haunted look didn't leave Tobias's eyes, nor did his limbs stop trembling. *You know I don't like them.*

Terrified would be a better description for how Tobias felt about storms, but even so, none of his past reactions had been like this, not even after he'd been forced to spend an entire night out in one. "I do," Jasper agreed. "But you've never reacted like this before. This was different."

Tobias peered up at him defiantly from under wet curls plastered to his forehead, but his expression gradually faded to one of resignation as Jasper met his eyes. Tobias's shoulders slumped, his whole body seeming to deflate, though his hands were still trembling where they rested in his lap. *It was the tree,* he sent, closing his eyes and letting his head rest against the door. *When it broke, the way it fell, it was... it reminded me of something.*

"Of what?" Jasper kept his voice calm and rubbed his hands up and down Tobias's legs as he willed Tobias's shaking to stop.

When I started looking for Samantha. Tobias tugged, guiding Jasper forward and urging him to sit with his back against the wall, his shoulder pressed against Tobias's. *Let me show you?*

Jasper nodded as he settled in next to Tobias. "All right."

TOBIAS ran, slipping and sliding on the piled leaves and moss. As he pushed through them, branches whipped back and ripped his clothes, leaving scratches on his exposed skin. He didn't know where he was going, just knew that he had to move, had to get away from the darkness he could feel behind him—the same darkness he'd felt when Samantha had disappeared. It had sensed him, was following him, and he needed to get away, needed to lose it. He didn't want to find his sister by being taken as well.

Samantha had been missing two weeks already. The storms were close, the air heavy with the threat of rain and thunder and the impending washout of the trail Tobias had been following for the past seven days. Not that he had much chance of finding it again. He'd gotten close, he knew it, but as he'd stretched his mind out to Samantha, someone—something—else had sensed him and he'd fled, abandoning the south-easterly trail he'd been following and heading deeper into the southern forest.

His sense of his sister was growing fainter, but the darkness was gaining, growing closer and stronger with every step. He stumbled again and again, tripping over exposed roots and catching his feet in cracks, but he couldn't stop despite the weariness of his bones and the blinding sweat that dripped down his forehead and into his eyes.

The first drops of rain went unnoticed. Light and tiny, they blended with the lashing branches and his dripping sweat, but Tobias was concentrating too hard on putting one foot in front of the other and finding the path of least resistance through the trees to notice.

The darkness surged forward with a desperate sense of want *and* need *and* mine. *Tobias bolted, jumping over downed limbs and ignoring the increasingly heavy rain drops that splattered his face and stung as they lashed at his bloody skin. The darkness, the* thing, *whatever it was, was gaining, he could feel it, and he was sure that if he looked over his shoulder he'd see it through the trees, eating up the distance between them with a speed Tobias could never hope to match.*

He wasn't going to look. Didn't need to look. He needed to keep going, keep running, keep his eyes ahead of him on the branches and logs that were in his way, on the holes through the trees, and on the rocky cliff he saw ahead where he might be able to climb, to lose it in a cave, or maybe lose himself until it no longer mattered if the thing found him or not. Looking was a bad idea, a dangerous idea. He'd have to slow, stop maybe, lose his momentum as he was engulfed by fear. He shouldn't look.

He did anyway, his feet moving of their own volition, momentum carrying him forward even as his mind registered that he couldn't see anything behind him despite the dark pressure in his head and the sense of impending doom. He whipped his head back around, half afraid that it had somehow gotten in front of him, and only had time to register the absence of any other being before he tumbled forward and hit the ground hard.

The rain began to fall harder, soaking through Tobias's clothes as he lay on the ground, his ankle throbbing. His jacket was ripped in several places and he could feel water—or blood—running down his arm, but it was too dark to see. The clouds covered the setting sun and the angry flashes of lightning were too brief to be of use. He staggered to his feet, wincing in pain as he took his weight onto his right leg, but managed to stumble onward. He leaned on trees and kept his eyes focused on the cliff ahead and a fissure he could just make out when lightning cracked near enough to illuminate the area.

The sense of being followed had faded, the darkness withdrawing to the edge of his mind, perhaps waiting to see what he would do or perhaps driven to seek shelter from the heavy rain now liberally laced with hail. It didn't matter; Tobias would be lucky to get to the rock face that evening, he wasn't running anywhere until morning at least. Even if he'd dared brave the storm, his ankle hurt too much to consider the idea.

His movement was painfully slow, the two hundred or so yards to the fissure seeming to stretch out to two or three times as far. When he reached the last of the trees, his ankle was throbbing and the rain had all turned to sleet and hail, lashing at his face and hands, soaking through his jacket. The pack on his back was heavy with water and the straps that slung over his shoulders were encrusted with ice. The fissure looked wide and deep enough that he'd be able to hide in it at least for the night, but it was ten feet away, ten feet he'd have to cross without support.

He took a deep breath, stepped out, and lighting struck, arcing up to hit the top of the tree. A branch broke and tumbled to the ground in slow motion, shards of wood pelting Tobias as he raised his arms to protect his face. It hit another branch on the way down, cracked in two, *and the larger piece flung outward, spinning as it fell, hitting Tobias in the shoulder, and sending him crashing to the cold, muddy ground.*

Pain shot through his ankle, and his vision narrowed to a hazy tunnel of gray and black. He shook his head, struggling to see, and slowly inched forward, dragging himself laboriously along the ground. There was no way he could stand—he could tell that without even trying—so he settled for crawling, his ankle held awkwardly in the air as he tried to keep his weight off it. The storm raged around him, bolts of lightning startling him as they flashed in the sky and cast flashes that briefly illuminated the open ground between him and the fissure. With each flash he could see he was a little closer, and he clung to that, pushing through the pain and pushing back the darkness that threatened to engulf him.

It was only the lack of rain on his face that let him know he had safely reached the fissure and crawled clear of the dangerous storm. He dragged himself on a few more feet, unsure if his legs were inside yet or not, and collapsed. His eyes closed as pain and exhaustion overwhelmed him.

JASPER blinked and shook his head, one hand reaching down to rub imaginary pain away from his right ankle. "That was…." he started, but stopped without finishing the sentence. There weren't words for the terror and pain.

Yeah. Tobias agreed, pressing closer, his hand stroking Jasper's arm as though Jasper were the one who'd run inside, terrified, and needed calming. It was soothing, and Jasper unconsciously leaned into the touch, his shoulder slipping under Tobias's arm. *When the branch broke, I panicked.*

"Understandable," Jasper murmured, his head rolling to rest on Tobias's shoulder, his eyes focused on the underside of Tobias's jaw.

I suppose. Tobias shrugged and Jasper's head was leaning in a little more when the motion stopped. *Comfortable?* He turned so he could look Jasper in the eyes, his shoulder sliding a little from under Jasper's ear.

"Yeah." Though he shouldn't be comfortable the way he was slouched down on the hard wooden floor, his back pressed against the unevenly plastered wall.

Good. And then Tobias twisted; his shoulder slipping out from under Jasper's ear as his hand came up to cup the back of Jasper's head. Jasper blinked, opened his mouth, and closed it as cool, rain-wet lips pressed against his.

CHAPTER TWELVE

TOBIAS tasted of rain and sage, of cloves and fallen leaves, deliciously dark and earthy. The moist warmth of his tongue in Jasper's mouth was a direct contrast to the cool rainwater that covered their lips and dripped from their hair. The hand that slid under wet cotton to press against Jasper's back was warm against his skin.

He leaned into the kiss, tilting his head and sliding his hands up to tangle in Tobias's hair. He pushed his tongue forward to wrap around Tobias's, stroked and teased as he tried to crawl into Tobias's mouth. He needed more, needed to taste the rain and the sage and the... apples? And cinnamon?

His brow furrowing, Jasper deepened the kiss, sliding his tongue along the roof as he searched for the lighter, fruitier flavors he'd briefly tasted. He found cloves and fallen leaves, a bit of slate perhaps, but nothing light and fruity, no apples or cinnamon, not even when he slipped his tongue back and... Sleet!

He only tasted the lighter flavors when Tobias's tongue was in his mouth or, like now, when it was brushing against his. With his tongue in Tobias's mouth, Jasper could taste the dark, earthy flavors of Tobias, but when Tobias's tongue caressed his, he tasted apple and cinnamon again.

Jasper slid his hands to Tobias's shoulders, pushed. "No," he whispered as he pulled back, his bottom lip catching between Tobias's teeth. "Stop."

Why? Tobias tilted his head to the side, his confused, lust-darkened brown eyes fixated on Jasper's.

"We can't."

Tobias's hand descended from the back of Jasper's head to his shoulder. *But—*

"No." Jasper climbed to his feet, shrugged off Tobias's hands as he stood, and moved across the room. He tried to say he wasn't interested, to convince Tobias—and himself—that it was just some fleeting rush of adrenaline that meant nothing, but the flip-flop feeling in his gut wouldn't let him.

Tobias followed, lightly resting his hand on Jasper's shoulder as Jasper crouched and dug in the duffels for dry clothes. *Please.*

"We can't," he said again, ignoring the twisting in his chest. He didn't know that the feeling was his, not after tasting himself on Tobias's tongue, feeling himself in Tobias's mouth. It could be what Tobias wanted him to feel, and he wouldn't give in. Tobias was someone he'd taken in, agreed to help, someone who would be gone from his life once they reached Shaleton, someone he'd been ready to abandon only hours earlier.

Whatever this feeling was, whoever it came from, it wasn't something Jasper could act upon. It could only end badly.

THE road forked five miles beyond the house, a narrow path on the left heading directly east while the main road continued in a southeasterly direction. Jasper tapped the brake pedal as he approached the split, glanced once at his silent passenger, and guided the truck down the left fork.

The map shifted and fluttered to the floor as Tobias's hand slid across the seat to touch Jasper. *Where are we going?* The words were clipped, frantic with the worry Jasper could see written in Tobias's furrowed brow and pinched lips. *The map says... we were supposed to... this isn't the right way.*

Jasper slowed the truck to accommodate the more frequent potholes in the narrower road. "We're just taking another route."

But.... His eyes darted around the cab, flickered to the pockmarked road before fixating on the speedometer. *We're going slower. They'll catch us. You have to turn around.*

Jasper stopped the truck on the side of the road and turned in the seat so he was facing his passenger. "Calm down." He placed his hand over Tobias's and squeezed the trembling fingers. "We'll get to Shaleton just as quickly this way. I looked at the map last night, after... after you fell asleep." Jasper hadn't been able to sleep, his mind replaying the kiss again and again until he'd finally climbed from the blankets and searched desperately for some sort of distraction. The map had been the best he had been able to come up with on short notice, but it had proved effective when he'd found an alternate route, one the men looking for them likely wouldn't be taking. "It's not the most direct way, but it won't make much difference in our time."

That's not.... Tobias shook his head, his brown curls falling into his exasperated eyes. *That's not what I meant. Those... those men, they'll find us, they'll be able to catch us. We need to go quickly, not on this small road.* His gaze took on a desperate intensity. *Please, just turn us around. Take the main route.*

"They're not following us, Tobias." He kept his voice low and calm, infused it with more conviction than he really felt. The men did seem determined to capture Tobias, but they couldn't have known Jasper and Tobias had reached Folsom's Hollow, and wouldn't know what route they were taking out of town.

Why were they in that town, then? Some of the panic had drained from Tobias's expression, replaced by confusion. There was a layer of trust there too, which tore at Jasper's heart as he tried to convince them both that his theory was right.

"There aren't many ways to get from Brightam's Ford to Shaleton, Tobias," he said quietly, hoping that he sounded more certain than he suddenly felt. It was the most likely scenario, but there was still a risk he was wrong. "They're following the most logical route, just like we were. That's all. They should stay on the main road."

Tobias regarded him for a long moment, and Jasper tried to lock his doubts far beneath the surface of his mind, where Tobias wouldn't be able to read them without prying further than he claimed to be willing to do. It worked, or else Tobias was choosing to ignore the worried thoughts, for he nodded, slipped his hand out of Jasper's grasp, and slid back to the other side of the bench seat.

Jasper pushed away the vague sense of misgiving and guilt coiled in his gut as he laid the map on the seat between them and restarted the truck. He was right about the men's route coincidentally aligning with theirs, he had to be, and if he wasn't, this route still gave them a better chance of avoiding the men chasing them than the main road. He just couldn't let Tobias see his doubts.

THE storm came up suddenly, the clear, sunny sky darkened and raindrops pelted the windshield with unexpected force and swiftness. Tobias jerked his head away from where it had been resting on the window, the sudden movement startling Jasper more than the unexpected shower. He peered at the sky, frowning when he saw an unending line of dark clouds and distant flashes of lightning. Swearing under his breath as he started scanning the road for a turn off that might lead to shelter.

Jasper?

He hadn't noticed Tobias scooting closer, his eyes wide as he peered out the windshield at the rapidly falling drops. "Get the map," he answered, his fingers clenched tight around the wheel and his eyes fixed on the road in front of him. This was the one flaw in his plan—he hadn't thoroughly studied the route, hadn't planned where to turn off when the daytime storms started. He had been planning on doing that in the next town, had thought he had a few days to figure it out.

Mother Nature had proved him wrong.

Tobias struggled to unfold the crinkling paper of the map, his hands shaking and the folds catching as he tried to spread it out over his lap. They lost long minutes, the truck creeping forward in the torrential downpour, the headlights barely illuminating the road a few feet ahead, the tires slipping in the mud even at the snail's pace.

Finally, after what seemed like an eternity, Tobias lay the map over his thighs and found Folsom's Hollow and the route they'd taken. *What am I looking for?*

Jasper couldn't spare a second's glance from the road ahead, but he could imagine Tobias's wide, terrified eyes, could feel Tobias trembling where their elbows were pressed together. "A turn off. A town. A place we can stop." The chances of anything close enough being marked on the map were slim—the road they were on was barely big enough to warrant inclusion—but it couldn't hurt to look. Maybe there were caves or some other site of interest for people who had the time to take trips during the dry season.

The map rustled as Tobias's finger traced the line of the road, his movement slow and careful. *Nothing. I don't... I don't see anything.* The map crinkled again, louder this time, and Jasper had to fight the urge to pull his eyes from the road and his hand from the wheel to help Tobias peer at the map in his clearly desperate search for shelter.

His mind was so divided, the urge to turn to Tobias so great, that he almost missed the tiny trail, just wide enough for the truck to turn down. Slowly, he backed up and eased the truck down the muddy path a few hundred yards until the undergrowth made it impossible for the truck to go any further.

The headlights illuminated only branches and pine needles, any true leaves long fallen to decompose on the forest floor. The path continued in front of them, narrow and slick with pooling water and decaying leaves, but Jasper couldn't tell where it led, if it led anywhere at all.

Tobias's trembling increased, his eyes wider than Jasper had imagined as he stared into the pouring rain, peering into the darkness past the edge of the headlights range and flinching at the flashes of lightning that illuminated nothing more than trees and a narrowing path. *Jasper?*

"This leads somewhere," he answered, peering intently into the rain, hoping that a flash would illuminate something they could use for shelter.

No. Tobias shook his head vigorously as his hand clutched tightly at Jasper's arm. *Keep driving.*

It was at least as great of a risk, especially since he'd have to back out of the narrow path, but Tobias's whole body was quivering now, and Jasper knew without asking that there was no way he was getting

Tobias to get out of the truck without a destination clearly in sight. "Are you sure?"

The terse nod was all he needed to put the truck in reverse and begin carefully backing down the slick, muddy path.

THE next turn off was a few hundred yards down the road, but they drove past it when a chance flash of lightning failed to illuminate anything more than trees and bushes along the side of the path, branches threatening to overwhelm it in a few places. The truck wouldn't have made it far, and Tobias had shaken his head before Jasper had even thought about turning the wheel.

The following turn off was on the left, another three hundred yards down the road, and substantially wider. Fallen leaves covered the ground and weeds and grasses poked up between stones, but careful examination in the dim glow of the headlights and brief flashes of brighter illumination showed that it had once been paved with gravel. Jasper turned the wheel without looking at his passenger; they didn't make gravel roads that led nowhere and they couldn't keep driving. The lightning was getting closer and closer and it would soon be too dangerous to be out in the open. If they didn't find something soon, they'd have to hole up in the truck and hope that this first daytime storm of the season was a relatively mild one.

Tobias stiffened as the truck turned, but no protest ghosted across Jasper's mind, and Tobias remained still, his muscles taut and his eyes fixed on the ever closer flashes of lightning.

The old, broken road looped through the trees, though Jasper was forced several times to veer around places where fallen trees and buckling roots made it impassable, but it maintained a general northerly direction as it wound into denser and tighter woods. Branches scraped at the sides of the truck, clacking against the paneling and windows, and twice Jasper thought they'd have to stop, that he'd have to try to negotiate the path backward or turn the truck around on the narrow path, but both times they made it through, the scratching of thick branches against metal paneling sending shivers down Jasper's spine.

Lightning crashed closer, the rumble of thunder almost simultaneous with the flash. Jasper twitched, more surprised by the thunder than the lighting, his mouth twisting into a grimace as he felt Tobias jump next to him. Any closer and they'd have to stop, have to hope that the lightning would be drawn to the taller trees and that the metal frame of the truck would direct any hits around rather than through them.

The next flash was even closer and Jasper twitched again, but this time he saw something—a low, squat structure fifty or so yards away. It was surprisingly close, but in the half-light of the storm it was the same color as the rest of the forest, and the trees and thick torrents of rain kept him from seeing much beyond the end of the hood.

Slowly and carefully, unwilling to hurry despite the pressing danger of the storm, Jasper eased the truck forward, turned it off the path where it passed the building, and brought it to a stop as close to the lone door as he could get. Half-rotted wooden poles kept the truck several feet away and the awning over the door had long since blown away, leaving only the stubs of a metal frame attached to the stout wooden wall above the door.

"We'll have to run for it," he said, eyeing the distance between the truck and the door and wondering if there was time to unload anything from the back and get inside between the increasingly frequent flashes of lightning. Two flashes in quick succession nixed that idea and he pulled the truck forward a little more, aligning the passenger door with the entrance to the building. "Do you want to wait for me to get inside?" The building could be locked up, or inhabited, though the empty parking lot and remote location made that theory unlikely.

No. Let's go. With a tug on Jasper's wrist, Tobias slipped from the truck, slammed the door, and dashed across the open space before Jasper even got the key out of the ignition. By the time Jasper reached the building, Tobias had gotten the door open and was inside, hovering just at the edge of the dim light cast by the open door.

"Is there—" Jasper started, but stopped when he realized Tobias wasn't within touching distance and wasn't likely to come any closer to the open door that Jasper couldn't close until he'd located another source of light. He diverted his eyes to the wall, searching for a light switch, running his hand up and down the wall close to the door, and cursing when the only switch he found did nothing. Either the electricity was off or the bulbs were burnt out, and it would take further exploration to determine which. For that, they needed light.

"I'm going to grab a flashlight," he said, turning back toward the truck, already mentally counting the time since the last lightning strike. One flashed, the rumble of thunder so close as to be almost simultaneous, and Jasper stepped out, confident he could get in the truck before the next one hit.

No!

The word sent sharp pain through Jasper's head and he stopped, his knees buckling and his right hand flying to his forehead as his left gripped the door frame in a desperate attempt to stay upright. "Tobias," he managed to grind out between clenched teeth, unsure what he was asking and half afraid he'd get an answer that would drive another spike into his skull.

A tentative touch on the small of his back eased the last fear and took away some of the pain. *Stay inside. Please.*

Jasper didn't have to turn to know that Tobias was blinking wide, worried eyes and chewing on his bottom lip, but he did anyway, returning Tobias's nervous gaze with one as steady as he could manage through the throbbing in his skull, and attempting a reassuring smile that felt like it failed. "We need light. The switch doesn't work and I—we—can't just sit here in the dark." It would be too much like that day in Crittendon, huddled in the cellar, the day that had convinced him that moving inland was a good idea and that he never wanted to see the coast again.

The irony of waiting out another storm in a dark, unfamiliar room while on his way to the other coast wasn't lost on him.

Tobias swallowed, his eyes roaming Jasper's face, flickering to the open door and cloud-filled sky. The thunder crashed again and Tobias jerked his hand and curled his fingers against Jasper's hip before he took a deep breath, slowly straightened them, and rested his hand flat against Jasper's side. *Hurry.*

It was harder to gather his courage this time, and his hand shook as he fumbled for the key, wanting to have it ready before he stepped out into the cold, hard rain. He watched the sky carefully, ready to move as soon as the lightning flashed, but it was Tobias's hand on his back that propelled him out the door, and instinct that kept his feet moving over the wet gravel until he reached the truck.

He struggled to get the key into the lock, adding new scratches to the already horribly damaged paint job. After several tries, the key slid in, the lock clicked, and lightning flashed in the sky, making Jasper jump as he pulled up on the handle. He'd never scrambled into the truck faster.

The flashlight was behind the seat, in his box of emergency supplies. The ones in the truck bed were bigger and better, but the storm was too fierce to risk standing out under the biting rain rummaging through the jumbled mess to find the lanterns or larger lights that he'd packed there. This was just a daytime storm, one that would end in an hour or two, and they'd be back on the road. Even if the electricity had long since been cut off in their shelter, they could manage an hour or two with the small light.

He reached down behind the seat and searched blindly, his eyes focused on the sky, the clouds, and the vision-obscuring rain that fell from them. Tobias was hovering, Jasper knew it, but when he looked back all he could see was a vague outline of the building, a darker shape behind the curtain of never-ending water.

The need to get back inside—back to Tobias, though he wouldn't admit that to anyone—grew stronger, and Jasper's fumbling became increasingly frantic. He was groping now for the handles that would let him lift the bag without dumping the contents so he could bring it back inside with him, or at the very least dig with it in his lap where he could see what he was doing. His fist closed around the slick handles, and he yanked upward, barely taking enough care to make sure the bag didn't spin or catch on the back of the seat and dump everything out through its open zipper.

The flashlight was on top, right where he'd thought it would be, and he grabbed it, leaving the bag open on the seat as he turned to the door and again began to watch the sky, gauging the lightning flashes and gathering his courage for the dash back to the building. Two small flashes were followed by a large one and Jasper pushed open the door, then slammed it behind him without bothering with the lock in his haste to cross the wet gravel between the truck and the building.

He was almost there, close enough to see Tobias hovering just inside the building, when the sky flashed, the crack so loud and immediate that Jasper froze, his muscles locking in terror as his brain realized that the storm was there, the lightning truly on top of them, and that right between the metal truck and the metal remains of the awning, he was in danger.

Another flash lit up the sky, the accompanying crack even louder than the first, and this one was followed by ominous groaning. Jasper turned and peered into the rain, but all he could see was sheets of water and dark shapes that he assumed were trees. A hand grabbed his wrist and tugged him backward, and he let out a startled yelp before he realized it was Tobias urging him back into the dubious safety of the building. He moved backward, his eyes fixed on the shadowy trees, Tobias guiding his every step.

Lightning flashed again as the door shut, and as darkness descended, Jasper realized the noise had likely been a tree hit by lightning. His stomach dropped.

Sleet.

CHAPTER THIRTEEN

THE storm stopped as quickly as it had begun. One moment, the pounding of rain on the corrugated metal roof of the building was near-deafening, the next it was gone, replaced with a heavy silence that felt unnatural. Jasper stayed still, his eyes closed in an attempt to ignore the darkness of the enclosed room and focus on his other senses.

The air was thick and still, full of moisture even inside the building. It was heavy and oppressive and left Jasper feeling as though he should just lie back against the cold concrete beneath him. His body lay motionless as his mind wandered, listening for more rain, for animals, for anything to make a noise.

It wasn't as if they were going anywhere.

Tobias stirred, the rustling of denim bringing Jasper's attention back to his immediate surroundings. His eyes snapped open and in the dim light of their lantern he could see Tobias peering at him, his expression a mixture of confusion and concern, his hand outstretched and hovering just short of Jasper's knee.

It made contact a second later, making Jasper jump even though he'd been half-expecting it.

Jasper? Tobias's mental voice was quiet, his eyes still puzzled. *The storm stopped.* He glanced to the door, then back to Jasper. *Shouldn't we go? While there's still daylight? Before....* He paused, and Jasper felt the subtle shudder that ran down Tobias's back through the hand on his knee and in his mind.

He twitched, ignored the urge to let the tremors run down his own spine. "Before what?" he asked, his voice carefully quiet.

Before it starts storming again. The corner of Tobias's mouth twitched up into a half-smile. *I'd rather not spend the night here. It lacks... well, everything.*

Tobias's smile blossomed into a full grin as he shook his head, and Jasper smiled as well, though he was unsure if it was due to the joke or the simple fact that Tobias was smiling. Either way, it made warmth pool in the bottom of his stomach as he climbed to his feet and held his hand out to Tobias. "Come on." Maybe it wasn't as bad as he thought.

IT WAS. And yet, it wasn't. The tree lay across the road, blocking all access to the direction they wanted to travel and cutting them off from their route back to the road they'd been following. It was big—wider around than the span of Jasper's arms—and even with the tools that Jasper had in the truck bed, it would take days they couldn't spare for them to cut through and drag a chunk off the road. They couldn't return to their route.

They could, however, keep driving along the road that had led them to their shelter and hope that it led somewhere, that it wasn't blocked farther down.

Jasper heaved a sigh of relief, shaking his head in fond amusement at Tobias's worried, questioning look. He'd been afraid that they'd be trapped in the gravel lot, that he'd be forced to try to cut through the tree or hack another path through the woods. Through the storm, it had looked as though it had fallen against the only way out of the lot, and Jasper had spent the entire storm wondering how he was going to tell Tobias.

Deciding to take a road that led who-knew-where when they were on a tight schedule might not have been ideal, but it was far better than he'd expected. "We'll keep going. The road has to lead somewhere."

He hoped it wasn't just to some other abandoned building farther down. "We'll connect with a paved road again and figure out where we need to go."

Tobias nodded and climbed into the truck, his expression unreadable as he leaned against the window, one knee bouncing up and down. He glanced over as Jasper climbed into the driver's seat, but he kept his hands in his lap and fidgeted.

They drove in silence. The road curved through the trees, worsened in several spots, but remained passable, surprisingly clear of downed branches or other insurmountable obstacles. More importantly, it kept going. They made good time, the miles flying by with surprising speed, but the roadside remained clear of anything other than trees and bushes. The building they had sheltered in seemed to be an anomaly, a lone outpost amongst miles of wilderness.

Dark clouds were gathering overhead when Tobias finally moved, unfolding his hands and taking the map from the glove compartment. One hand reached out and lightly touched Jasper's knee while the other traced the route they'd been following. *I think... I don't....* He turned to look at Jasper in the rearview mirror. *There's no towns or anything marked. Not for miles. Not on this road at all.*

"If it's small, it might not be on the map." The response was automatic, but even as he said it, Jasper knew it was a hollow assurance. The building they'd sheltered in had clearly seen use at one point in time, but it was just as clear that the road had been intended strictly as an access route to it, and that they weren't likely to encounter any towns or other buildings along the way. He briefly wondered what it had been used for, out so far from everything else, but pushed the thought aside to concentrate on the issue at hand. "How far until we hit a main road?"

Tobias's eyes moved back to the map and Jasper focused on the road while he waited for the other man to respond. The trees were growing closer and the pavement rougher, branches occasionally breaking through the road and bouncing the truck as it barreled over them. When the storm started again, they would be facing more danger than merely the rain and lightning.

The hand on Jasper's knee twitched. *It's too far. We won't—*

The whisper-quiet thought cut off with a suddenness that had Jasper looking toward his passenger, heedless of the danger on the road ahead. "What's wrong?"

Tobias remained still, his eyes unfocused. His lips parted in a soundless gasp. *We have to go.*

Inexplicable dread churned in Jasper's stomach. "We are."

Faster!

There was nothing Jasper could see on or around the road to explain the sudden urgency in Tobias's tone, but Jasper could feel the panic through the hand on his knee and see the anxiety in Tobias's eyes. He pushed harder on the gas pedal, sending the truck surging forward at a reckless speed.

"What's wrong?" he asked again. He didn't take his eyes off the road, didn't slow, but he needed to know what the sudden urgency was. The storm wasn't close enough to merit a blind run, and they were more likely to find shelter at a sedate pace.

They're coming!

"Who?"

The sudden tight grip on Jasper's arm almost pulled his eyes from the road. *Those men! The ones who have Samantha! Who-Who took me!*

Sleet. Jasper tightened his grip on the steering wheel, narrowed his eyes to better focus on the road, and pushed his foot farther forward. The engine rumbled and the cab shook as the truck careened ahead, bouncing over pot holes and narrowly missing low-hanging branches. "How close are they?" he asked through clenched teeth, his stomach souring with the knowledge that his gamble had failed.

I don't know. Tobias turned in the seat, pressing his shoulder against Jasper's as he peered through the back window. *I can't see them.* He twisted, sat down again, and directed his gaze toward Jasper. *But I can feel them. They're looking for me. They know we went this way.*

The confirmation that they had been followed not only on their alternate route but also on their detour was like a stab in Jasper's gut. "We have to… wait." He stopped, his eyes flickering to Tobias's as a seed of hope took root in the back of his mind. "They won't be able to get past the tree."

For a moment, Tobias calmed, his eyes growing distant. *No.* He shook his head, his eyes impossibly wider. *They did. I don't know how, but they got by… and they're gaining on us.* He clutched at Jasper's arm, his grip painfully tight. *We have to stop, hide, get off the trail… something. We can't keep going this way!*

"I don't—" Jasper began, but paused, his eyes scanning the road. Just ahead the road split. The right hand path was narrow and unpaved, a treacherous risk, but a better option than simply staying on their current route, sitting ducks for the men who were inexplicably gaining on them if Tobias was right.

Jasper had no doubt that he was.

The tires slid on the partially dried mud and broke through the crust to expose the wet soil beneath. Branches clattered against the windshield, bending and breaking as the truck forced its way through. Jasper didn't look behind them, didn't look at Tobias, didn't look anywhere but the narrow road in front of them as he pushed the truck to the limit.

THE paved road they came to was a surprise, the sign for the next town an even bigger one. Tobias scrambled across the bench seat as soon as they passed it, his hand wildly grabbing for the map that had fluttered to the floor during their wild ride. He spread it over his legs with shaking hands, ran a trembling finger over their approximate location as he tried to match the sign to the map. *Oh, sunny day.*

Jasper tore his wild gaze from the road to stare at his awestruck passenger. "What is it?"

We're… that's…. Tobias waved the hand he didn't have pressed against Jasper's thigh aimlessly in the air. *We're back on track. Haversdon was one of the towns we were going to stop in.*

"Clear skies," Jasper breathed, too shocked to muster the breath for a louder exclamation. If the rain held off for another twenty minutes they'd be safe, sheltered for the night in an actual room with an actual bed, able to rest and regroup before running again in the morning.

Yeah. Tobias nodded as he folded the map, carefully bending the paper along the established folds until it was compact enough to fit back in the glove box. *We should hurry, though.* His gaze darted to the rearview mirror. *They're still back there. Still coming. Still gaining.*

Jasper didn't need Tobias to project his fear to feel the urgency behind his words. They weren't in the clear yet, and the faster they reached shelter, the better. Once they stopped, the storms would provide their protection.

THE first drops of rain splattered on the pavement outside the inn as they unloaded their bags from the back of the truck. Tobias hurried ahead, then bounced on his toes as he waited by the door for Jasper to join him. *Hurry!* He pressed a palm to Jasper's shoulder blade as Jasper fought with the lock, struggling to juggle the bag, the key, and the anxious man next to him.

He grinned as the tension faded from his muscles with the knowledge that they'd reached shelter just in time. "It's barely starting. We timed this perfectly."

Tobias studied the sky for a moment, then settled his gaze on the road approaching town. *I guess.* He didn't sound nearly as relieved as Jasper felt.

"They haven't stopped yet?" Jasper's muscles twitched and tightened again. The men should have stopped at the first sign of rain, but then again they shouldn't have made it past the downed tree. Clearly, Jasper had to stop thinking of them the way he thought of everyone else.

No. Tobias pushed Jasper though the door as soon as it was open, removed the key, and slammed the door shut behind him before Jasper caught his balance inside the room. *They will soon, though.* He caught his bottom lip in his teeth. *I think.*

Jasper reached past him and flipped the lock. "They'll have to."

Yeah. Tobias didn't sound convinced, but said nothing else; instead he crossed the room to sit on the bed, his hand falling away from Jasper as they parted.

Jasper let his bag drop to the floor next to Tobias's. "Hey." He sat on the bed, nudged Tobias with his shoulder. "We'll move again in the morning."

Tobias nodded, the corners of his mouth twisted downward in a frown. *I know.*

"So what's wrong?"

Just.... Tobias shrugged, his shoulder rubbing against Jasper's. *I can still feel them. It's… distracting.*

Jasper laid his hand on Tobias's shoulder, rubbing up and down over his tight muscles. "Try not to think about it."

That's easier said than done. Curls bounced as Tobias shook his head, but there was a glimmer of… something… in his eyes as he peered at Jasper through lowered lashes. *What should I think about instead? 'Cause, you know, if you don't give me something else to think about, I'll just keep thinking about that thing you told me not to think about.*

Jasper didn't even try to wrap his mind around that sentence. "Well, um…." And then he stopped, leaned forward, and slipped his fingers under Tobias's chin, lifting it so he could press their lips together.

That'll work. Tobias smirked against Jasper's lips as he shifted, bringing his hands up to tangle in Jasper's hair as he turned on the bed, angling his body toward Jasper's. *Are you sure, though? Last time....* He pulled back ever so slightly as he trailed off, unable or unwilling to finish the sentence.

They both knew how it ended.

Jasper pulled Tobias back closer, slid his tongue across Tobias's lips as he deepened the kiss, letting his actions speak for him. Tobias's lips parted, and their tongues brushed together.

THIS time, the kiss tasted only of Tobias, the dark, earthy flavors untainted by the lighter flavors Jasper knew must be the way he tasted to Tobias. It was delicious, perfect and wonderful and exactly what Jasper had wanted the first time... only not. Tobias was holding back, Jasper could tell, could feel the tension in Tobias's muscles that had nothing to do with the men following them or the storm raging outside, tension that wouldn't fade no matter what Jasper did with his tongue or his hands or anything else.

Reluctantly, he moved back and cupped Tobias's cheeks in his hands. "You're holding back."

I have to. Tobias's eyes darted around the room, focusing everywhere but Jasper's face. *Otherwise I can't.... You don't want....* His eyes slid shut, his expression forlorn. *You can't have it both ways. If I don't hold back, you'll feel... everything.*

"That's what I want." The words were surprising, but even as he said them, Jasper realized he really meant them. "I want to feel what you're feeling. This," he brushed his thumb across Tobias's lips, "without it, doesn't feel right."

Tobias withdrew, freeing his face from Jasper's hands. *It's not that simple.*

"Why not? You want this; I want this, what's the problem?"

You can't... I can't.... Tobias sighed, let his head flop forward into his hand. *You can't just want it sometimes. I'll never know. And I'll mess up.* He looked up, met Jasper's eyes with a gaze so intense Jasper had to resist the urge to scoot away. *I know that what—what I do, with feelings and thoughts, projecting them, that it scares you. That it's not something you're used to. It's just... I can't stop myself just some of the time. It's too hard to stop, too hard to keep it from happening, and if I lose that concentration, I don't know that I'll get it back. I know I won't get it back if I have to try again and again and again.*

The tight desire in Jasper's gut uncoiled a little as uncertainty and fear wormed their way into his consciousness, but he pushed them aside, forced himself to meet Tobias's eyes. "What do you mean? I can't...." He let his eyelids fall closed, sucked in enough air to save a drowning man, and blew it out in one long huff. "I need to know that you're not going to make me feel things."

Then I can't—

Jasper held up a hand, cut off the desperate voice in his head. "Make me feel things like they're *my* feelings," he clarified, desperately trying to make Tobias see the difference, desperately trying to get it clear in his own mind. "When I can tell it's what *you're* feeling, it's—it's different."

But yesterday, you... when I...

"It surprised me. I panicked." Jasper shook his head and looked up, meeting Tobias's eyes with a steady gaze. "It's strange, okay? Different. Not something I'm used to."

But—

"I'll get used to it." Jasper let the corners of his mouth slip up into a smile. "I want to get used to it."

Are you.... Tobias looked down, licked his lips, and shyly looked back up into Jasper's eyes. *Are you sure?*

The last vestiges of Jasper's doubt fell away at the desperately hopeful look in Tobias's eyes. The hand on his thigh was trembling, and Jasper knew the look in Tobias's eyes barely scratched the surface of the hope and desire he was feeling. His smile widening, Jasper leaned in, his fingers catching Tobias's chin, and pressed his lips against Tobias's. "Yes," he whispered straight into Tobias's mouth before he deepened the kiss, his hand sliding back to stroke Tobias's hair.

The sudden flood of sensation—need, want, hope, desire, happiness—nearly sent Jasper reeling. He tightened his fingers in Tobias's hair, his grip on Tobias's shoulder and concentrated on the taste of Tobias on his tongue, on the taste of himself on Tobias's tongue. He could feel Tobias's fingers in his hair, too. It was different than Tobias's hair—coarser, less silky—but the sensation was familiar and sent tickles down the back of his hands where Tobias's curls didn't reach.

"Clear skies," he murmured straight into Tobias's mouth, unable—unwilling—to pull back just yet.

Yeah. It was a simple toss-off word of agreement, but Tobias deepened the kiss, pushing Jasper back to lie on the bed, his legs still hanging off the side as Tobias straddled him.

Jasper slid his hands under Tobias's shirt, ran his hands over the smooth skin and solid muscles of Tobias's back, and thrust his hips upward, rubbing their jean-clad groins together and eliciting a moan from them both. He touched and rubbed and lost himself in the sensations, his tongue delving and his hands stroking, knowing exactly how it felt to Tobias. He wasn't going to be able to hold back much longer. He didn't want to.

CHAPTER
FOURTEEN

JASPER woke with a start, gasping as he sat up and blinked into the darkness, his heart racing with unidentifiable terror. Outside, wind and rain pounded against the building. Apart from the drone that everyone who lived through wet seasons learned to ignore, the room was silent. Even Jasper's ragged breathing was drowned out by the noise from outside, and he couldn't hear Tobias at all.

Carefully, so he wouldn't wake Tobias if he were still sleeping, Jasper twisted and leaned down. "Tobias?" he said, pitching his voice so it was just audible over the pounding rain. "Are you awake?"

The lump that was just visible in the dark room shifted and a warm hand pressed clumsily against Jasper's arm. *Yeah. Sorry. I didn't mean to wake you.*

Jasper fumbled with the lamp, blinked as light filled the room, and turned to look down at Tobias. "What happened?"

Nightmare, I think. Tobias sat up, brought his knees to his chest, and wrapped one arm around them. The other hand stayed pressed to Jasper's arm.

"You think?" Jasper blinked. "What else could it be?"

Messages? Tobias shrugged. *I don't know if we're close enough to Samantha for her to send to me or not.*

Jasper didn't know what the range was, but they still had at least a week's journey. "How far can you send? We're still about twenty-five hundred miles from Shaleton." Their route wound a little and thus was slightly longer, but Jasper didn't think that the psychic connection between Tobias and his sister would be affected by the landscape that forced the roads to twist.

Probably not that far, but maybe? Tobias sighed and leaned against Jasper as he pulled his knees in closer. *If she's hurt or in pain, she could maybe send further. I don't know. Maybe they're hurting her.*

He looked up at Jasper with a wide, worried gaze that cut straight to Jasper's heart. He looked young and vulnerable, more like a boy than he had since Jasper had first seen him, and it brought out Jasper's protective instincts. "Do you want to tell me about it?" Based on Tobias's reaction, Jasper didn't think he wanted to know, but he couldn't let Tobias just fret if telling him would help.

There isn't anything to tell, really. Tobias sighed and rubbed his hand over his face before returning it to his knee. *It was just pain, mostly. Samantha was worried about something—I don't know what— and she hurt and she was scared and I don't even know what else. There wasn't anything specific.*

Jasper wrapped his arm around Tobias's shoulders and tucked him in a little closer. It felt comfortable having Tobias tucked under his arm like this, and though Jasper regretted the circumstance— particularly since it was a far cry from how they had both been feeling before they fell asleep—he was glad he was able to provide the comfort. "Maybe it was just a nightmare. It's been a long few days and we were exhausted."

Maybe. Tobias didn't sound as though he believed it. *Why would I dream about Sam though? I had other things on my mind when I fell asleep.* He glanced up at Jasper, a teasing smile on his lips. *I don't think I'd dream about my sister after that.*

Jasper returned Tobias's grin. The memory of what they'd done before falling asleep wasn't fresh in his mind after his rude awakening, but it was close enough to the surface that he could easily recall the pleasant lethargy he felt as they'd curled up in bed together. They hadn't gotten beyond fondling, both of them coming in their pants before they'd had a chance to do anything else, but it had ensured Jasper fell asleep with a smile on his face.

"Maybe it wasn't, then," Jasper said, his grin fading. "It could have been her, and you were more receptive since you were so relaxed?" He wasn't sure how Tobias's abilities worked, but the idea seemed logical enough.

I guess. Tobias sighed, slumping further in Jasper's arms. *I don't know which I'd prefer, to be honest.*

"I know." There were downsides to both, ones Jasper didn't care to think about. "We'll figure it out, though, whichever one it is."

Tobias made a soft snorting sound. *How?*

Jasper shifted his grip on Tobias and lay down with him. "You can start by trying to send something back."

What if she doesn't answer? Tobias shifted so he was lying stretched out along Jasper's side and lifted his head so he was looking worriedly at Jasper. *What then?*

"You try again when we're closer." Jasper gently pushed Tobias's head down so it was resting on his shoulder and started carding his fingers through Tobias's dark curls. He put his other hand on Tobias's back and gently stroked as he tried to soothe the tension he felt there. "If she doesn't answer right away, it could just mean that you're not strong enough. Or she could be asleep." It was a stretch, he knew, but he had to give Tobias something to cling to.

Maybe. Tobias sighed and the tension slowly started seeping out of his muscles. *I wish there was some way to know for sure.*

"I know," Jasper whispered, stilling his hands. Tobias was relaxed now, lying limp against him, though Jasper could still feel the worry he was projecting. "I wish there was more we could do."

Thanks. Tobias let out a final sigh and let his eyes slip closed. *I do too.*

"We'll move in the morning," Jasper promised as he gave into his exhaustion and reached for the light. He closed his eyes as soon as it was dark, relaxed under the comforting weight of Tobias and let sleep claim him. If Tobias answered, Jasper never heard.

IN THE morning, the alarm woke them early, though it turned out to be pointless for them to even get out of bed. Though the sun should have been peeking over the horizon according to the clock, Jasper could still hear the hard patter of rain against the walls and the roof, and it didn't sound as though it would be letting up any time soon. "Hailstones," he muttered, eyeing the outside door and wondering if the inn's proprietor would unlock the interior one or if they'd be forced to run through the storm to get any news.

Tobias stretched out and brushed his fingers against Jasper's leg. *Is something wrong?*

"The storm isn't letting up." Jasper went over to the door directly opposite the one they'd used, and tried the handle. It was locked, as he'd expected. Most inns had small hallways that led to the main office and the proprietor's living quarters, but they were only used during the worst of the wet season. The rest of the year, the doors that accessed them were kept locked for security and the guests would use the outside doors.

Tobias sat up, held out his hand, and waited patiently for Jasper to take it. *How long will we have to wait?*

"I don't know." Jasper ran a hand through his hair as he sat down. "If that door is unlocked, I might be able to get some news from the office. Otherwise, we'll just have to wait until we hear it let up."

So then we're stuck. Tobias fell back on the bed and flung an arm across his eyes. *Sleet. I need to get closer to Samantha.*

Jasper lay back next to Tobias with a sigh. "You didn't reach her?"

No. Maybe I fell asleep too soon, but.... He sighed. *What do we do now?*

"I guess we should get cleaned up, since we're stuck," he said after a few minutes of companionable silence. "We can wash our clothes, too, if the storm hasn't let up after we shower." By then, there wouldn't be any chance for them to reach the next town if they didn't leave immediately, so access to the weather tracker would be a moot point. They'd be stuck for at least a day, and though Jasper wasn't thrilled about it, they could take advantage of their secure stopping place to get some rest and wash the clothes they'd been using since they started out. Yesterday's particularly needed to be cleaned.

For a moment, Tobias looked like he was going to protest, but instead he rubbed a hand over his face, and sighed. *All right. Do you want to go first?*

It didn't much matter to Jasper, but he could tell that Tobias wasn't ready to get up yet, so he pushed himself up and swung his legs out of bed. "Sure. Thanks."

Welcome. Tobias stretched again, exposing a bare strip of stomach that made Jasper want to stay in bed so he could touch and taste.

He deliberately looked away, standing and placing his hands at the small of his back. It cracked as he leaned back a little, and he sighed as his bones settled into a more comfortable position.

Tease, Tobias said, looking at Jasper with a raised eyebrow. *Don't make sounds like that if you don't want me to do something about them.*

"I'm not the one lying there with my stomach exposed," Jasper retorted, poking at the exposed skin with one finger.

Tobias squirmed away, huffing out a soft laugh that completely ruined the glare he directed Jasper's way. *I'm not teasing, though,* he said as he stretched again, pulling the thin material of his T-shirt up farther. *If we're not going anywhere today...*

"Let's wait and see what the weather does." Tobias's change in attitude, though welcome, was too sudden for Jasper to believe it. "I don't want to miss our chance if we can leave."

Right. The teasing smile fell from Tobias's face and Jasper could again feel his worry. *Hurry.*

"Relax," Jasper said, regretting his words already. "Even if the rain stopped right now, we'd still have time to shower." Cleaning their clothes would be another story, but that was why they were going to wait on that.

I know. Just, hurry. Please. Tobias's smile was tight, his tone a clear dismissal.

Jasper nodded and grabbed the last clean set of clothes out of his bag. "Of course." He couldn't tell Tobias to calm down, not after riling him up, so there wasn't much else to say. "I'll be out in a few."

TOBIAS scurried into the shower as soon as Jasper left it, moving as fast as Jasper had ever seen. *I'll be out in a few,* he sent, brushing his hand against Jasper's arm. *Then we can go if the weather clears.*

It didn't sound as though it would, but Tobias wouldn't be able to hear him over the shower anyway, so Jasper sat on the bed and pulled on his shoes and socks. He'd just finished putting them on when there was a knock on the interior door and he heard the sound of a key turning in the lock. "Yeah?" he asked, heading over and opening the door when he reached it.

The inn's proprietor stood on the other side, looking rumpled and apologetic. "Sorry," he said, flashing an uneasy smile at Jasper. "I meant to unlock this last night, after you checked in, but my wife made a late dinner and by the time I was done, I forgot."

"It's all right," Jasper assured him easily, his earlier worry forgotten. "We knew better than to go anywhere."

The proprietor nodded. "Thank sunshine. I've had idiots who tried to go outside in a storm because I was slow getting to the door, and they want to blame me."

"It's their own fault for going out in it," Jasper remarked.

"Yeah, well, try telling that to them." The proprietor held out his hand. "I'm George. Don't think I introduced myself last night. If you need anything, feel free to come down and ask."

"Thanks," Jasper replied. "I'm Jasper and my friend is Tobias." He waited for George to release his hand and tucked it into his pocket as he leaned against the door. "You know what the storms are doing?"

"Sticking around today." George rocked back on his heels. "I looked before I came down and it's pretty much a solid wall. They're saying we might get a break tomorrow, though."

"Hope so," Jasper said with a sigh. "This is a little much for this early in the season."

George nodded, and Jasper allowed himself a sigh of relief. At least he hadn't underestimated how bad things got. He'd been basing his guesses on how the storms had been in Crittendon and Brightam's Ford, but the geography was different here. Eventually, they'd reach the point where the storms that swung up from the eastern ocean and looped over the land would clash with the ones that crossed the continent from the west, creating an exceptionally dangerous wet season for people who lived in their path, but they seemed not to be there yet.

"You can come down to the office and look whenever you'd like" George volunteered. "We have laundry equipment too, if you want to take advantage of the downtime."

Jasper nodded. They'd have to pay, too, further stretching Jasper's resources, but they'd deal with that later. "Thank you," he said, stepping back inside and starting to close the door. "We'll do that."

"I'll see you in a bit, then," George said as he turned to go. "Take care."

"You too." Jasper shut the door before George was completely gone and turned to gather their clothes. Tobias wouldn't like that they were stuck—neither did Jasper for that matter—but at least they were safe and somewhere they had the opportunity to take advantage of the situation. It could have been much worse.

IT ALMOST seemed like it was ten minutes later when Tobias rushed out of the shower, hastily dressed in the last of the old clothes Jasper had lent him before the trip. He skidded to a stop just inside the room, looked between Jasper and the pile of dirty laundry he'd gathered on the bed, and stalked over to Jasper with an accusatory look on his face.

What are you doing? He asked, pressing his hand to Jasper's arm. *We need to go, not wash our clothes!*

"We can't go." Jasper picked up one of their bags and started stuffing the dirty clothes back into it so he could carry them to the laundry machines. "It's still storming. The manager came by and said it doesn't look like it's going to let up today. We can't leave."

We have to. Tobias planted his feet firmly and glared at Jasper. *Samantha hasn't answered me. I need to get closer.*

"You will." Jasper set the duffle down on the bed and turned to face Tobias. "Tomorrow, or the next day if tomorrow doesn't work. It's not late enough in the season for the storms to be this bad all day every day. There will be a break in them, and we'll go."

What if there's not? What if I can't get to Samantha? What if we're stuck here until the wet season is over and—

"Hey." Jasper cut Tobias off. "That's not going to happen. I promise, the first chance we get, we'll leave, okay? We just need to be sure we're safe when we do, or we won't be able to help her."

Tobias sighed, sat on the bed, and stretched out his leg so his foot brushed Jasper's ankle. *What if those men find us while we're waiting? They were right behind us, and they're coming. I know they are. I can feel them.*

"Are they here, right now?" Jasper started to rethink his plans about doing laundry. If the men chasing them were actually in town and actively looking, they would have to brave the storm anyway, taking their chances against the elements in the hopes that the rain would protect them from the human threat.

No. Tobias shook his head. *They're close, though, and I think they're moving. It's hard to tell.* He leaned over to put on his shoes and socks, but lifted his head after a moment and looked up at Jasper again. *We can't stay here if they come.*

"We won't." Jasper sat on the bed next to Tobias and pushed his hand back through his sandy hair. "The storms should keep them from getting too close today and—"

The storms should have kept them from getting Samantha! Tobias balled his hands into fists and jumped up to pace back and forth in front of Jasper. He stopped after a minute, taking a deep breath, and sank back down on the bed so he could press his shoulder against Jasper. *They know how to travel in them. They have to. How else would they have been able to find me? How else could they have gotten Samantha to Shaleton?*

"They took her during the storms?" Jasper tilted his head to the side. He hadn't realized Samantha had been gone that long. "How? And from where?"

Just before the storms last year. And north. Over the mountains. Tobias shrugged. *I don't know where, exactly. It wasn't on the map you showed me.*

Jasper blinked incredulously, revising his entire view of how far Tobias had traveled. He'd known it had to be far—he'd never encountered anyone who communicated the way he did before—but it had never occurred to him that Tobias would have crossed the northern mountains. They were steep and jagged, believed by most to be impassible, and covered with snow from the wet season for the vast majority of the year. Jasper hadn't even known that there was anywhere suitable to live north of them.

"You crossed the mountains?" he asked, just to be sure he'd heard correctly. "How?"

Walked. Tobias folded his hands in his lap and looked down at them. *It took a long time, most of the dry season, to get across them. That's why I had only gotten as far as your place when the storms started.*

"You walked." It was hard to believe, but Tobias was here, sitting next to him, so Jasper had to accept it. "What about the people who took Samantha? How did they get across? And how would they get her to Shaleton and make it all the way back for you?"

They had a head start. Tobias didn't look up. *Samantha was— away from town. We thought that maybe she would find her way back, but she didn't, and then when I couldn't sense her anymore, I tried to follow. I think someone stayed back from the people who took her, waiting to see if anyone would come, and I got all turned around trying to hide from them and I got stuck in the mountains when the wet season started. If they knew their way and had someplace to hide from the weather...*

"They could have made it," Jasper finished, trying to work out the timeline in his head. "This was before the last wet season, right?" In that case, they might not have traveled during the storms at all. If they'd kept Samantha subdued, they might have waited out the wet season and taken her to Shaleton during the dry.

Tobias picked at a loose thread in his pants. *Yeah. Samantha was chosen to perform the ritual to appease the forest spirits last year. I don't know what she did—no one does until they're chosen—but she had to spend several days in the forest, away from our town. She was happy and excited, but when she was supposed to come back, something happened and—*

"And that's what you showed us in my safe room," Jasper guessed, finally putting the pieces together. The forest spirit Samantha had gone to appease couldn't have had anything to do with her abduction. There were men coming after them now, so men had taken Samantha. Even if the spirit had been malevolent, those creatures were tied to their homes, and the most it could have done was keep Samantha there.

Yeah. Tobias flashed a grateful look at Jasper then immediately returned his gaze to his hands. *I followed as soon as I knew she wasn't coming back, but they almost caught me too. Those men, they're not right. They feel dark. Dangerous. I ran and hid and then the storms started and I had to find shelter. I spent most of the last wet season in caves, trying to move as best I could, but I got lost, and didn't get out of the mountains until into the dry season, and then I had to walk.*

Jasper filled out the timeline in his mind. It would have taken Tobias most of the dry season to walk from the closest place in the mountains to Brightam's Ford. Adding on the time he'd likely spent wandering around in the mountains, it was a miracle he'd made it that far. "Hailstones," he murmured as the true amount of time Tobias had spent traveling dawned on him. "They've had your sister for a year."

That's why I have to find her. Tobias finally looked up and met Jasper's eyes. *I can't let them capture me too.*

"They won't," Jasper promised. "Even if they can travel during the storm, they won't know where we are. They can't knock on doors, they'll just be pulled inside the first place they try." He squeezed Tobias's knee. "If we leave as soon as the storms break, we'll be fine."

Are you sure?

"As I can be." Jasper stood and grabbed both bags full of their dirty clothes. "Come on. Let's start the laundry and check the radar." It wouldn't do much good yet—the storms that could keep them in tomorrow wouldn't show up for hours yet—but it seemed to make Tobias feel better, because he nodded as he stood and took one of the bags from Jasper.

Okay, he sent, forcing a smile Jasper could tell was fake.

He ignored that, though, focusing on the fact that Tobias was smiling, and hoping that the radar would show them good news before their laundry was done. He didn't think Tobias would stand for anything less than leaving as soon as the sun rose in the morning.

CHAPTER FIFTEEN

THE streets glistened under the early morning sun. The storms had stopped sometime around sunrise, waking Jasper with the sudden silence. He'd lain in bed, listening to the town wake up, until the alarm went off an hour later. Tobias had slept through it all, or at least seemed to, not stirring until the tiny clock had started making noise, but once he was awake, he'd practically dragged Jasper from bed in his haste to get back on the road.

It had taken every bit of Jasper's persuasive powers to convince him that they at least needed to stop for supplies first. Once he had, Tobias had taken to that with enthusiasm as well, and had goaded Jasper down the street toward the shops clustered around Haversdon's town square.

"Easy," Jasper said, digging in his heels a little when the pace got too fast. "We don't need to run."

We need to get on the road, Tobias protested, tugging on Jasper's arm again. *We need to get to Shaleton while we still can.*

Travel would be hard with the worsening storms, but it wasn't impossible, and likely wouldn't be until after they'd reached Shaleton. "We need to make sure we don't forget anything, either. I don't want to be stranded without something we need."

Tobias sighed, but let Jasper lead him into the first shop at a more sedate pace. *Fine, but then we're going, right? There's nothing else we need to do?*

"Nothing else," Jasper said with a laugh. "Now calm down. We don't want to attract attention again."

Tobias immediately straightened and stepped away from Jasper, breaking contact with him and obviously trying to look like a normal shopper on a normal day. He did an all right job, mimicking Jasper's walk and even managing to nod at the other people in the store as they passed by, but they still managed to attract attention. It was impossible not to as the only visitors in a small town and the fact that they were traveling in the wet season just added to the curiosity the townsfolk had about them.

They made it through the hardware store without being stopped and talked to the gas station owner without interruption. Halfway through the grocery store an old woman—likely one of the town gossips—touched Jasper lightly on the arm. He was so used to Tobias touching him that way that he only noticed someone else was nearby when Tobias bumped against his other shoulder. *Jasper. Company.*

"Sorry," Jasper said, flashing an insincere smile at the woman. "Can I help you with something?"

"I just wanted to welcome you to town. See if there's anything I can do to help you out." She patted Jasper's arm. "Most people have been hiding because of the weather, but we do like seeing new folk around here, and I wanted to make sure you knew you were welcome."

Jasper's smile became even more strained. "Thanks, but we're just passing through."

"Oh? Really?" She titled her head curiously. "Where are you headed to?"

"Shaleton. We're hoping to get there before the weather gets too bad."

The woman took a step back, her welcoming expression fading to wary as she eyed both Jasper and Tobias suspiciously. "Shaleton? Really? What for?"

"His sister is there," Jasper tilted his head toward Tobias. "We're going to see her, try to get her to come back with us to Brightam's

Ford." And beyond, if they were successful, but Jasper wasn't going to tell her that, not when he didn't want to think about it himself.

"Oh." The woman relaxed visibly. "Well, good luck then. I hope you can beat the storms and find a safe place to stay this wet season." The way she said it implied that Shaleton wouldn't be safe. Jasper couldn't disagree.

"Thank you," he said, stepping around her to continue on his way. Tobias was getting antsy beside him, pressing close though not saying anything, and the encounter just illustrated what a bad idea it was to try to get Tobias to pass as normal in a small town. There was too much else on his mind and too many prying eyes to make it work.

The rest of the shopping trip was uneventful, with Jasper quickly grabbing the items they needed off the shelves and dropping them in the basket Tobias was carrying. They made it all the way to the register without anyone else stopping them—a small miracle considering the number of townspeople who were in the store, presumably stocking up after the storms yesterday—and Jasper breathed a sigh of relief as Tobias swung the basket up onto the counter.

The girl behind it smiled at them and flipped her hair as she looked at Tobias. "How are you doing today?"

The question was clearly directed at Tobias, but for the first time, Jasper was glad that he couldn't answer aloud. Jealousy wasn't like him, but as the cashier continued to look straight at Tobias while punching the register keys slowly, a bit of it curled in the pit of Jasper's stomach. "We're good," he said, attempting to keep his tone normal. "Just getting supplies so we can get on our way while the weather is still good."

"Oh. You're leaving?" The girl blinked and started punching their purchases into the cash register a little faster. "We don't usually get people traveling out this time of year."

She was clearly fishing for information, a thought shared by Tobias as he bumped his shoulder against Jasper's. *She can't really think we're anything but travelers.*

Jasper nodded. "We're just passing through. Headed toward Shaleton."

The girl stopped punching the register. "Really? You're the second group I've checked out today who's headed there." She leaned in, looked between Jasper and Tobias, and lowered her voice. "The other group looked like they belonged there, though, if you know what I mean. You two look like you could belong here, but those men, they were dressed crazy. All sorts of fancy green and purple."

They're here! Tobias clenched his hand hard around Jasper's arm. *Come on! We have to go or they'll see us!* He stepped toward the door, trying to drag Jasper along with him, but Jasper held his ground.

"Hold on!" Jasper tensed his arm and yanked Tobias back. "You don't want the whole town coming after us because we didn't pay, do you? We don't need that kind of attention when we're just trying to get on our way."

Tobias kept tugging. *We need to go. Now!*

"Hold on." Jasper looked at the stuff on the counter, figured that the girl had rung up everything that they absolutely needed, and pulled out his wallet. "We don't want to cause a scene."

That got Tobias to calm down and step back toward Jasper. *Sorry.* He flashed a sheepish smile as he tucked his hands in his pocket and shifted so his elbow was against Jasper's. *I wasn't thinking.*

There was a lot Jasper could say to that, but they were in public, and the last thing he needed at the moment was to give the people of Haversdon further clues about the strange way Tobias communicated. Instead, he waited with as much patience as he could muster while the girl behind the counter finished ringing up the last few items, and paid her as quickly as he could while Tobias stuffed their purchases into bags. "Thanks," he said, once they had everything, and he grabbed one of the bags and placed his hand on Tobias's back, hoping that they could both stay calm long enough to get back to the inn and pack the truck.

THE town square was bustling, people strolling between the shops and children darting around, laughing as they played, so Jasper felt fairly safe as they stepped out of the grocer and headed back toward the inn. The men after them had already shopped for food, after all, and they clearly hadn't been staying in the inn or the van would have been in the parking lot along with Jasper's truck. The only other vehicle had been a run-down station wagon that probably belonged to George, the proprietor, and couldn't possibly have made it between towns, even in the dry season.

Jasper glanced over the square as they walked through it, taking in all the people just in case, but no one stood out the way men in emerald trench coats would have. "Maybe they already left," he offered quietly as they stepped away from the noise of the square onto the quieter side street that lead to their inn. "If they thought we were ahead of them, then—"

No.

The fear that accompanied the word was enough to chill Jasper's bones. He shuddered as he slowly turned his head, intending to look at Tobias but stopping halfway when he realized what Tobias must be staring at. "Sleet!"

Two men in bright emerald green were moving around a van parked in an alley between two houses. It was a narrow area, practically covered by the overhanging roofs of the houses on either side, and though it wouldn't have been ideal to survive the storms, it would have sufficed in the windowless van as long as the windshield was protected. Their backs were to Jasper and Tobias, fortunately, but based on the position of the stuff they were loading into the van, it likely wouldn't stay that way for long.

Jasper grabbed Tobias's shirt. "Just keep walking," he said as he steered Tobias toward the inn. They had to pass the men, there was no way around that, but they were on the opposite side of the street, and if they moved quickly and quietly, they had a chance. "Stay quiet."

No. We need to go back to the town square. Circle around. He spun, his shoes scraping against some loose gravel as his shirt pulled free of Jasper's grip, and grabbed Jasper's wrist. *Hurry! They're going to turn and then—*

It was too late.

The taller of the two men turned and froze as his gaze landed on Jasper and Tobias, and then time seemed to slow. The bag the man had picked up fell to the ground, its contents spilling everywhere as the man turned and grabbed his companion by the shoulder. He said something that Jasper couldn't hear, and they both lunged forward. Their hands slipped into the pockets of their coats as they dashed across the street, their gazes narrowed and their feet hit the pavement with unnaturally loud thuds.

It was only when they pulled their hands back out of their pockets, revealing the same guns they'd held earlier, that Jasper was able to move again, his brain suddenly kick-started by a surge of adrenaline. "Sleet, hail, and fog!" he cursed, spitting the words out with venom as he tried to direct Tobias toward the hotel. The only chance they had was to get away from the men long enough to get to their hotel—and that would be easier if they were closer—but he couldn't take the time to explain that, not with the men moving toward them guns at the ready and angry yells coming out of their mouths.

No! Tobias tugged his hand free of Jasper's grip. *This way!* He took off the way they had come, leaving Jasper no choice but to follow.

It was hard to keep up. Tobias was fast, his panic lending him speed that Jasper couldn't match. He didn't dare yell, didn't dare do anything but try to keep up, but the men were gaining on them and Tobias was racing ahead, swinging around corners faster than Jasper could track. His lungs burned and his feet ached as he ran, unaware of where he was or where he was going or anything other than the fleeting presence of Tobias in front of him and the ever-looming presence of men and guns at his back.

He stumbled, not quite falling, but slowing enough that he lost Tobias around another corner and had to blindly guess which direction Tobias had taken as he rounded the bend. The men were still close behind him—closer now that he'd tripped—and though he knew they were still too far away for it to be possible, he imagined he could feel their hot breath on the back of his neck.

Jasper put on a burst of speed, calling forth every reserve of energy he had left, and took two corners in quick succession. The second led him into an alley with no way out, but there were trash cans in it, clustered close together near the back, and Jasper slipped behind them and crouched down as low as he could. The moment he ducked, the two men who had been chasing him came running past without so much as glancing his way.

Jasper let out a sigh of relief, but it was short-lived. Before he could stand up, the men came back, walking this time, and they stopped just outside the alley, their guns held loosely in their hands as they looked around. Jasper trembled in place, struggling to control his loud breathing and doing his best to focus on what they were saying. He couldn't hear more than snippets—mostly curses, though he did catch something about their van and Shaleton and time—but he didn't dare creep any closer. The knowledge wouldn't do him any good if they spotted him and captured him, or worse.

By the time they left, still cursing loudly and kicking at the loose rocks on the wet pavement, Jasper had almost caught his breath. He stood slowly, ready to duck down again at the first sign of anyone coming by, but when he gathered the courage to approach the end of the alley, there was no one there. The street he'd turned off was deserted, as was the one before that, and Jasper had no hope of tracing his route back any further than that. He didn't know where he was, where Tobias was, or where the men were, and he didn't dare search for anyone out of fear that he'd find the wrong group.

Instead, he walked, turned onto a larger street three blocks down, and stopped a young boy who was tossing a ball with his sister in the yard. "Excuse me," he said once the boy had the ball and was in no danger of being hit if his sister wasn't paying attention. "Do you know how to find George's inn?"

Jasper couldn't remember the name of the inn—wasn't sure he'd ever known it, to be honest—but it didn't matter. The boy rolled his eyes, assumed the universal expression children got when they thought adults were being stupid, and pointed down the street in the direction Jasper had come from. "That way. Turn right onto Blossom, go down two blocks, then left on Fallen Oak. You can't miss it."

"Thanks." Jasper flashed a smile at the kid, turned around, and started in that direction. He walked at first, the bag he'd been carrying held loosely in his hand, but he couldn't shake the desperate need to find Tobias and get out of town or the feeling that he was being followed despite the empty street, and by the time he reached Orchard, he was jogging. He would have been in a flat-out run by the time he turned on to Fallen Oak, but his muscles still hurt from earlier and his legs refused to push him any faster than a jog.

By the time he reached the inn, he was winded, each breath hurting a little more than the last. It made moving painful, but Jasper only allowed himself to stop long enough to check that the office was locked, George nowhere to be found, before he went on to the room they'd rented to gather up their things.

That didn't take long at all, though Jasper kept glancing over his shoulder as he loaded their bags as well as the one from the store into the back of the truck. Only once was there someone watching him—a young couple with their dog—but with each passing moment the feeling of being watched increased. By the time he got everything into the truck, including the filled gas cans he'd dropped off that morning and asked to be delivered, he was starting to understand Tobias's nervousness. It felt as though there was someone hiding behind every tree and building, as though someone was going to jump out at him every second, and even going inside the room to leave the key and the money didn't help. There was nowhere to hide. No one could possibly be inside, yet Jasper dug the money out of his wallet as fast as he could and set it on the bed under the key without counting it a second time. "Sorry, George," he said to the empty room, as he looked around one last time. "I hope it's enough."

The feeling didn't go away, not even when Jasper climbed into the truck and started it up. He was safe here, safer than he'd be anywhere else in town, and yet he couldn't shake the feeling that he needed to move, to go, to get away from the town and the men who had somehow managed to slip into it.

The problem was that he didn't know where to go.

"Where in stormy weather are you, Tobias?" Jasper asked as he shifted the truck into reverse. He had to hope that toward Shaleton was the right answer, that Tobias had managed to figure out how to get out of town on the right road, and that he was somewhere that Jasper could find him before he got too far.

There was always the possibility that Tobias was still in town, still trying to make his way back to the inn, but Jasper didn't have time to wait. He refused to consider that idea, just as he refused to consider that Tobias could have gotten lost and left town on the wrong road or, worse, that the men had found him after they'd given up on finding Jasper. If Jasper let himself consider that anything other than finding

Tobias walking along the road toward Shaleton was a possibility, he'd be frozen with indecision and that wouldn't help him or Tobias.

An engine rumbled nearby, startling Jasper out of his reverie, and he looked out the window to see the van pulling into the lot next to him. "Sleet!" he cursed, banging his elbow into the lock on his door as he slammed his foot onto the gas, sending the truck shooting backward just as the men started to climb from the van. Jasper couldn't spare much attention for them as he jerked the transmission into drive, but out of the corner of his eye, he saw two of the men climb back into the van while the third—who hadn't been chasing them earlier—stayed in the lot, waving them on.

He only had a split second to wonder why before the truck raced forward, quickly reaching speeds that were unsafe in town. The van bolted forward as well, only a few seconds behind him, and a quick glance in the rearview mirror killed any thought Jasper had of slowing for the safety of the townspeople. Instead, he pressed his foot harder against the gas pedal, pushing the truck to its maximum speed, and hoped that he would be able to lose the van before he had to risk innocent lives in order to get away.

CHAPTER SIXTEEN

JASPER whipped the truck around another corner and floored it again, forcing his eyes to focus on the road ahead instead of the rearview mirror. He thought he knew where he was now, thought he knew which roads he needed to take to get on the main road out of town, but he didn't dare take that last turn without being certain that he'd lost the van. He hadn't seen it in two turns, but the desperate need to drive faster and faster hadn't left him and he didn't dare start searching for Tobias until he was certain that the men weren't still behind him.

A quick glance in the mirror as he approached his turn showed him that the road was still clear, and he slowed the truck a little before swinging it around the corner. This time, there were no squealing tires to give him away, and when the truck was fully around the corner, Jasper let himself breathe a tiny sigh of relief.

It didn't last long. He still had to find Tobias, get out of town, and figure out how to lose the men again while they were traveling along the same road to the same destination, but at least he'd overcome the first hurdle. Or so he hoped. He drove the truck at a more sedate pace, using caution as he got closer to the center of town where all the people seemed to be gathered, but he couldn't stop himself from glancing in the rearview mirror every few seconds, and the one time he saw a vehicle behind him, his heart rate jumped.

It wasn't the van, just a car that presumably belonged to one of Haversdon's residents, but the sight brought back the tingling along

Jasper's spine and the unavoidable urge to press the gas pedal all the way to the floor until the car was left in his dust.

He resisted, barely, his foot twitching over the pedal every time he glanced in the rearview mirror, even after the car turned onto another street, leaving the view behind Jasper clear once more. By the time he reached the main road out of town, he was sweating, his hands threatening to slip on the steering wheel.

There was a figure ahead, silhouetted in the sunlight, and Jasper forgot the danger as his heart leapt. Before it occurred to him that it might not be Tobias, he had already covered half the distance between them.

"Tobias!" he called, rolling down the window and leaning out as far as he could while still keeping his hand on the wheel and his foot on the gas pedal. The figure stopped, stiffened, and slowly turned, looking back at Jasper while still silhouetted in the sunlight. Jasper couldn't see his face, but he knew even before the figure started walking toward him that it was Tobias, and he hit the brakes.

The truck coasted to a stop about ten feet away from Tobias, and Jasper slid out, the tension melting from his shoulders as Tobias broke into a run. When he was close, Jasper stepped forward with his arms outstretched and closed the distance between them so he could tell that Tobias was unharmed. They collided about three feet from the truck, Tobias hitting Jasper with enough force to send him stepping back for balance.

You're all right! Tobias slung his arms around Jasper, hitting him in the back with the grocery bags. *You got away!*

"Yeah." Jasper hugged Tobias back, surreptitiously checking him for injuries, and stepped back, holding Tobias by the shoulders so he could give him a visual inspection. "I lost them not long after I lost you and managed to find my way back to the inn. Figured I ought to get our stuff so we could leave once I found you."

They didn't follow you? Tobias gazed toward Haversdon. *I thought about going to the inn, but then I thought they would look there and I didn't know if you would make it back or if I would be able to get into the truck or hide or anything. I figured heading out of town would be safer—they might not think of that right away, especially if they were chasing you.* He ducked his head. *Sorry.*

"It's all right." Jasper patted Tobias on the shoulder. "I figured you'd headed out of town when you weren't at the inn by the time I got everything in the truck. Good thing, too," he added, his tone sobering. "They showed up in their van just as I was ready to leave, so I didn't have time to wait or look anywhere else. I just drove."

Tobias's shoulders tensed. *Did they follow you?*

"I lost them." Jasper slid his hand down Tobias's arm and took one of the bags.

Are you sure?

"They weren't behind me when I turned onto this road." Jasper shrugged. "I hadn't seen them in a few turns, actually, but it won't take them long to figure out where I'm going." He glanced back up the road as the tension between his shoulder blades increased, again urging him to move. "We should go."

Tobias followed Jasper's gaze and handed him the other bag. *Yeah. If they're on the road, it won't take them long to get here, even if they think we're in town. They'll just wait for us in the next one instead of trying to find us here.*

Or they could do both. The man they'd left behind suddenly made sense to Jasper, and the knowledge sent a chill down his spine that urged him to move even faster. Whatever these men wanted with Tobias, they were clearly willing to do whatever was necessary to get it, and they had access to resources that Jasper didn't.

They needed to move.

THE feelings of urgency and terror faded as the day progressed, but Tobias didn't stop looking over his shoulder, and Jasper found himself unwilling to stop for more than a few minutes all day long. Even though he knew intellectually that the men were far behind them and that they'd likely had their own issues getting out of Haversdon, he couldn't completely shake the feeling that they needed to put as much distance between the men and them as possible.

As it turned out, that was a good thing.

The sky stayed clear, but when they were about an hour out from Needa's Crossing, the weather tracker they'd picked up at the hardware store beeped from its place behind the bench seat, and Tobias twisted around to peer down at it. *There's a storm,* he said, pressing one elbow against Jasper's shoulder as he continued to peer down at the screen behind them.

That much was obvious—the tracker wouldn't have beeped otherwise—but it didn't give Jasper the information he needed. "How close?" he asked, pressing his foot down a little harder on the gas pedal. Regardless of how close it actually was, if it was close enough to make the tracker beep, they needed to get in sooner rather than later and Jasper wasn't pushing the truck to the limit just yet.

Close. Tobias shrugged, his elbow moving against Jasper with the movement. *I can't really tell, but it's moving fast.* He pulled the tracker out from behind the seat and handed it to Jasper as he turned around.

The road was clear and lined by fields, so Jasper eased his foot off the pedal slightly and risked a glance down at the tracker. The storm was a large dark spot in the lower corner, moving closer and getting bigger with every refresh of the screen. Even with this less-than-accurate portable tracker, it was clear that this storm was a big one, and that if they didn't beat it to Needa's Crossing, they would be in trouble.

Is it bad? Tobias asked, settling in next to Jasper and peering down at the tracker as well.

Jasper handed it back to him so he could put both hands on the wheel, pressed down hard on the gas again, and nodded. "Could be. We might beat it, but if it picks up any speed or we run into any problems, it'll be close."

Can we go faster?

"Not much. The road's bumpy and we're carrying a lot right now." Plus, if he pushed the truck too fast, the gas mileage would drop and they might be forced to stop outside of town to fill the tank again. Jasper thought they had enough to get to Needa's Crossing—he'd filled the tank when they'd stopped to eat lunch—but he was afraid to drive it too hard with the approaching weather.

Hailstones. Tobias shifted, pressing closer to Jasper as he pulled his legs up onto the seat. It was the same position he'd assumed many times during the drive thus far, but after the tentative kisses they'd exchanged in Haversdon, it was far more distracting, and Jasper suddenly found it hard to focus completely on the road.

"We'll be all right," he said, forcing his gaze, at least, to stay where it belonged. "We're only about an hour out. Even if we get caught in it, we should be close enough to town that we can make it in."

At least, he hoped they could.

IT TURNED out he didn't need to worry.

The storm came on quickly when it started, but they were already walking back from dinner at a local diner in Needa's Crossing when the first raindrops hit the ground. The first one Jasper saw splashed on the sidewalk in front of him, the second hit the bridge of his nose. He looked up to see the clouds that had been absent all day gathering in force, the sky darkening with alarming speed, and grabbed Tobias's hand without thinking about it. "Come on!"

Tobias followed, his feet pounding against the wet pavement in time with Jasper's, his eyes wide as he stared at the sky, letting Jasper do all the navigating. *It was clear ten minutes ago!*

"I know! That's how. These storms. Happen." He had to gasp out every word, but he didn't dare slow or stop to catch his breath. These storms that swung inland from the east coast before heading back out to sea tended to come on more suddenly and violently than the ones that crossed the continent west to east, and this one was clearly going to be typical. From the suddenness of the rain and the way everyone else who had been out was suddenly dashing for cover, Jasper doubted they had long before the full force of the storm hit. "Come on! We need to. Hurry!"

Rain pelted them harder as they ran, the tiny drops that first fell quickly growing in size and falling faster. By the time they reached the end of the block and rounded the corner, they were soaked, and the rain was hitting hard enough to hurt.

Tobias put forth a burst of speed as they approached the inn, dragging Jasper along with him. They stumbled under the inn's overhanging roof together and pressed close to the wall to take advantage of the small amount of shelter it offered. The wind still whipped the rain under the overhang, pelting them with tiny droplets, but the heavier raindrops fell mostly straight, only bouncing to hit their feet rather than lashing at them so it was a slight improvement.

"Sleet," Jasper gasped, tripping over a rock and pulling Tobias back a little. "Slow down a little. We're safe."

Almost, Tobias agreed, but he eased the pace a little as he pulled Jasper to the main door of the inn, yanked it open, and dragged him inside. *Now we are.*

This inn didn't have outside access to the rooms, a fact for which Jasper was grateful as they walked through the lobby and down the hall toward their room. It was easier to dig in his pocket for the room key without the rain and wind and the threat of lightning or hail, and the thick walls protecting them from the weather made it easier to breathe even with Tobias maintaining his fast pace. He moved past the other rooms so quickly that Jasper couldn't read the numbers on the doors, and only stopped when they reached the one they'd been assigned.

Come on, Tobias said, bouncing on his toes as Jasper struggled to slide the key in the lock. It was old and a little rusty, and though both the key and the lock had clearly survived years of use, it was a struggle to get the key in and a fight to make the lock turn.

"Calm down," Jasper admonished softly, grinning as they key finally slid into the hole. "We're just as safe here as we will be in the room."

I know. Tobias pressed close, resting his chin on Jasper's shoulder and watching as Jasper fiddled with the door. *Doesn't mean I want to stay in the hall all night.*

There was something in Tobias's tone that shot through Jasper, making his whole body sit up and take notice. The way that Tobias was pressed against his back was part of it too, as were the emotions Jasper could clearly feel projected along with Tobias's words, and the realization of what he wanted made Jasper's hand slip on the key.

Tobias's hand covered his, guiding it back. *Come on. We need to—*

Bang! Bam bam! Bang!

Jasper's hand slipped again as he jerked away from the door. He pushed Tobias out of the way and turned to look down the hall. There was no one there, and for a brief moment, Jasper was afraid that they hadn't gotten enough of a lead on the men pursuing them. They'd been in town for at least an hour before the storm started, and it wasn't as though there had been anywhere else to go once they'd gotten on the main road out of Haversdon. Their only hope was to leave Needa's Crossing heading straight east or south and turn later instead of taking the southeast road that lead directly to Shaleton. It would take longer and both alternate routes held their own dangers, but either should keep them from being followed.

If they could remain undetected in Needa's Crossing, that was.

The chances of the men making it in before the storm and picking the same inn were slim, particularly since Needa's Crossing was big enough to provide a choice, but that knowledge didn't stop Jasper's heart from clenching as he stared down the hall. Tobias stayed pressed close behind him, the contact meaning something completely different than it had a moment earlier, and peered over Jasper's shoulder.

What was that? Tobias asked, his tone soft as though there was a chance someone could overhear him.

"I don't know," Jasper started, but he trailed off in the middle of the last word as the inn's manager appeared at the end of the hall, herding a small boy holding a large ball in front of him. "Sorry!" he called, flashing an apologetic smile as he laid a hand on the boy's shoulder. "The ball got away from my son, here. We didn't mean to startle you." He looked down at the child. "Did we?"

"No." The boy scuffed his toe on the floor and sighed. "Sorry." He didn't look or sound sorry, just annoyed at being caught and made to apologize, but Jasper nodded anyway.

"It's all right. No harm done."

The manager sighed, looking relieved. "Thanks." He patted the boy's shoulder. "Come on. It's time for you to head to bed."

The moment they were out of sight, Jasper let out a deep breath, slumping against the door as tension drained from his body. "Hailstones. That was—"

A ball. Tobias's eyes sparkled with mirth and his lips twitched as he looked at Jasper. *We were afraid of a ball.*

"It could have been—" Jasper started, but he stopped himself, and shook his head. There really was no excuse that made the whole situation anything less than completely ridiculous and bringing up the men chasing them would just ruin both of their good moods. "Never mind."

Tobias reached around Jasper to fiddle with the key and titled his head to the right as he asked the question Jasper didn't want to answer. *Could have been what?*

"The—"

The lock clicked and the door swung open, sending Jasper tumbling. His head knocked against the door as he went down, which threw off his attempt to catch himself, and he landed in a heap on the floor, the air knocked from his lungs and his head feeling like it was spinning. "Sleet!" He tried to push himself up, but before he managed to sit, Tobias was there, looking down at him.

Are you all right?

"I'm fine. Just a little winded." Jasper caught Tobias's hand in his, stopping it from fluttering around, and pressed it against his chest. "See?"

Tobias tilted his head to the side and looked Jasper up and down. *Yeah,* he said after a minute, a smile blossoming on his face, *I do.* He leaned down then, moving so quickly that Jasper couldn't process it, and pinned him to the floor. His lips brushed against Jasper's, tentatively at first, but with increasing enthusiasm as Jasper first gasped at the unexpected contact and then moaned at its loss.

"Clear skies," he whispered, wrapping one hand around the back of Tobias's neck and holding him down. He pushed his tongue forward, sliding it over the crease of Tobias's lips until they parted, letting him inside where he teased and stroked, then curled his tongue around Tobias's before pulling back and parting his lips in a clear invitation to follow. Tobias took it, mimicking what Jasper had just done as he slid his hands over Jasper's body.

Nimble fingers brushed lightly against Jasper's side, reminding him of Tobias's earlier desire, and he moaned into the kiss, thrusting his hips up as Tobias's hand crept lower. It brushed over Jasper's groin, pressing just enough to taunt him before moving back up, sliding under his shirt and bushing lightly against his stomach. Jasper made a soft sound of protest, shifting to draw attention to the area he wanted Tobias to touch, but Tobias just swallowed the noise with a kiss and continued to slide his hand upward.

It felt good, despite the hard floor beneath him, and Jasper moaned again as Tobias's fingers brushed over his nipple. He arched his back, instinctively looking for more contact, and slid his hand down to tug at the hem of Tobias's shirt. "Off," he whispered, trying to pull it up over Tobias's head without breaking the kiss for longer than it took to ask.

Trying, Tobias replied, breaking the kiss. He ducked his head as he sat up to let Jasper pull the shirt off over his head. *Now you,* he said as he tossed the shirt toward the bags piled against the wall. Jasper took advantage of the opportunity and sat up and pulled off his own shirt before climbing to his feet and drawing Tobias up with him.

"Come on," he said, pushing the door shut and kicking both their shirts toward the bags before pulling Tobias in so they were standing chest to chest. "The bed's more comfortable."

Tobias made a soft noise of agreement as he wrapped his arms around Jasper's neck and went in for another kiss. This one was soft and tender, full of promise, and Jasper smiled as he kissed Tobias and slowly turned so Tobias's back was to the bed.

It was only a few steps to the bed that dominated the small room, and Jasper guided Tobias across the space without ever breaking their embrace. *Seducing me?* Tobias asked as Jasper eased him down onto the bed, amusement coloring his words.

Jasper had to grin as he climbed onto the bed and straddled Tobias's hips. "Maybe. But you started it."

CHAPTER SEVENTEEN

ME? TOBIAS blinked up at Jasper, his innocent expression ruined by the smirk on his lips and the amusement coloring his tone.

"Yes, you." Jasper grabbed Tobias's wrists, pinning them to the bed above his head, and leaned in so their lips were almost touching. "Don't give me that innocent look."

Tobias's smirk flashed into a wide grin as he tipped his chin up and pressed his lips against Jasper's. *Okay,* he said as he slipped his tongue into Jasper's mouth. *I won't.*

His tone was still mischievous and teasing, but Jasper couldn't reply without breaking the kiss, so he settled for growling low in his throat and pushing their tongues into Tobias's mouth. For a moment, it became a battle of wills, their tongues curling around each other as they moved back and forth, but then Tobias acquiesced, parting his lips further as Jasper's tongue slipped between them.

Jasper relished the victory, grinding his hips against Tobias's as he curled their tongues together and moaning into the kiss as his cock hardened further. Tobias pushed his hips up, increasing the friction, slid his hands down Jasper's back, and moaned as well.

Sleet, Jasper, he said, never breaking the kiss.

Their tongues and lips moved together with ease that felt fantastic. He could feel the echo of Tobias's feelings as well as his own, the sensations muted, but still present and growing stronger with each stroke of their hands and roll of their hips. "Sunny day," he whispered, pulling back from the kiss to take a breath. If this was what he was feeling now—more than he'd felt that first night—he could only imagine what it was going to be like when this went further.

The mere thought was almost enough to get Jasper to stop, but then Tobias lifted his chin, tangled his fingers in Jasper's hair, and pulled him back into the kiss. He slid his tongue into Jasper's mouth, twisted it, and thrust his hips up, and Jasper forgot everything except the sensation of Tobias moving beneath him.

Sliding one hand down and pushing it between their bodies, Jasper whispered, "More." Tobias's pants were buttoned securely, as were his, and neither wanted to come off easily, but after a few minutes of acrobatics that ended in his sitting up and Tobias laughing, Jasper managed to get both pairs unbuttoned. He pulled his own off quickly and kicked them to the floor at the bottom of the bed before tugging at Tobias's and tossing them aside as well.

"Perfect," he said when Tobias was lying naked in front of him, looking more beautiful that Jasper had imagined. He was still gaunt from the months of traveling and foraging he'd done before finding Jasper, but their time together had brought some tone to his muscles, and Jasper let his gaze roam over his body appreciatively.

Tobias bumped his thigh against Jasper's. *Look later. Sex now.*

He said it in such a serious tone that Jasper couldn't help but laugh. He tried to hold in the chuckle and almost managed, but then he met Tobias's eyes, saw the almost petulant expression on his face, and couldn't keep it in. "Demanding," he managed, still laughing as he crawled up Tobias's body to kiss him again.

Tobias made a soft sound of protest as he slid his tongue into Jasper's mouth. *Tease.*

"Am not," Jasper protested before kissing Tobias again. He didn't stay on his lips this time, but placed tiny pecks along Tobias's jaw until he reached his ear, then back down along his neck to his collarbone. As he peppered Tobias's skin with kisses, he fumbled on the table by the bed, blindly groping for the lotion he'd seen there when they first arrived. It wasn't perfect, but since he hadn't planned on this happening, the lotion would have to do for tonight. They could stop at the store and grab something better before they left town in the morning.

Prove it. Tobias pushed his hips up, pressing his hard cock against Jasper's thigh, and scratched his fingers down Jasper's back. *Please.*

It was an easy request to grant. Jasper's fingers closed around the bottle just as his lips reached the junction between Tobias's shoulder and neck. He sucked the soft skin there into his mouth, relishing the salty taste as he pulled the lotion a little closer. The skin was red when he pulled back, and he kissed it gently before placing another kiss on Tobias's lips and sitting up to kneel between his legs. "You ready?"

Yes. The amount of impatience and desperation Tobias managed to convey with that one word was amazing. Jasper wanted to do this— needed to do this—and though he knew the impatience driving him was more Tobias's than his, he didn't fight it. Instead, he gave Tobias what he wanted, urging him to bend his knees and sliding one lotion-slicked finger inside.

Tobias was tight even around Jasper's one finger, but he moaned as Jasper wriggled it. When Jasper hooked it just so, hitting that sensitive spot, Tobias gasped. *Sleet!*

The pleasure and pain that accompanied the word hit Jasper like a sudden downpour. He almost fell forward from the intensity of it, but he caught himself at the last second and straightened his finger. He pulled it back, intending to back off until he could adjust to the unaccustomed sensations or Tobias could figure out how not to overwhelm him, but the feeling of emptiness and loss that hit him the moment his finger pulled free convinced him to slip it back in, accompanied by a second, before Tobias could even say anything.

This time, Jasper braced himself before he scissored his fingers, and the wave of sensation that hit him wasn't nearly as overwhelming. It felt good, actually, better than anything he'd experienced with any partner before. Part of that could have been time—he hadn't been with anyone since moving to Brightam's Ford—but he knew part of it was Tobias. As Jasper scissored his fingers once more, again letting

Tobias's feelings wash over him, he wondered why he'd been afraid of this at first.

"Clear skies, Tobias," Jasper whispered, leaning up to kiss him briefly before adding a third finger. The sensations were much the same there, just stronger and more intense, but it was nothing compared to what he felt when he pulled his fingers out completely and lined his lotion-slicked cock up with Tobias's hole. "Are you ready?" he asked again, though he knew the answer from the almost uncontrollable urge to move that he felt. Jasper wasn't giving in, wasn't letting Tobias control this just by sharing his feelings, and wasn't going to move until Tobias gave him an answer.

Yes, it came, soft and desperate as it echoed in Jasper's mind. *Please. Jasper. Need you. Now.* The wanton look on Tobias's face matched the desperation in his words, his brown eyes wide and pleading as he looked at Jasper, and his pink lips parted enticingly.

It was all the permission Jasper needed, and he slowly pushed forward, closing his eyes as the dual sensations enveloped him. He could feel the tightness and heat of Tobias around him and the undeniable pleasure that accompanied it, but it conflicted with Tobias's slight discomfort, just as his desire to move conflicted with Tobias's need for him to stay still. Jasper gave in to what Tobias needed, holding himself frozen in place as he felt Tobias relax around him. He breathed carefully through his mouth as he struggled to stay still, muscles trembling with the effort.

Move, Tobias said what felt like it could have been hours later, though in reality was only a few minutes. *Now.* He was desperate for it too, Jasper could feel it along with the urge to thrust that replaced the need to stay still.

He pulled back, almost slipping out completely before he thrust forward again, slamming into Tobias with desperation. Tobias grunted and moaned, urging Jasper on with a litany of, *more, please now,* and slipped his hand between their bodies to wrap it around his cock. He picked up a rhythm that Jasper soon matched with his thrusts, fast and steady and almost too much for Jasper to take. His mind was filled with Tobias's pleasure and his own, making coherent thought impossible. His world narrowed to just Tobias beneath him and around him, as

Tobias chanted in his mind and urged him on by sending feelings in a way that Jasper still didn't fully understand.

Jasper didn't think he would last long, but Tobias came first, orgasming with a cry that echoed inside Jasper's mind and sent a wave of pleasure that overrode the last bit of control Jasper possessed. He cried out Tobias's name as he came, threw his head back, and collapsed forward when it was over. He lay bonelessly across Tobias's chest for a moment, his breathy gasps echoed by Tobias as they both tried to ground themselves again.

"Wow," Jasper managed, and the sentiment was echoed by Tobias.

Yeah, he said, smiling softly as he squirmed, forcing Jasper to pull out.

Jasper rolled over, wiped them both with the corner of the sheet, and pulled Tobias closer, out of the wet spot. Staying on the dry sheets required that they lie close on the tiny bed, but it worked with Tobias resting his head on Jasper's chest and tangling their legs together. "Night," Jasper said, once they were settled.

Tobias only hummed sleepily in return, but Jasper could feel the contentment coming from him as they both drifted to sleep.

IN THE morning, Jasper woke before the alarm. The covers he'd pulled up to his shoulders before falling asleep had pooled around his waist and Tobias was lying half on top of him, leaving his left side warm and his right side chilly. Goosebumps puckered the flesh of his exposed arm, but the covers were tangled underneath Tobias, and Jasper couldn't free them without waking him up.

He considered it for a minute, glancing over at the clock before looking down at Tobias. The only illumination in the room came from the clock face, which cast an ethereal blue light over the room. The blue hue made Tobias look paler and accentuated his prominent cheekbones and long, straight nose. Jasper was entranced. He wanted to run his fingers over Tobias's cheek and card them through his hair, but that would wake Tobias up, so instead he rested his hand on his chest and contented himself with looking.

Tobias woke slowly, even when the alarm started beeping, wrinkling his nose and trying to bury his face in Jasper's chest. *Make it stop*, he said, covering his exposed ear with one hand. *It's loud.*

"That's the point," Jasper chuckled, though he rolled them both and stretched until he could reach the clock on the table to turn it off. "It's supposed to wake you up."

I know. Tobias sighed as they rolled back so he was again half on top of Jasper. *It's not how I wanted to wake up, though.*

Jasper took his cue. "How did you want to wake up?"

Slowly. Tobias smiled as he started kissing Jasper's chest, working his way to Jasper's collarbone and then up his neck.

Jasper tipped his head back, giving Tobias better access, and moaned as Tobias slid his hand down his chest. "We won't get on the road early if you do that," he warned, trying to mentally calculate how long it would take them to get to the next town if they drove south and how early they needed to leave if they wanted to be sure to beat the storms. There really was no safe bet, not with the storms starting earlier and occurring during the day. South would give them a little more time than east, as the coast got the worst of it, but they weren't so far north that they would be protected from the weather that hit the southern coastline for long. They had a day, maybe two, and then it would be impossible to predict when the storms would hit.

Does it matter? Tobias stopped moving his hand. *We're not going to be able to go further than one town before the storms start again.*

"We won't," Jasper agreed. "But we want to make sure we get that far. We're only a few days drive from the coast, no matter which way we go, and the wet season is really starting. I'd rather leave early and have more time in the next town than get trapped on the road."

Me too. Tobias frowned as he sat up, climbed over the crusted spot on the sheets, and headed toward the shower.

Jasper hurried after him, scooting out of bed as quickly as he could get untangled from the sheets and padding over to the bathroom just before Tobias closed the door. "Hey," he said, putting his palm against the wood to keep it open and grabbing Tobias's arm with his other hand. "We'll pick this up tonight, okay?"

Okay. The disappointment that Jasper had felt from Tobias before he climbed out of bed faded and Tobias grinned. *Promise?*

"Promise." Jasper matched Tobias's grin as he leaned in and cupped Tobias's chin in one hand. "As soon as we're settled for the night." He kissed Tobias gently, catching his bottom lip between his teeth as he pulled back.

Tobias rested his forehead against Jasper's and smiled. *Sounds good.* He was smiling when he stepped back, keeping his hand on Jasper's arm so he could talk without hurting Jasper. *What's the plan, then? Besides get out of here as soon as possible.*

"Head south." Jasper pushed his hair back, sweeping a few stray reddish blond strands from his eyes. "We'll be less likely to encounter big storms that way, at least for a day or two, and if we get out of town without being seen, the people chasing us will probably think we headed straight for Shaleton."

They'll beat us, then. Tobias bit his lip and looked aghast. *Won't they?*

"Maybe." It was a risk they'd have to take. "But they might double back looking for us, or search the towns along the way. If we head straight for Shaleton, we know they'll be on our tail. If we go south and turn east in Briars Grove, we might be able to slip into Shaleton." It was an admittedly risky plan that would add at least two days, possibly more, to their journey, but Jasper couldn't think of any other way to avoid the men pursuing them.

Tobias nodded. *Okay.* He didn't look certain and there was worry beneath his tone again, but he forced a smile to his face. *I'll shower, you pack?*

It was hardly a fair trade, but Jasper agreed anyway. "Sure. But you get to haul everything out to the truck."

The look on Tobias's face made it clear that he knew he wouldn't do it alone. *Okay.* He leaned in and kissed Jasper again. *I'll hurry.*

IT ENDED up being one of their faster departures. Even though they both took their time in the shower, the sky was barely clear when Jasper pulled the truck out of the secured parking, and Needa's Crossing was still sleepy as they drove through it. Even the diner that had been so busy the night before and promised breakfast in its windows was closed, and it was with regret that Jasper drove by.

"We'll eat on the road," he said, catching Tobias's look out the window as well. They'd talked about getting breakfast as they packed, but while stopping to grab something quickly might have been an option, waiting for the diner to open was not.

Tobias cast a longing glance over his shoulder as he slid his hand along the bench seat to bump it against Jasper's leg. *Okay. Can we stop if we see something else?*

Jasper doubted they would, but his stomach growled at the idea of a hot breakfast, so he acquiesced. "Keep an eye out. And watch for the van too."

The look Tobias gave him told him that he didn't need to mention that, but Tobias kept it at just a look and dutifully turned his gaze out the passenger side window. They passed another diner as Jasper weaved his way through the town, mostly guessing at which streets would take him to the main road south, but it wasn't open either. Neither was the restaurant on the next street or the slightly more upscale one around the following corner. There were a few people sitting outside a coffee shop where they might have been able to get pastries, and the lights were on in the bakery, but the first was too uncertain and the second was too far away for them to stop.

Instead, Jasper kept driving, and before they'd seen an open place serving hot breakfast, they'd reached the road south and Jasper swung the truck onto it. "We'll stop in a half hour or so."

Okay. Tobias twisted around so he was kneeling on the seat and peered out the back window with an intensity he hadn't devoted to finding food.

"Do you see anything?" Jasper wanted to look too, but he didn't dare take his eyes off the road ahead. It was paved and fairly well traveled during the dry season, but that didn't mean the recent storms hadn't damaged the pavement or knocked trees across the asphalt.

No. Tobias kept looking until the truck rounded a curve and Needa's Crossing was completely out of sight. *I think we got away.*

Jasper grinned as Tobias turned around. "Good. Now if we can just stay ahead of the storms, we should get to Shaleton in five days. Six if the weather is bad."

CHAPTER EIGHTEEN

THE forests outside Shaleton were dark and lush, thicker than any Jasper had seen before. The one near Brightam's Ford was old and big, but it had been thinned by the storms and had as many saplings as towering trees. It had amazed Jasper when he'd first moved out from Crittendon, as most of the forests near the west coast had been logged and tamed, but it was nothing compared to this. Here, evergreens outnumbered the deciduous trees ten to one, and the thick vegetation made the road dark even when the sun was at its zenith.

The stories about the crazy things that happened in Shaleton were often accompanied by mentions of the forest, and driving through it, Jasper understood why. He'd scoffed before, thinking that forests were places of life, not terror or madness, but as he peered through the windshield at the battered wooden sign that read, *Shaleton, 50 miles,* he actually shivered.

You feel it too? Tobias scooted closer, pressing himself against Jasper's side. *There's something here. Something bad.*

Jasper wasn't sure what he felt, but the forest looked far darker and more forbidding than the heavy vegetation should account for. "Maybe." It didn't matter if he really did, or if it was his imagination or Tobias's fear that was causing the dread in the pit of his stomach. It still made it hard to keep his foot on the gas pedal.

Tobias flashed a wan smile that did little for Jasper's nerves. *It's not far, right? We won't be here for long?*

"An hour, probably, if that sign was right," Jasper said, slowing the truck a little as the road got rougher. This close to the coast, with the thick vegetation all around, the road was bumpy and broken, so he couldn't maintain the speed he'd kept for the past five days. The roads been the best around Briars Grove, the sprawling town where they'd turned from south to east, but even an hour ago, before they'd gotten truly into the forest, the road had been passable. This was chancy.

Good.

That was a matter of opinion. Jasper wasn't looking forward to reaching their destination any more than he was looking forward to driving through the dark forest, but he hadn't come this far to give up. "Yeah. If the weather holds, it shouldn't be too bad."

Tobias nodded, seemingly content, though his expression was wary and his posture remained tense. The further they got into the forest, the wider his eyes got and the straighter he sat. Five miles in, he was perched on the edge of the seat, and at ten, he gasped, squeezing Jasper's arm tight enough to bruise. *Jasper! I think—*

Whatever he was about to say was lost as the truck shuddered and groaned, bouncing them apart as it jerked to a stop, with smoke spewing out from under the hood. Jasper slammed his palm against the steering wheel, hissing at the sharp pain as he watched the smoke continue to billow out from the front of the truck. "Hailstones!"

Can you fix it? Tobias caught his bottom lip between his teeth and looked around worriedly. He was practically radiating tension, his whole body taut as he scooted across the bench seat toward Jasper again.

"I don't know," Jasper lied, sliding out of the car and heading around to the hood. He knew even before he opened it that whatever was smoking was something he couldn't fix without a secure shop, several parts, and tools that he didn't keep in the truck, but Tobias would question him if he didn't at least look.

The ball of smoke that floated up to the tree tops when Jasper opened the hood confirmed his suspicions, as did the broken belt. That alone would be enough to strand them, as he didn't have a spare, but it wouldn't cause the smoke he was seeing. "Sleet," he murmured, grabbing a flashlight from the seat before lying down on the ground and pulling himself beneath the truck. It was hard to see, even with the flashlight, but when he finally saw the damage, his fears were confirmed.

"I can't fix it," he said after he scooted out from under the truck. "A belt's broken, and the radiator is busted."

Tobias frowned as he gave Jasper a hand and helped him to his feet. *So what do we do?* He looked back up the road, which was empty and had been for days. They'd only seen one other car outside of the towns since leaving Briars Grove, and only two besides the van following them before that. *We can't stay here. It's going to storm.*

"Walk, I guess." That wasn't a much better option, but Jasper didn't know what else to do. If they stayed in the truck, they'd be vulnerable, exposed to the storm through the glass. Walking, at least, they'd be able to look for a place to shelter for the night, one that might afford them slightly more protection than a truck that looked like it was about to catch fire or might be swept away if the road got washed out.

We won't make it before the storm starts, Tobias pointed out, though he didn't try to stop Jasper when he opened the back and started pulling things out of the various bags he'd packed them in. They'd stocked up on a lot in Briars Grove, unsure how the trip to Shaleton was going to go and what they'd find when they got there, and over the last few days, the things Jasper had bought had spread out in the back of the truck.

"I know." Jasper sighed, digging through the back of the truck, trying to figure out everything they'd need to bring. "We'll find somewhere to hide. There have to be safe places animals use."

Tobias looked around, his expression dubious, before he started helping Jasper with the bags. *Big enough for us?*

"Probably." Jasper wasn't fully versed on the common fauna of this forest, but there had to be some larger animals around that needed shelter from the storms. Vegetation this lush would attract animals, and the animals would need to find shelter from the storms. It couldn't be that hard to find.

TWO hours later, when the first drops of rain started to fall, Jasper was starting to question his decision. The thick canopy above kept the worst of the drops off at first, but as he looked up through the few gaps, he knew it wouldn't stay that way for long. They needed to find shelter, and quickly.

Tobias clearly felt the same way. He clutched Jasper's hand tighter, crowded close despite the rough terrain and the packs they'd slung over their shoulders, and looked around with wide eyes as the first drops began to hit them. *We need to stop.*

"I know." Jasper sucked in a deep breath, trying to hold in his irritation. He knew they needed to find a place to stop, had *known* they needed to find a place to stop since they abandoned the car. He didn't need Tobias to remind him. "I'm looking."

Tobias flashed a small smile. *Sorry. I know you are. I just—*

"I know," Jasper said again, softer this time. He didn't like the idea of being caught out in the storm at all, and his experience was limited to that fleeting glimpse in Crittendon and their brief encounters after leaving Brightam's Hollow. Knowing that Tobias had actually been caught in one, Jasper couldn't blame him for the sudden spike of fear he felt every time the rain began to fall. He took another deep breath, blew it out, and focused again on peering into the trees. "We'll find somewhere. Just keep looking."

There had to be places for the animals to hide, but try as he might, Jasper couldn't find them. The forest appeared to be a solid mass of trees, none of them hollow. All the animals they might have been able to follow to safety were long-hidden, protected from the oncoming weather they surely sensed long before Jasper or Tobias did.

I am looking, Tobias groused. *There's just nothing to see. There's nowhere to hide.*

"Then we'll do the best we can." There was a particularly close group of trees off to the left and Jasper guided Tobias toward them, figuring they could at least block the worst of the weather by hiding in the circle of their trunks. It was far from perfect, but it was certainly better than standing in the middle of the forest with no protection at all. "Come on."

Tobias followed with his head ducked against the rain falling through the forest canopy and his hand still curled around Jasper's, but at the last minute he stopped, jerking Jasper to a halt. *Over there,* he said, pointing toward another bunch of trees off to the right. It was farther away than the one where they were heading, and not as closely grouped, so Jasper had dismissed them in favor of the other group. Now that they were closer, though, he could see that one of the trees toward the back of the clump had a dark spot in the side of it and his hopes began to lift.

Immediately, he changed course, tugging Tobias behind him as he stumbled toward the trees. The canopy was too thick for there to be much underbrush in this part of the forest so late in the year—it would grow early in the dry season and gradually die out as the holes left in the canopy by the storms healed—but the ground was uneven and littered with fallen branches and leaves. Jasper's instinct was to run, but he refrained, knowing he'd fall, or Tobias would, and then they'd never make it to Shaleton.

The search felt like it took forever. The rain pounded against their skin. It ripped leaves from the trees and sent them fluttering down to stick uncomfortably to the two men wherever they struck. Eventually, they got close enough to the tree to see that it was indeed hollow, and Jasper felt the weight that had been pressing on his shoulders since they'd left the truck lift a little. "Good catch," he said, picking up the pace slightly now that he could see they were heading toward potential safety. It looked big enough that if it was empty, they'd both be able to huddle inside.

When they reached it, Jasper placed his free hand on the tree and leaned down, cautiously peering inside. All he saw was black, a deeper darkness than the gloom of the twilight forest that hid anything that might be inside. "Sleet."

Tobias's hand immediately moved to his shoulder when Jasper dropped it, and Tobias leaned in, frowning as Jasper dug in the bag he'd let slip from his back. *What are you doing? We need to get in there!*

"We need to make sure it's empty, first," Jasper replied. He pulled out the flashlight he'd been looking for and pointed it at the ground before turning it on. The beam cut through the gloom and darkness, illuminating the leaves and sticks on the forest floor and casting a haze into the hollow of the tree.

In that light, Jasper still couldn't see anything, so he risked angling the light toward the tree a little more, let the edge of the beam land inside the hollow, then slowly moved it around until he could see the entire thing. The hollow was small, but empty, and though it would be an uncomfortable place to spend the night, it looked as though he and Tobias would just fit. "Go on," he said, gesturing with the light for Tobias to crawl in first. "If we huddle in the back and put our bags in front of us, we should be safe from the worst of it."

Tobias didn't hesitate, his hand slipping from Jasper's shoulder as he scurried inside. He pressed his body against the back of the tree and drew his legs in to his chest, leaving just enough room for Jasper to wriggle his way inside and twist around until he was seated in a similar position, his body touching Tobias's from shoulder to hip. Without speaking, they piled their bags in front of the entrance, Jasper's bigger one on the bottom and Tobias's smaller one on top, and shifted around as they tried to find the most comfortable position possible. The bags blocked all but the very top of the opening, but they left no room to stretch out at all.

Tobias sighed as he let his head fall back against the tree wall. *We're not going to be able to move in the morning.*

Jasper laughed, the sound echoing up through the hollow of the tree. He'd never asked Tobias's actual age, or cared after figuring out that he wasn't the boy he'd first seemed to be, but he guessed that Tobias was in his late twenties. Jasper was fast approaching forty, and if Tobias thought that his bones were going to ache, Jasper could only imagine how much pain he would be in. "It could be worse."

I know. Tobias shifted and rested his head on Jasper's shoulder. *Thanks.*

Jasper had turned off the light as soon as they'd had the bags arranged, but he could sense Tobias's smile. "For what?" he asked in a whisper, wishing for the first time he could communicate the same way

Tobias did. The sounds of the rain and wind hitting the tree were eerie yet beautiful, and it felt almost profane to disrupt them with his voice because he wasn't sure Tobias was actively scanning his thoughts. After asking him just to think, Tobias had explained that he could pick up on people's thoughts, but unless those thoughts were accompanied by strong emotion, he had to actively look for them.

Coming with me. Tobias let out a soft sigh and relaxed against Jasper. *Helping me. You didn't have to.*

"I wanted to." Jasper kissed the top of Tobias's head and let himself relax as much as he possibly could in the confined space. If there had been room, he would have wrapped his arm around Tobias's shoulders, but there wasn't, so he settled for finding his hand in the dark and lacing their fingers together. "I couldn't just let you try to travel alone."

Still. Tobias squeezed Jasper's hand. *Almost everyone at home told me I should just give up on Sam, especially once we figured out that she was across the mountains. We don't ever cross them, and the idea was too much for everyone else, I guess.* He sighed softly. *I thought I could do it by myself, but obviously I was wrong.*

"I'm happy to help," Jasper said, and though he'd meant it more as a platitude than anything else, he was surprised to find that it was true. The trip had been stressful and at times terrifying, but looking back on it and comparing it to his life before he met Tobias, Jasper realized he hadn't felt so passionate about anyone or anything in a long time, and that was all thanks to Tobias.

Really? Tobias grinned, his cheek moving against Jasper's shoulder as a wave of warmth and awe washed over him.

"Yes. Really." Jasper grinned as well, overwhelmed by the force of Tobias's unexpected happiness. "Now go to sleep," he added, fondness he couldn't deny coloring his tone. "We have a long day tomorrow."

A long day the next few days, Tobias corrected while he yawned. *We still have about forty miles to get to Shaleton, and that's probably the edge of town. Samantha could be all the way on the other side of it.*

Jasper hoped not, but finding Tobias's sister in a city the size of Shaleton was a bridge they'd have to cross when they came to it. They had to get there first, and Tobias was right. They had at least three, probably four more days of walking just to reach the city, and they weren't likely to have an easier time finding shelter from the storms they'd have to endure than they did tonight.

"Yeah," he agreed, letting his eyes close. "The next few days. So sleep."

Okay, Tobias said, his hand relaxing in Jasper's grip. If he said anything else, Jasper didn't hear it and he fell asleep almost immediately, despite the cramped quarters and the wind howling outside.

MORNING dawned bright and early, the sun filtering through the tree canopy at just the right angle to penetrate the gap left in the entrance to the tree hollow and shine in Jasper's eyes. He blinked, raised one hand to block it, and groaned as Tobias stirred next to him. "Morning."

Already? Tobias stretched, or tried to anyway, his arm hitting the side of the tree before he could straighten it and his legs only managing to jostle their bags. *Feels like I just fell asleep.*

Jasper could relate. Logically, he knew he had been asleep for several hours, that he'd slept through the storms that had likely raged all night long, and that it was probably midmorning, given how late in the wet season it was, but he felt no more rested than he would have if he'd just sat there all night listening to the weather. Less rested, perhaps, because at least if he'd been awake he would have consciously shifted some instead of keeping his arms and legs in the same tight ball that he'd fallen asleep in. "Me too."

Tobias grabbed his bag, pushed it out through the hole in the tree, then did the same with Jasper's, freeing up enough room in the tree hollow that they could both uncurl from the tight balls they'd spent the night in. Neither of them could straighten their legs all the way without putting their feet through the hole as well, but it was a start, and Jasper sighed in relief as he straightened his knees a little.

"Sun, that feels good," he said, extending his arms straight up and moaning as his shoulders and spine popped.

You'll stretch better out of here, Tobias said, shaking his head fondly as he twisted around, his limbs bumping against Jasper with every move, until he was on his hands and knees. *Come on.*

Jasper watched as Tobias crawled through the opening before slowly shifting onto all fours as well. He probably could have stood up in the hollow—it seemed to go high enough, but the opening wasn't that tall, and he'd just have to bend over again to get out. Staying mostly curled up seemed like the best idea, given the kinks in his muscles. So, undignified as it was, he crawled out, trying not to wince as the stones and sticks on the forest floor dug into his palms and knees.

His back popped the moment he stood, and he bent over, popping it again and sighing just before he noticed the unnatural stillness. Their bags were at his feet, right where they had landed when Tobias pushed them out, but Tobias wasn't nearby, and there were no animals to be heard, only the slight rustling of a gentle breeze through the trees. "Tobias?" he asked, turning slowly. The sharp rustle of leaves on the forest floor told him what he would see before it came into view, and his stomach sank.

Two of the three men who had been chasing them were standing on either side of Tobias, holding him securely despite his struggles. They looked like the same two who had broken into Jasper's house all those weeks ago and started this whole adventure. Jasper definitely recognized the one with the amethysts on the back of each hand, but couldn't be sure about the other. Briefly, he wondered what had happened to the third man. Before he could start to formulate a plan, the leader—or at least that was what Jasper assumed the man with the amethysts was—pulled something from his pocket while still holding Tobias with his other hand, and squeezed it.

Pain shot through Jasper, his whole body shaking as he fell to the ground. The last thing he was aware of before darkness claimed him was the shocked look on Tobias's face and the voiceless cry of denial that echoed in his skull.

CHAPTER NINETEEN

"STATE your business."

The walls of Shaleton loomed above Jasper, seeming larger than their two stories as he peered up into the barrel of a gun. The guardsman holding the gun scowled down at him, frowning at his disheveled appearance, and Jasper had to resist the urge to run his hand through his matted hair in what would be a futile attempt to tame it. "Visiting. A friend's sister moved out here last year, and I promised him I'd make sure she's okay. We're hoping to get her to come back inland once the wet season is over," he said, using the same lie he'd told the woman back in Needa's Crossing as he hefted both bags on his shoulders so the guard could see them.

"You walked?"

Jasper couldn't blame the man for the suspicion in his tone, but his heart still jumped when the gun moved closer, pointing directly at his head. "Truck broke down about forty miles from here," he said truthfully. "I'd hoped to find someone else on the road, but I had to hide from the storm that first night, and I didn't really get back to the road much. Seemed safer in the trees with the storms popping up all day." He'd only rejoined the road a few hundred yards before the trees gave way to the paved ground separating the forest from Shaleton on the inland side.

The guard's eyes narrowed as he looked at Jasper, but after a moment, he nodded and lowered the gun. "Wait there. I'll let you in."

It wasn't as though Jasper had any choice, so he nodded his thanks and tried not to shuffle from foot to foot as he waited for the guard to descend. After what felt like an eternity, the door in the wall blocking Shaleton from the woods opened slightly, and the same man who had been peering at Jasper down the barrel of his gun looked out through the tiny opening. His eyes roved over Jasper once again, and he nodded, stepping back as he pulled the door all the way open.

"Thank you," Jasper said, hefting both bags up on his shoulders. Over the past four days, he'd discarded as much as he dared, but he needed some stuff to survive and some to blend in once he arrived in Shaleton, and he hadn't been willing to discard anything Tobias might need either. It would have been too much like admitting defeat.

"You'd better find your friend's sister quick," the guard said as he secured the door behind Jasper. "Or see if one of the inns will take you in. You don't want to be on the streets once the storms start."

It was never advisable to be in the open once the storms started, but something in the man's tone told Jasper that he was referring to more than the danger from the elements, so he refrained from commenting. "Do you know of any inns that might have openings?" he asked, glancing up at the sky. It was still sunny, but on the west coast they often rolled in with no warning at all, and he doubted it was any different here on the east coast.

The guard didn't look too pleased to be providing the information, but he did point down the street and give Jasper directions before stomping back up the stairs to resume his post. "Thank you!" Jasper called up, but the grunt he got in reply was no friendlier than the directions had been, and he shrugged as he started down the street. At least he'd made it this far.

THE residents of Shaleton proved to be as brusque as the guard at the gate had been—more so in most cases. On his way to the inn, Jasper had been given wide berth by the few people he saw on the streets, and the innkeeper greeted him with a gun he only lowered when Jasper said the gate guard had sent him. That was the only concession to courtesy Jasper got. Even in the morning, when he'd showered, shaved, and put on clean clothes so he looked and felt like a real human being again, the residents of Shaleton showed no sign of wanting to talk to him.

"I'm looking for—" he would start, but the moment he'd start to describe the men who took Tobias, people would shake their heads and stammer out that they didn't know before suddenly remembering something they had to do immediately far away from Jasper. Just mentioning the emerald green dusters was usually enough to make most people pale and turn away, but the few times he described the tattoos, people practically ran in the opposite direction.

He was about to give up when a hand closed around his arm, and he looked down to see a one-eyed man who looked crazier than Jasper had when he'd arrived tugging him toward an alley. "Wait—" he started, but the man put a finger over Jasper's lips and shook his head.

"I know who you're looking for," he said in a low tone after glancing up and down the street several times. There was no one near, but that didn't seem good enough for the man, who jerked harder on Jasper, scowling when he resisted. "I'm not talking about them out here!"

Jasper followed him to a dark alley and leaned down despite the man's rancid odor. "Who are they?"

"The Order!"

"The Order of what?"

The man looked at him as though he were the crazy one. "You really aren't from around here, are you? They're just The Order. Or they are now, anyway. They had a name, once, a long time ago, but no one uses it anymore. No one who's not a member, anyway. No one talks about them, either."

"So why are you?" Jasper narrowed his gaze as he started calculating whether he could pull his arm free from the old man's grasp. He had no doubt that if it came to it, he could outrun the guy, but the man's thick nails were digging into his arm and his grip was stronger than Jasper would have guessed by looking at him.

"Because you're makin' people talk, and that's never good." The man leaned around Jasper to peer out at the street. "You'll get their attention. Bring it on all of us. We don't want that."

"Right." Jasper drew out the word. The man was sounding crazier by the second, and Jasper was starting to understand the reputation Shaletonites had. If men like the one in front of him were the only ones willing to talk to anyone, of course people thought the whole town was crazy.

"You don't know, because you're not from around here, but trust me on this. Don't ask anyone else." The man's grip tightened enough to make Jasper wince. "If your friend is with The Order, he's in the temple in Center Square, but don't go there. You're better off just hoping that your friend gives them what they want."

Jasper didn't know exactly what The Order wanted from Tobias, but he knew that it wasn't something Tobias could give, or something he was willing to let Tobias give. "I can't do that."

The man grabbed Jasper's shirt with his free hand and pulled him down so their noses were almost touching. The look in his eyes was wild, and his breath was even viler at this distance, but his tone was serious enough to hold Jasper's attention despite the stench. "Then don't mess up, or we'll never see the dry again." He released Jasper with a push, which sent him staggering backward.

"What?" Jasper regained his balance with effort, catching himself against the stone wall for support as the man approached him again.

"Remember," he said, poking his finger into Jasper's chest as he walked past, leaving Jasper standing, speechless and wondering what had just happened. Little of what the man had said made sense and he didn't know if he could trust it at all, but it was the first clue he'd gotten, and if he knew anything, it was that he needed to get to Tobias as quickly as possible

The temple in Center Square seemed like a good place to start.

THE idea seemed to lose its merit when Jasper actually saw the building. The Order's temple dominated Center Square, its polished black stone rising eight stories into the air, and the mere sight of it from across the square sent a stab of fear through Jasper's heart. It was obvious he was in the right place at least—the green swirls that Jasper recognized from the tattoos were mounted above the double doors, a large purple stone in the center of the swirling arms—but the building was so big he couldn't imagine searching it and finding Tobias without being caught.

As he watched, a steady line of people walked in through the doors and walked back out only a few minutes later, clearly having accomplished whatever it was they went to do. Most of them left the square immediately, hurrying away with their heads down and their hands tucked into their pockets. The few people who didn't leave right away bustled across the open space to the opposite side, where they purchased food from the few booths open there. The rest were boarded up, just as the benches remained empty and the fountains dry. What had once clearly been a busy gathering place was nearly lifeless despite the number of people walking through it.

"You can't put it off forever," a voice at Jasper's side said, and he looked to see a young woman, her hair bound back in a braid and her expression as wary as Jasper's. "They'll know."

"Who will?"

"Them." The woman pointed toward the temple with her chin. "Don't know how, but they always know if you skip. It's better to just get it over with than get a visit. Unless you want to be the talk of the town, of course." She shuddered dramatically.

Jasper laughed and shook his head. At first glance, the woman reminded him of Carla, though there was a weariness about her that years of hauling goods between Crittenden and Brightam's Ford hadn't given Carla, and his friend would only put on a long dress like this woman was wearing if she had no other choice. "No, I'd prefer to avoid that."

"Me too." The woman sighed, her body deflating in a way that made Jasper feel even wearier, and shrugged. "Well, come on then. Let's get it over with. Maybe it's better if you're not alone."

Jasper didn't know what they were going to do, but based on the looks of the people walking in and out of the temple, he doubted anything would make it better. "Maybe," he said dubiously as he fell into step with the woman. "I doubt it, though. They probably have some secret way to make it worse."

He'd hoped she would give some clue about what they would be doing inside, but instead, she just nodded her head and led the way to the line walking into the temple. No one else in line was talking either, and he took his cue from them, watching everything the people in front of him did so he wouldn't make any mistakes. His clothes didn't stand out—Brightam's Ford fashion apparently fitting in with the variety in Shaleton—but he couldn't help but feel that the men standing on either side of the door were going to notice something off about him and stop him before he crossed the threshold. Instead, they gave Jasper the same impassive stare they gave every person entering the temple, and he barely contained a sigh of relief as he passed through the doors and out of their sight.

Inside, the building was no less foreboding. Candles flickering in sconces along the walls provided the only light, leaving the center aisle in near darkness and hiding most of the details from Jasper's view. Those that he could make out were baffling, unlike any place of worship he'd ever entered. Those were usually open and airy, designed to let in as much sunlight as possible and to move with the storms rather than stand strong against them. This was a fortress, with rows of benches separated by a narrow aisle, and thick poles reaching up to the ceiling that reminded Jasper of trees. Perhaps it was his recent experience, but the place felt uncannily like the forest, and with each step he took, his unease grew.

The altar, for lack of a better term, was the stump of a tree large enough that Jasper couldn't stretch his arms across it, and behind it stood an ornate wooden chair. It was unoccupied, something the people in front of Jasper seemed to take as a good sign, and a man and a woman, both dressed like the men who had taken Tobias, tattoos and all, knelt on either side of it. They watched with sharp gazes as each person knelt in front of the altar in turn, clasped their hands behind their back, and stretched their neck out over the wood so they could press their lips against it.

When it was his turn, Jasper mimicked the pose, leaning forward as far as he could and feeling horribly exposed as he waited for the knock that signaled he was allowed to move. Again, he felt as though the pair could see right through him and knew he was an impostor only looking for a way into the secretive parts of the temple. He could feel their scrutiny, his spine tingling as their gazes bore into the top of his head, but just as he was certain that he'd been discovered, the knock came.

Jasper rose to his feet as swiftly as he could without seeming rushed, trying to keep his body from shaking as he fought hard against the urge to run as quickly as he could. He had to force his feet to move slowly as he followed the line of people along the outer wall toward the door, and it wasn't until he was halfway there that he noticed the alcoves between the flickering candles and the men and women positioned in each of them. They were dressed like all the others, their tattoos not quite as elaborate as the ones on the pair by the altar, but visible, and as he looked as well as he could without turning his head, Jasper noticed that the ones with the more elaborate tattoos were stationed in the prime positions.

The journey out seemed to take twice as long as the journey in, the gaze from each alcove boring into him as he walked past. The line was spaced farther apart going out than it had been coming in, the time each of them spent with their heads on the altar ensuring that there was only ever one person in front of each alcove at a time. No distractions that way; no chance to team up, no hope that someone else would distract a guard and give Jasper a chance to slip by. However he got to the back of the temple, it wouldn't be through the main doors.

By the time Jasper made it outside, the sky was overcast with another brewing storm, but it still felt like a breath of fresh air. He paused the moment his feet hit the cobblestones of Center Square, sucked in a deep breath, and forced his muscles to relax as he tried to will away the tension that had built up just by being inside.

"Keep moving," a voice said, and Jasper started as he noticed the woman from earlier. "You know this isn't the place."

Jasper didn't, but he remembered seeing everyone hurrying away from the temple and thought about how he'd feel if his exit was blocked by someone taking deep breaths right where he needed to walk, and he flashed her a sheepish smile. "Sorry," he said, keeping his voice low as they started to walk back toward the edge of the square. "It feels so good to leave that I forget sometimes."

"We all do, but I heard they're looking for a sacrifice. Don't give them a reason to make you one." The woman paused and looked up at Jasper when they reached the edge of the square. "If I were you, I'd go straight back to wherever you need to be. Today isn't a day to hang around."

It didn't seem like any day was a day to hang around, but with the storm threatening and the temple looming over the square, Jasper could see how today was particularly bad. "I will," he said, nodding at her and tipping an imaginary hat. "Thank you."

"Stay safe," the woman said, and then she vanished down a side street before Jasper could return the sentiment.

JASPER took her advice to an extent, heading straight back to the inn, but he only stayed long enough to wait out the afternoon storm. By the time night fell, bringing with it more storms, Jasper was tucked into one of the abandoned stalls in Center Square, watching as the last of the Shaletonites filed out of the temple and headed toward the safety of their homes. He stayed through the first rumble of thunder, watched as the temple doors closed against the rain, and steeled his nerves when a flash of lightning revealed that the square was completely empty and the temple front devoid of anyone who might be watching.

Pulling his jacket up over his head as meager protection from the rain that lashed against his exposed skin, Jasper ran across the square. His feet slid on the water-slick stones, making it hard to gain ground, but he pressed forward, ignoring the rain and the thunder and focusing on getting across the square before the water turned to ice. He made it, barely, reaching the building just as another flash of lighting lit up the sky and the drumming of rain was joined by the clicking of hail hitting the cobblestones.

The temple provided a little shelter from the storm, its towering height working with the slight angle of the precipitation to create a small, sheltered area. Jasper huddled in it, one shoulder pressed up against the polished black stone as he slowly made his way around the building, looking for a service door or a window or anything that might gain him entry into the temple. Tobias was inside—Jasper could feel it—but the knowledge did him no good without a way to get in and, more importantly, a way to get Tobias out.

The front of the building yielded nothing, just as Jasper had expected, but there were alleys along either side of the building and a street along the back. There had to be another entrance somewhere. The room Jasper had been in was huge, but it hardly took up the whole building, and he doubted that members of The Order took deliveries or did daily business through the main temple doors. He just had to find where they did and then maybe he could sneak through.

He'd deal with the issues of finding Tobias and getting back out once he got inside.

The rain whipped directly into Jasper's face when he rounded the corner, and he squinted against it, searching more by feel than sight. His right hand pressed against the stone while his left hand shielded his eyes as best he could manage. The building on the other side of the alley worked with the temple to create a wind tunnel, and Jasper was forced to bend almost double under a sudden onslaught of water and ice which threatened to push him back several times as he tried to continue his search.

It yielded nothing, though in the dark and rain he couldn't be sure he hadn't missed something. If he didn't find anything along the back of the building, he'd try again, but at the moment he was too relieved that the rain was coming from his side instead of falling directly into his face to notice much else. Holding up his left hand to protect his eyes, Jasper started along the back of the building, looking for openings in the stone.

Ten steps in, he found one, a small depression in the wall that was barely visible in the darkness. Even in daylight, the shadows of the building would make it difficult to find for anyone who didn't know the location, and Jasper's heart sped up when he pressed his hand against the depressed surface and discovered that it was metal instead of rock. This was the entrance he was looking for.

Slowly, Jasper reached for the handle, a slight groove in the metal that drew no more attention than the door did. He was so close, and with Tobias on the other side of that door, Jasper could practically taste his victory. The rain and sleet ceased to matter as he turned, putting his back toward the street and curling his fingers around the handle.

He was just about to pull when hands landed on his shoulders, yanking him away from the door, and a low voice growled into his ear. "Don't!"

CHAPTER TWENTY

JASPER lashed out, swinging his arm in a wide arc as he tried to twist away from his captor. His fist connected with something solid, and he cursed as another set of hands grabbed it, stopping it midswing. "Get off!" he yelled, struggling as the first pair of hands slid down to wrap around his chest and pinned him against the solid body of the person behind him.

He struggled more, kicking out in the hopes that he could slide from the man's grasp, but the arms just squeezed, lifting him up instead of letting him slide down. "Jasper!"

This time, Jasper recognized the rough voice, and stopped struggling. "Darius?"

"Yes!" The arms loosened and Jasper stepped away to peer at his friend. Carla was hovering by his side, one hand pressed to her cheek where Jasper's flying arm had clearly hit her. "What are you two doing here? How did you get here?"

"Train." Darius grabbed Jasper's arm and tugged him toward the empty street. "Come on."

"But they aren't running now. How—" A crash of thunder cut Jasper off.

Darius narrowed his gaze and tugged harder on Jasper's arm. "We'll tell you when we're somewhere safe and dry," he said, glancing up at the sky and frowning as water pelted his face. The storm was getting worse, more hail mixing in with the rain and the wind whipping furiously down the empty street. "We can't stay here."

Jasper wanted to protest, but before he could, Carla took his other arm. Between them, she and Darius all but dragged Jasper across the street, down another alley, and around a corner, where they paused in front of a building that seemed to be another inn. Carla kept hold of Jasper's arm while Darius unlocked the door with a large key, and together they pushed him inside, sending him stumbling ahead of them as though he might run back to the temple if they didn't force him inside.

They weren't entirely wrong.

The moment the door clicked shut behind Darius, Jasper whirled on his friends. "What in clear skies are you doing? Where are we?"

"Our inn," Darius said, locking the door from the inside. "Come on."

Carla put her hand on Jasper's back and started to guide him down the hall. "We'll explain once we're in our room."

Her touch and tone were soothing, but they weren't the ones Jasper wanted, and as he followed Darius down the hall, Carla by his side, her hand felt more like it was holding him back then urging him forward. He understood why they didn't want to talk here—the hallway was as empty as the foyer had been but it would only take one door opening at the wrong time for them to be overheard—but that didn't mean he liked it. He itched to move faster, chafing at Carla's shorter strides and Darius's calm pace, and as he watched his friend fiddle with the lock, he thought that maybe he finally understood some of Tobias's impatience with him.

The moment the door shut behind them, Jasper looked Darius straight in the eyes. "Explain. Now."

"Patience." Carla patted Jasper's arm before going over and pulling drinks out of the small refrigerator in the corner of the room. "Sit, both of you," she instructed as she set the beverages on the low table in front of the couch. "There's no need to be uncomfortable while we talk."

The room Darius and Carla were sharing was bigger than the one Jasper was using, though it wasn't as if he had needed much space. A bed and protection from the storms were all he'd required, and he'd gotten that, though little else. This room, he noticed as he followed Carla's instruction and sat on the couch, not only had the tiny kitchen and seating area, but also had a tiny window above the bed. It was secured now, of course, covered with heavy shutters, but in the dry season, it would be a premium feature. "Nice room."

"Convenient, too," Carla added with a soft smile as she sat next to Jasper on the couch.

"And expensive." Darius took his drink and sat on Carla's other side. "But it was the closest inn to that damn temple, so we took it anyway."

"But why?" Jasper took a sip of his drink and wished that it were something stronger than just juice. "All you knew was that we were coming to Shaleton, not what we'd find here. You thought it was a stupid idea to come."

"We got your message. The one you sent from Durrysville," Darius said, putting his arm around Carla's shoulders.

"Durrysville?" Jasper blinked. "But you were in Brightam's Ford. How did you get here? And when?"

"I told you, train." Darius grinned. "We bought the one that Carla was looking at the day I delivered your supplies and drove it out here ourselves."

"We got here four days ago," Carla added in response to Jasper's other question. "We've been looking for you ever since."

"But why?" Jasper tried to remember what he'd sent, but the past weeks had been so busy with running from The Order, figuring out his relationship with Tobias, and then just trying to get to Shaleton alive that he couldn't remember sending a message, much less what he'd said in it. "What did I say?"

"You said that the van following you was from ClearSky Industries." Carla put her drink down on the coffee table and twisted so she was leaning against Darius and looking at Jasper. "I remembered reading a news story about them right before I left Crittenden. They were trying to establish locations on the west coast, but people were pushing back because they were associated with The Order of the Storm Quellers."

A knot formed in Jasper's stomach as the pieces started to fall into place. "Is that...?"

"The Order that's in that monstrous temple there?" Darius snorted. "Yeah. Took us a day to figure it out, 'cause no one here seems to know about the Storm Quellers part, but that's their official name. They're a fringe religious group that believes the correct sacrifice to the nature spirits will stop the wet season for good."

Fear coiled in Jasper's gut. It wasn't hard to figure out what they thought the correct sacrifice was, and they'd had Tobias for five days now. There was a possibility that he was too late, that he'd been too late since waking up on the forest floor and—

"Breathe." Carla's hand on his arm jerked Jasper out of his terrifying thoughts and he sucked in a deep breath as he tried to focus.

"They've had Tobias for five days," he said softly, somehow managing to keep his voice steady. "Did they—do they have a special time they believe they have to make this special sacrifice?"

"The first full moon of the wet season," Carla said, squeezing Jasper's arm lightly before letting go. "Tomorrow."

Relief flooded through Jasper and he slumped back against the couch with a sigh. "So we still have time, then."

"Not much, but yeah," Darius said. "It's good we found you when we did, though. We need you with us tomorrow."

"We can't just walk in the temple," Jasper protested. "I tried that already. All you can do is offer yourself up as a sacrifice." That ritual made more sense now too, though Jasper wondered if the benches were ever used to host any sort of worship service. "There are guards to keep people from getting curious and wandering off."

"True, but we're not going to the temple."

Jasper narrowed his gaze and glared at Darius. "I'm not leaving Tobias there. If you're not going to help—"

"We are." Carla said, meeting his glare with an even gaze. "But we can't just walk in there and get Tobias out. There's no way. We have to wait."

"Until when?"

"Sundown." Darius's look dared Jasper to object. "They have a clearing out in the woods that they use for their rituals. It's one of the reasons the people here don't go out there."

"So, what? We're just going to wander out to the woods? Won't that look suspicious?" Jasper rubbed his hand over his face as he tried to gather his thoughts. "We can't exactly pretend to be out for a stroll if no one but that Order goes out to the woods, especially not if it's storming."

"We're not going to pretend to be out for a stroll," Carla said, looking smugly at Jasper. "We're going to pretend to be initiates. They'll think we're supposed to be there."

"People just walk out to the forest and want to join?" It sounded too easy.

"No." Carla shook her head. "People sign up beforehand and join the morning of the full moon every month. We picked up robes yesterday and today, so when they go out to the forest, we'll join them and blend in."

"Why don't we join them in the morning?"

"You want to spend the entire day inside that temple, listening to their babble?" Darius raised one eyebrow and cast a doubtful look at Jasper. "Really?"

"No." Jasper glared at Darius. "I want to rescue Tobias and his sister, if she's still alive. If we can get to them sooner, why are we waiting?"

"Because we need to be able to get out, Jasper!" Carla sucked in a deep breath and blew it out slowly, visibly calming herself. "If we get into the temple, how do we get out? How do we get away from the group? We'd be stuck in a locked-down building that we don't know. As soon as they figured out what we were trying to do, they'd catch us. At least in the forest, we have a chance."

Her argument made sense, but it galled at Jasper to have a means to get to Tobias and not use it. "I don't want him in their hands any longer than he has to be," he said in a soft tone. "I need to try to get to him."

"We will get to him, I promise." Darius reached over Carla to squeeze Jasper's shoulder. "We're just going to do it the smart way instead of rushing off."

Jasper closed his eyes and nodded. "Okay," he said, trying to ignore the twisting in his gut that was telling him this was a bad idea. There were no good ideas in this situation, and Darius and Carla were right, trying to rescue Tobias in the woods was a much better one than barging into the temple and getting trapped themselves. "We'll wait."

"It'll be okay," Carla said, patting Jasper's knee. "We'll get him back."

"Okay." Jasper just wished he could believe it.

HE STILL didn't believe it the next night when he found himself standing in a forest clearing with a line of initiates. He swayed back and forth, doing his best to stomp his feet and make it seem like he was singing along with the song he couldn't quite make out. In front of them, emerald-clad members of The Order of the Storm Quellers led the chant, their tattoos glistening in the rain and the amethysts on the backs of their hands shining in the torchlight.

Above, the clouds shifted, allowing the moon to shine through and illuminate the heavily tattooed man standing in front of the whole group. He raised his hands, revealing three amethysts embedded in the back of each, and silence fell over the group. "Bring forth the sacrifices."

Two emerald-clad men stepped into the clearing, lugging a third man between them. For a moment, Jasper thought he'd found Tobias, but then he realized the man was too short. He was dressed in a purple robe with sleeves that fell past his fingertips. His head hung forward, his dark curls hanging over his blindfold, and he struggled weakly against his captors. From the fight he put up, it was obvious he had little strength left, and as he stumbled along, his bare feet occasionally peeking out from the bottom of his robe, he never once lifted his head.

As they secured him to a tree behind the leader, the next group came forward, carrying a woman with dark hair that fell halfway down the back of her purple robe. She too was blindfolded, but unlike the man, she didn't struggle. Instead, she hung limply in her captor's grasp, her head hanging forward like the man's and her bare feet dragging through the mud. They secured her to another tree behind the leader, leaving one in between her and the man, and let her sag limply in her bonds.

The moment she was tied up, the men stepped away and something dark stepped out of the forest. It was humanoid, walking upright with two arms and two legs, but there was no way anyone who saw it would mistake it for a human. It was small and lithe, its head barely reaching the shoulder of the tattooed man standing in front of it. Its slender legs bent oddly as it walked, and even with the distance and the rain obscuring his view, Jasper could see that its body was covered with short fur.

"The forest spirit!" Carla whispered, the words almost lost in the pounding rain. "It's real!"

It was obvious that the creature was flesh and blood, but Jasper didn't correct her. The creature was ethereal enough that he could easily see how someone just catching a glimpse of the light fur and skin would think the same way, particularly if they glimpsed its wide blue eyes or the cat-like ears that stuck out from the side of its head. The Order seemed to believe it too, a murmur rippling through the crowd as the creature looked out over them. When its gaze reached Jasper, he had to fight the urge to step back, the second of scrutiny feeling longer and more intense than any he'd ever experienced before.

When it moved on, he breathed a sigh of relief, slumping forward like many of the other initiates and focusing so much on his own relief that he almost missed what happened next. The creature, apparently done surveying the crowd, turned to the man and woman tied to the trees behind it. It walked around them, its movements predatory as it let its piercing gaze roam over their bodies. It sniffed, pressing its nose against their necks, and its tongue darted out to press against the skin of the woman.

Without warning, it whirled, its eyes flashing as it glared at the leader of Storm Quellers and hissed something Jasper couldn't hear and probably wouldn't have understood anyway. Jasper did hear the growl that rolled over the clearing like a low rumble of thunder, and he shuddered as the creature stepped forward, squaring off with the man despite its disadvantage in height.

The leader, to his credit, met the creature without flinching, saying something to it that Jasper couldn't make out before turning to the crowd and exposing his back to the angry being behind him. Again, he raised his hands, and again, the crowd quieted, the murmurs of discomfort and awe that had been reverberating through it ceasing immediately. A rumble of thunder filled the silence, and when it quieted, the leader took a step forward. "Bring him!"

The resulting commotion was loud enough that the entire crowd turned. Again, two men dragged a third into the clearing, but this one was fighting, twisting and writhing in his captors' grip as his legs kicked out. His bare feet slipped in the mud, which sent him tumbling down until the grips on his arms jerked him up short, but he clambered to his feet again, scrambling to keep up as he tried to twist away.

His face, too, was covered by a blindfold, but, though his face was obscured, Jasper immediately recognized him. He recognized the shape of his body and the healing cut on his right hand from the last morning they packed the truck. It was that cut that erased any doubt from Jasper's mind, and he moved without thinking, raising his arm to push the initiate next to him out of his way.

"No!" Darius grabbed Jasper, yanking him back just before his hand made contact. "Whatever you're thinking, stop," he said, his voice low in Jasper's ear. The sound was almost lost in the noises of Tobias's struggle. "It's not a good idea."

"It's better than just standing by and watching!" Jasper hissed as he tried to wrench his arms free of Darius's grip. "I'm not letting them give him to that thing!"

"We won't!" Darius held on tight. "But we can't do it this way!"

"Then how?" They were running out of time. The clearing wasn't large, and Tobias had already been dragged more than three quarters of the way up the aisle. "We're not going to save him standing here!"

Darius pushed up onto his toes, looking over the crowd, then tugged Jasper backward. "I know. Just wait a minute. We have to be smart about this."

"We don't have time for smart." Jasper yanked his arm away, freeing it from Darius's grip. Before he could move, however, the men reached the edge of the clearing, and he was forced to watch as they tied Tobias to the middle tree and stepped back to let the creature sniff at him.

It seemed more eager with Tobias than it had with the other prisoners, its tongue darting out several times to lick at his skin. Tobias flinched each time, but his bonds were too secure for him to do more than jerk his head, and the creature soon stopped that by grabbing Tobias's chin with its hand.

The mental whimper that echoed in Jasper's skull was his undoing.

"Get off him!" he shouted, ignoring the pain in his head and pushing forward through the crowd before his friends could stop him. He had no idea what he was going to do next, no plan or course of action in mind except get to Tobias. Nothing else mattered, not Darius and Carla yelling at him to stop, not the initiates staring at him wide-eyed or staggering aside as he shoved past, not the strange creature touching Tobias nor the angry leaders gathering in front of their prisoners. Jasper's brain registered all of it as he moved, getting through several rows of initiates too stunned to resist, but he ignored it, focused instead on the one thing he'd wanted for the past five days: Tobias.

The leader stepped forward, turning his back to the forest spirit as he glared out at the crowd. "Stop him!" he shouted, pointing at Jasper, the amethysts on the back of his hand flashing as lightning forked across the sky. "Bring him to me!"

The crowd in front of Jasper rippled as initiates and Storm Quellers alike realized what was happening behind them. Jasper managed to force his way through two more rows of people before he encountered real resistance, then hands started grabbing at his arms and robe, trying to hold him back. Jasper whirled and ducked, dodging as many as he could and jerking away from those he couldn't avoid. His cloak tore as he struggled, but he ignored it just as he ignored the rain pounding down on his shoulders and the lightning flashing overhead.

The commotion grew as Jasper wriggled through, breaking free of initiate after initiate and using the fact that there were so many of them to his advantage. It wasn't easy, but he got through the last line of initiates before hands took hold of both his biceps and he found himself staring into a terrifyingly familiar face. He didn't need to look down to know that there was a single amethyst embedded in the back of each of the man's hands. The tattoos on his face and the snarl that had haunted his nightmares since waking up on the forest floor were enough.

"You," the man spat, stepping forward so he was standing chest-to-chest with Jasper. "I should have killed you instead of trusting that the storms would do it for me." He reached up and curled his hand around Jasper's neck, squeezing hard enough that it cut off Jasper's air. "He's ours and nothing you do will change that!"

His smirk was the last thing Jasper saw as his vision started to gray out.

CHAPTER TWENTY-ONE

THE pressure eased a second later and Jasper gasped desperately for breath, his whole body sagging in his captors' arms. He blinked to clear the gray spots from his vision, but when they faded, he almost wished he hadn't. The man was still in front of him, still smirking, only rather than choking him, he was using a fistful of Jasper's robe to pull him up and forward. The people holding his arms loosened their grips as he was hauled forward, but the man's grip on his robe was tight enough that he doubted he'd be able to break free, even if he had the strength to try.

He could still hear a commotion behind him—initiates regaining their footing, he guessed, and maybe a few of them turning on Darius and Carla if they'd been stupid enough to follow him—but he didn't turn to look. He could barely tear his gaze away from the snarling face of the man holding him, and when he did, it went straight to Tobias.

The creature was still inspecting him, sniffing and tasting and making Tobias squirm despite the commotion in the crowd, and it looked pleased. Its ears twitched as it circled him with predatory steps, one hand stroking over his chest and lingering on his shoulder as it walked behind the tree. When it emerged on the other side, it stroked across his collarbone and up his throat, its fingers lingering on his chin as it lifted Tobias's head and turned it back and forth. Then it sniffed again, leaning in so close that it might have been biting Tobias... or kissing him.

The creature's tongue darted out again to lick along the curve of Tobias's jaw, and Jasper saw red. Adrenaline filled him with renewed vigor, and he pushed forward, pulling his arms free of the men holding them and forcing the one in front of him to take a few steps back. Their bodies collided, but Jasper barreled forward. He had to get to Tobias.

The man stumbled, pulling Jasper down with him, and rolled when he hit the ground, forcing Jasper onto his back. "Do you really think you can defeat me?" he asked as he straddled Jasper's waist and used the hand tangled in his robe to pin him to the ground. "You're an idiot," he said as he leaned in to put his lips close to Jasper's ear. "You don't stand a chance."

The man's hold on Jasper's robe loosened a little as he straightened so he was sitting on Jasper again instead of leaning over him. Jasper grinned desperately. "Maybe not, but I'm still going to try." He drew his knees up toward his chest and hit his opponent squarely in the back, knocking him off balance, then pushed him and used their momentum to roll them both to the side.

The man fought back, rolling until they hit the legs of the Storm Quellers standing around them. Jasper landed on top of his antagonist, but tattooed hands pushed at him, toppling him over and forcing both men to roll in the other direction. Jasper grabbed the man's duster, holding onto it as tightly as he could so that he wouldn't be dislodged if the man decided to suddenly let go of his cloak. He gained the advantage again, and landed a vicious blow to his opponent's jaw, using the duster to jerk him into the punch. For a moment, he thought he'd won.

The feeling of victory was short-lived. Someone's foot connected with his spine, and as he fell, they rolled again. This time Jasper landed on his back, with the tattooed man grinning maniacally down at him. "He's brainwashed you," the man said as he spat blood. "You actually think that leech is worth this? He's what's keeping us trapped! He's why these storms are here!" Thunder crashed overhead, emphasizing his words, and Jasper flinched as the rain started to fall harder.

"He's not responsible for anything." Jasper snarled as he blinked water out of his eyes. "He can't control the weather."

"He's part of the problem. Him and everyone like him. The storms are our punishment for letting people like him live." The man pressed his free hand against Jasper's throat again, pushing down with enough pressure that his vision began to gray around the edges once more. "The right sacrifice will stop the storms."

Jasper blinked furiously to clear his vision. "The storms are natural," he said, the words barely a whisper as he gasped for breath. "Nothing will stop them."

The man laughed, sounding delighted as he pressed down harder on Jasper's neck. "You're wrong." The grin that spread on his face sent chills down Jasper's spine. "Soon, the sacrifice will begin, and when the storms stop, I'm going to kill you."

"They won't." Jasper pushed against the man with both hands, but gravity was on his opponent's side at the moment, and Jasper couldn't budge him.

"We'll see," the man said, his smile growing. "Right about—"

A horrific scream drowned out the man's words, so loud that it took Jasper a moment to realize he wasn't hearing it with his ears, but with his mind. Tobias's voice was piercing into all of them from a distance. The man holding Jasper down let go, pressing his palms to his ears and wincing in pain as he tried futilely to block out the sound and the agony that accompanied it. As Jasper's vision cleared, he could see that everyone around him was doubled over, their hands pressed to their ears and their own moans of agony adding to the noise only Jasper knew was just in their heads.

Stunned, he pushed the man off him and scrambled to his feet, fighting against the urge to double over, block his ears, and curl up. Tobias was in pain, and when Jasper looked up, he saw why. The creature had both hands pressed to Tobias's temples, doing what, Jasper didn't know, but it was obviously hurting him. That knowledge alone let Jasper fight against the agony that had overtaken everyone else to stagger forward one excruciating step at a time.

The Storm Quellers crumpled to the ground at the slightest touch, leaving a clear path for Jasper to stumble along as he tried to get to Tobias and the creature. A few of the Storm Quellers grabbed at his cloak, but he pushed them away easily. Their hands covered their ears as they tumbled to the ground and hit it with soft noises that were lost in the mental sounds of Tobias's screams. Everyone was moaning, but the only sound Jasper cared about wasn't a sound at all, but an echoing of feeling inside his skull, nearly driving him to his knees with pain even as it urged him forward.

He tripped when he reached the podium, landing on all fours near the incapacitated leader of the Storm Quellers, and muttered a curse under his breath as he tried to regain his footing. The leader smirked when Jasper staggered again, looking pleased despite the hands pressed to his ears and the pain showing in his eyes. This was what he wanted, that much was clear to Jasper, and he used the knowledge to force his legs to move. They wouldn't win. Not now. Not when he was so close.

Jasper lurched to his feet, grabbed the knife from his boot as he straightened, and covered the remaining distance in a few swift steps. The creature had its back to him, its hands still pressed to Tobias's temples, and Jasper shoved at it. The knife slid into its back easily, stopping only when the hilt hit rough skin. Jasper pulled it out and stabbed again, pushing harder this time, and the creature let out an inhuman scream as it tumbled to the ground and rolled into the underbrush.

Silence fell over the clearing and for a moment, Jasper couldn't move. He stared at Tobias, unable to process what had just happened, unable to think in the echoing silence. Then Tobias slumped, sagging against the ropes that held him tied to the tree, and the hold over Jasper was broken. "I gotcha," he said, taking Tobias by the shoulder and pushing him upright. "I'm getting you out of here."

He had managed to cut through one layer of the rope binding Tobias when suddenly it felt as though the ground was jerked out from under him, a powerful blow from the side sending him sprawling. The knife flew from his hand, disappearing into the storm and darkness, and the rain pelted down mercilessly as he looked up into the slitted eyes of the creature he'd knocked away from Tobias.

It growled as it leaned in, sniffing at him, and for a moment, Jasper thought it was going to try the same thing on him as it had tried on Tobias. It even went so far as to put one hand up to his temple before it growled again, claws extending from the tips of its fingers and prickling against the flesh of Jasper's skull. He twisted his head away, his eyes squeezed shut, and kicked his legs upward, trying to dislodge the creature. It didn't fall like he'd hoped, but it shifted, giving Jasper just enough room to roll and push the creature away.

He made it to his feet just as it charged again, growling in concert with the thunder rumbling overhead. It slashed out, slicing through the material of Jasper's robe, its claws scraping against his skin. He dodged, alert for both his knife and the creature, but it was too dark and the creature too fast. It closed the distance between them again and again, and the tatters of his robe provided no protection as its claws tore and slashed.

Jasper scrambled away, scooping up a fallen branch and swinging it wildly as the creature closed in again. He missed, and swung again, swiping madly at the creature he could barely see make out in the rain and hail. It dodged every one of his desperate blows, moving gracefully over the muddy ground. The roots and fallen branches that kept tripping Jasper proved no obstacle for it, as it stepped over them easily.

The storm grew stronger, pounding them with rain and hail big enough to bruise. Jasper raised one arm to shield his face as he continued to swing, near blind now as the storm clouds blocked the moon. The forest spirit was reduced to a light shape barely visible against the trees, while everything and everyone else faded away completely, washed out by the torrential downpour. Even Tobias, struggling nearby and screaming Jasper's name into his skull, was impossible to distinguish from the tree he was tied to.

The creature, by contrast, appeared to be in its element, and came at him unerringly, lunging forward almost faster than Jasper's eye could follow and slashing at him before darting out again, always evading Jasper's wild swings and easily keeping its footing on the treacherous ground. The creature grew bolder as the fight went on. It stayed close to Jasper longer as Jasper lost energy, and drove Jasper back toward the trees as he futilely tried to avoid its sharp claws. He was almost out of the clearing when he fell, sprawling on his back in the mud. The stick he'd been swinging flew away and the creature lunged, grabbing Jasper by the shoulders and shoving him against the nearest tree.

The growl that left its throat was low and menacing, and it sent a shiver down Jasper's spine even as he waited for the inevitable sensation of claws raking across his throat. He was beaten, defeated by the very creature he'd come to save Tobias from, and the worst of it was that Tobias would be next. He couldn't even do the one thing he'd promised.

As he closed his eyes, unable to watch the claws swinging toward his throat, lightning cracked overhead, hitting the tree Jasper was pressed against. Another crack echoed through the clearing, followed by the horrible sound of splintering wood. Jasper opened his eyes and looked up just in time to see the smoldering remains of a huge branch hurtling toward him.

Then everything went dark.

LIGHT returned slowly, in soft bursts full of gentle words and soft touches that did little to ease his agonizing pain. Jasper was never sure where he was during those periods, or who was with him, but the voices were familiar and comforting and they all urged him to do the same thing: sleep. So he did.

When he finally felt well enough to open his eyes and keep them that way, he was tucked into a bed with Tobias curled up next to him, one hand tucked under his cheek and the other resting on Jasper's heart. His breathing was deep and even, and Jasper smiled softly as he took Tobias's hand and squeezed it gently. "Hey."

"You're awake."

Jasper blinked at the unexpected response and lifted his head so he could see Darius sitting in a chair next to the bed. A book was open on his lap, but he looked as though he'd been watching Jasper instead of reading it.

"Uh, yeah." Jasper rubbed a hand over his face as he tried to reorient himself. The room was swaying and he didn't recognize it, which meant it wasn't the inn they'd stayed at in Shaleton. He couldn't figure out how they could possibly have gotten anywhere else. "Where are we? What happened?"

Darius let out a soft snort. "Before or after you got knocked out?"

"After." Jasper remembered most of the fight—the wind, the rain, the creature's claws scratching across his chest, the stabbing pain as Tobias shouted for him from a distance—and he had no desire to be filled in on anything he might have blocked from his mind. What he wanted to know was how he'd gotten from the forest floor to this comfortable bed, and how they'd managed to get Tobias as well. "I remember fighting that... whatever it was. I just need to know how we got here, wherever here is."

"Our train," Darius said, and suddenly the swaying made sense. "The station master in Shaleton tried to tell us it was too dangerous, but we decided to risk it. Only the engine has any windows, and Carla had them fitted with overhangs when we bought the thing. We're heading back to Brightam's Ford, or as close as we can get before the tracks wash out for the season, anyway. As for what happened, that's a long story."

"I think we've got time," Jasper said dryly as he turned on his side so he was facing Tobias. He let his gaze dart from Darius to Tobias and back again. "Is he all right?"

"He will be." Darius shrugged. "I don't know exactly what's wrong with him, but the other two say—"

"Other two?" Jasper asked, cutting Darius off. There were only the three of them in the room. He assumed Carla was operating the train, but he couldn't imagine who else could be onboard. "What other two?"

"The other two sacrifices being offered. It was Tobias's sister and a friend of theirs." Darius's gaze flickered to Tobias as he settled back in the chair. "We couldn't exactly leave them, not after everything he went through to find Samantha."

"Right." Jasper shook his head to clear the cobwebs from it. "What did they say about Tobias?"

"That he'll be fine." Darius leaned forward. "He just needs rest."

A weight felt like it was lifted of Jasper's shoulders and he breathed a sigh of relief as he nodded. "Good." He rubbed a hand over his face, trying to fight back the weariness that was threatening to overtake him, and sighed as he let his arm fall back to his side. "That's good."

"He's been awake," Darius said, looking seriously at Jasper. "It was you we were really worried about. You've been asleep for almost a week."

Jasper blinked, trying to reconcile the flashes of awareness with the passage of a week. He couldn't. "Really?" It felt like a day had passed, maybe two. Not seven.

"Yeah." Darius sighed as he sat back in the chair. "Some of it was drugs, but those ran out yesterday."

"Drugs?" Jasper couldn't imagine where his friends would have gotten any of those. They occasionally shipped some out to Brightam's Ford from the west coast, but they were always the first things offloaded as Dr. Parks was usually out by the time the next batch got to him.

Darius nodded. "We took you to a doctor after we got out of that clearing. He stitched you up and gave us some medication to give you so you wouldn't be in pain."

Jasper blinked, trying to wrap his mind around that. "Wait," he said as he pushed himself up to a sitting position and scooted back so he could lean against the wall behind the bed. It vibrated with the movement of the train, but it would keep him awake, and that was better than trying to figure this out while fighting off sleep. "You're losing me. Start where I lost consciousness."

"Tobias took that thing down," Darius said in a strangely impressed tone. "Somehow he got free and found your knife."

"He did?" Jasper remembered the knife flying away before he'd cut fully through all of Tobias's bonds. "How?"

"I wish I knew." Darius shrugged. "I didn't see anything. I was on my knees in pain from his screams just like everyone else. One second I'm in agonizing pain and wishing he'd shut up, and the next, he's silent and that thing was on the ground, bleeding green."

"Then what?" Jasper leaned forward, his weariness forgotten as he got caught up in the story. "Did he kill it?"

"I think." Darius pushed his hair back and slumped in his chair. "Tobias kept stabbing it. It was screaming—horrible noise, sounded like a tornado—and then it shriveled up. Tobias kept trying to stab it, but he couldn't get the knife in anymore."

"Sleet."

"Yeah. Half the people cleared out right then," Darius said with a nervous laugh. "And Carla and I were able to round the rest of them up. I think they were too stunned by their god or whatever they thought it was dying to protest. We cut Samantha and Aaron free, and Carla kept an eye on the Storm Quellers while I ran to the city and got the guards. They weren't willing to upset the status quo when Carla and I got to Shaleton, but they couldn't refuse to help when we had the Storm Quellers all tied up and rescued kidnap victims."

"So the Storm Quellers are gone?" Jasper couldn't quite believe it. They'd chased him and Tobias for weeks, completely uprooted him from his life, and forced him to do things he'd never have imagined before meeting Tobias. They'd also been indirectly responsible for his falling in love, but he wasn't going to forgive them the things they'd done to Tobias because of that.

"They might be back," Darius said with a shrug. "Some of the junior members of The Order turned on the leaders, but with that kind of power, they won't go down easily."

"No, they wouldn't," Jasper agreed. They'd cause all sorts of problems, he was sure. Thinking about it, he was amazed that Darius and Carla had managed to round them up to begin with, even with the help of Samantha, Aaron, and the city guards. "By the way, how did Carla hold them off?"

Darius chuckled, the sound both amused and proud. "You've never seen her wield a knife, have you?"

"No." Jasper hadn't, and based on the look on Darius's face, he didn't want to. "I'll just assume she's scary."

"Well, that and they were still stunned," Darius agreed. "Plus, I think Samantha and Aaron talked to them, so they were all in pain. The leader tried to attack Carla before I left. She kneed him in the groin and knocked him out with the hilt of her knife. None of them wanted to mess with her after that."

"I wouldn't either." That was a whole new side of Carla, and though Jasper was grateful, he was also glad he'd missed it. "So, then what?"

"That was it, really." Darius shifted, uncrossing and recrossing his legs. "The guards took the Storm Quellers into custody, we took you to a doctor, and everyone who could talked to the magistrates. Once we were sure you and Tobias could travel and they didn't need us anymore, we left. The train goes pretty well in the storms as long as we keep it slow enough to handle the curves on wet track, so we're hoping to get to Brightam's Ford before the rails are washed out for the season."

Jasper sank down a little in the bed as he tried to process everything. "Huh."

"Yeah." Darius stood. "I should go tell Carla and the others you're awake. You want anything while I'm up? I could heat up some soup or something, maybe."

The moment Darius mentioned soup, Jasper's stomach rumbled, reminding him that it had been several days since he could last remember eating. He assumed they'd managed to feed him somehow while he was drifting in and out of consciousness because he didn't appear to have lost much weight, but he was definitely hungry now. "That would be great."

Darius nodded and slipped out of the room, leaving Jasper alone with Tobias for the first time since Tobias had been captured in the forest. "Hey," he whispered again as he gently stroked Tobias's cheek with one finger. He didn't want to wake Tobias up if he needed the sleep, but part of him hoped that Tobias would respond. Jasper needed to see with his own eyes that Tobias was all right.

Tobias stirred slightly, leaning into Jasper's touch and smacking his lips a little. He settled then, and Jasper thought he might fall back into a deep sleep, but instead, he opened his eyes all the way and smiled softly when he saw Jasper looking down at him. He lifted his head, capturing Jasper's lips in a soft kiss, and when they broke apart, Jasper smiled too.

"How are you feeling?" he asked as he leaned down to kiss Tobias again. He fully expected that Tobias would answer while they were kissing, but Tobias remained silent. He wrapped his hands around the back of Jasper's head, holding him down, and slipped his tongue between Jasper's lips. The kiss was desperate, with Tobias holding on until Jasper pulled back, gasping for breath, and then Tobias drew him down again, kissing him just as frantically as before.

This time, when Jasper disengaged, he gently untangled Tobias's hands from around his neck and held them between their chests as he looked straight into Tobias's eyes. "Are you okay?"

Tobias still didn't answer. Instead, he pulled his hands free, rolled to the side of the bed, and fumbled for something on the ground. It was a pad of paper and a pencil, not at all what Jasper had expected, and neither was what he wrote on it. *No,* it read, the word sending a chill through Jasper's gut. *I can't talk.*

CHAPTER
TWENTY-TWO

"WHAT?" Jasper blinked and sat up as he snatched the notebook from Tobias's hand. The words on it didn't change, nor did the fact that, despite their close proximity, Tobias hadn't actually said a single thing to him. "What do you mean?"

Tobias shrunk back, looking as small and vulnerable as he had the first time Jasper had seen him. His eyes were wide, his lower lip trembling as he shook his head back and forth, back and forth, making his hair bounce on his forehead. He didn't reach for the notebook or make any attempt to explain and that, more than anything, terrified Jasper.

"Sleet!" Jasper dropped the notebook, turned, and put his hands Tobias's shoulders. "Easy, easy. I'm sorry. I wasn't trying to upset you." Tobias stilled, looking up at Jasper with a pleading gaze that cut straight to his heart. "I'm sorry," Jasper repeated as he slid one hand up to stroke Tobias's cheek. "We'll figure this out, okay?"

Tobias nodded and slowly reached for the notebook. His fingers shook a little as he curled them around it, pulled it up to his chest, and pressed it over his heart. Jasper watched, waiting for Tobias to write something, but when minutes passed without his doing anything but hugging the notebook to his chest, Jasper put his hand over Tobias's and gently squeezed.

"It'll be okay." The look on Tobias's face said more eloquently than anything he could have written or sent that he didn't believe a word of it, but that didn't matter. It still had the effect Jasper wanted. Tobias's hand stopped shaking under his as incredulity won out over fear, and Jasper found himself able to smile down at Tobias despite the disbelieving look on Tobias's face. "It will," he promised, and then grinned wider as Tobias glared and yanked his hand out from under Jasper's.

You don't know that, he scrawled, scowling at Jasper as he wrote. The words sloped sideways across the page and threatened to run off the edge toward the end, a stark contrast to the careful lettering with which he'd told Jasper he couldn't send his thoughts.

"Yes I do," Jasper said, stretching out on the bed again and pulling Tobias into his arms. "We're safe. Your sister is safe. Darius and Carla are safe. That's what's really important. We'll figure everything else out, all right?"

Tobias squeezed his eyes shut as he nodded, a tiny tear trickling out the corner of his eye. He wiped viciously at it with his fist as he pulled back and lifted the notebook and pen up once more. *It hurts when I try to say anything,* he wrote, once again using the neat letters he'd started with. *What if it doesn't stop? What if whatever that creature did is permanent? I can't—*

Jasper stopped him by taking Tobias's hand, keeping him from writing anything else. "*If* that's the case," he said, emphasizing the first word, "we'll deal with it. There are things we can try, other ways we can talk. And this works just fine for now." He met Tobias's gaze evenly, doing his best not to let his doubt show. Darius had promised that Tobias would be all right, which meant they believed that this wouldn't last forever, and Jasper had to cling to that, for both his sake and Tobias's.

Tobias stared back at him for what felt like forever before he nodded and dropped the notepad and pen. Jasper hugged Tobias tightly before tilting his head up for a soft kiss. "I love you," he said, his heart surging as Tobias deepened the kiss, slipping his tongue into Jasper's mouth and letting his actions show what he couldn't say.

They were still kissing, their hands roaming and their tongues dancing, when the door opened again with a rush of sound. Darius stepped through, followed by two people Jasper didn't recognized. He knew from Darius's explanation earlier who they were, but they looked different enough in the light with proper clothes and no blindfolds that Jasper wouldn't have known if he hadn't been warned.

Tobias broke the kiss when the door whooshed shut, but as he rolled over, he stayed in the circle of Jasper's arms, lacing their fingers together as he settled in with his back to Jasper's chest. Jasper squeezed Tobias's hand and pressed a kiss to the back of his neck before lifting his head. He could smell the soup from across the room, and his stomach grumbled loudly as he inhaled, taking in the tantalizing scent.

"Hungry?" Darius asked wryly as he held out the soup. Jasper was loath to let go of Tobias, but the soup smelled so wonderful and he was so hungry that he didn't really have any other choice.

"Yes," he said, squeezing Tobias's hand once more before gently untangling himself. "Sorry," he whispered, sitting up and scooting back so he could again lean against the wall behind the bed. It rattled with the movement of the train, making his hands shake as he curled them around the cup, lifted it to his lips, and took a tentative sip.

The hot liquid slid down his throat, warming him from the inside as it started to fill him up. He immediately took another sip, this one bigger, and hurriedly swallowed it as it started to get too hot for his tongue. He was halfway through the cup before it was cool enough for him to really taste it, but the chicken and rice filled him up quickly, and by the time it was cool he was full enough that he could sip slowly and savor the taste. It was wonderful, just a little spicy, with the rich warm flavors of the herbs and vegetables mixing well with the milder ones of the chicken and the rice. Jasper held one sip in his mouth for a moment, relishing the flavor, and when he swallowed, he nodded at Darius. "It's good."

Darius snorted. "I'd hope so, the way you were gulping it down. Are you going to want more? I heated up a whole pot."

"Maybe?" Jasper shrugged as he took another sip. "I'll let you know when I'm done." He didn't want to eat too much too quickly, not after the days he'd spent sleeping, and he had other things on his mind as well. "You going to introduce me while I eat?"

"Thought I'd let Tobias handle that," Darius said, smirking as Tobias shot up, blinking wildly. He looked frantically between Darius and Jasper, his gaze pleading, but Darius crossed his arms and gave Tobias a level look. "They're your friends."

The look Tobias shot Darius was comical, but he picked up the notebook and pen anyway, scribbling a sentence before showing it to Jasper. *This is Samantha and Aaron.*

It was short and terse, but Jasper smiled anyway, nodding at the two people standing silently off to the side. "Nice to meet you," he said, taking pity on Tobias and finishing the introductions himself. "I'm Jasper."

The woman stepped forward, holding out her hand, and Jasper took it without thinking. It was cool and small in his grip, delicate in a way he wasn't used to. *Nice to meet you,* she said, her voice sounding completely unlike Tobias's. Jasper wasn't sure why he'd thought they would sound the same—she wasn't Tobias after all, and people's speaking voices sounded different—but it surprised him, and his eyes widened a little as he blinked up at her.

Tobias, who was watching them carefully, narrowed his gaze and bumped his shoulder against his sister's arm. *Be nice!* he wrote, underlining the words several times as he showed the pad to Samantha.

"She is," Jasper assured Tobias, smiling slightly when Tobias narrowed his gaze and glared at Jasper. "Honest. I was just surprised at what she sounded like, that's all."

Samantha's eyes twinkled as her chuckle echoed in Jasper's skull. *Surprised? Why?*

"I thought you'd sound alike." Jasper shrugged self-depreciatingly. "Stupid, I know."

Not stupid, just.... Samantha trailed off, clearly searching for a word, and looked toward Tobias for help. She didn't say anything Jasper could hear and Tobias didn't write, but they were clearly communicating in some way.

As Jasper watched them, he started to notice the similarities in their appearance. They had the same deep brown eyes and dark curly hair, though Samantha's fell halfway down her back while Tobias's stopped mid-ear. Their noses and mouths were similar too, though Samantha's face was round whereas Tobias's was oval, and her cheekbones weren't nearly as prominent as his. Their mannerisms were similar too, both of them tilting their heads to the side as they looked at each other, unconsciously mimicking the other's pose, and Samantha's free hand picked at the hem of her shirt the way Jasper had seen Tobias pick at his clothes several times on their trip. She was nervous, though the palm pressed against Jasper's was still cool and dry, and he had to admit that if he hadn't known Tobias, he wouldn't have picked up on it at all.

Uninformed, Samantha said, startling Jasper out of his contemplations.

He blinked, trying to focus again on the conversation they were having, and failed to remember what she had last said. "What?"

Not stupid, Samantha repeated, her lips quirking up in amusement the same way Tobias's did, *just uninformed. You've only met Tobias. You couldn't know that we'd all sound different.*

"I should have," he said after he swallowed the last of the soup. "It makes sense."

"What makes sense?" Darius asked, stepping forward to take the cup from Jasper when he held it out. "You're having an entire conversation that I can't hear," he grumbled, crossing his arms over his chest as he stepped back. Aaron touched his arm briefly, a small smile playing on his face, and Darius's scowl deepened. "That doesn't make it better."

"Doesn't make what better?"

"See? It's not very pleasant, is it?"

Samantha rolled her eyes and looked at Aaron, who grabbed Darius's arm again, hauling him forward until he was close enough for Samantha to grab him with her free hand. *Better?* she asked, and Darius nodded as Aaron stepped up against the bed and put his hand on Jasper's shoulder, completing the circle. Only Tobias was left out, sitting in the center and only touching Jasper. It felt wrong to have him like that, deliberately excluded, but since he couldn't talk, there was no reason for him to touch Darius. Jasper could only assume that he could still hear Samantha and Aaron without any pain.

It's nice to meet you, Jasper, Aaron said, smiling slightly. *Thank you for coming to find us.*

"You're welcome." Jasper managed a strained smile as he tried to shrug off the discomfort of being thanked. He'd come because he couldn't let Tobias face the journey alone, not because he had any desire to save either Samantha or Aaron. Even Tobias had been focused solely on Samantha, and it was awkward to have thanks coming from the one person they'd barely thought about rescuing.

Yes, Samantha echoed, *thank you. And thank you for helping my brother. He needs it.*

Tobias rolled his eyes and stuck out his tongue, answering Jasper's question about his ability to hear Samantha and Aaron. *Yeah,* he wrote, *I'm the one who needs help.*

It was clearly the start of a typical sibling argument, but Jasper wasn't in the mood. He was tired and sore, and he wanted answers before he made everyone leave him alone to sleep some more, and this was the perfect opening. "Right now you do," he said softly, regretting that he had to call attention to the fact that Tobias currently couldn't talk. "Unless you already know why you can't talk."

It was that creature, Aaron said, scowling at the memory. His furrowed brow coupled with his dark coloring and stocky build made him look a little scary, and Jasper was glad he was on their side. He was still clearly weakened from his ordeal, but he had a heavier build than Samantha and Tobias, and even after being held captive for almost year, he still had some meat on his bones. It was no wonder he'd been able to struggle when Samantha hadn't.

"Do you know what it was?" Jasper asked, looking between Aaron and Tobias. "Or what it is?"

We call them tree guardians, Samantha interjected. *They live in all the forests, though most of the ones we've encountered before have been uninterested in humans. They live in the trees, and talk to each other the way that we do. Some people say they can talk to the trees too, but that's just a rumor.*

"What about the ones that are interested in humans?" Darius asked. "What do they do?"

Watch, Aaron said softly. *They can gather psychic energy from people, animals, maybe even the plants, and use it to help the forest. They'll heal a tree with it, or a sick animal, and they make sure that the forest stays healthy.*

"So then what was this one doing?" Jasper asked, shuddering as he recalled the way the creature had grabbed Tobias's head and made him scream. "That's not how they gather this energy, is it?"

No. Samantha let out a shaky breath. *They just watch. All living creatures give off psychic energy, and they can gather it in just by watching. Certain activities give off more and every year, a couple goes out from our town and, uh, lets them watch.*

It took Jasper a moment to fully grasp what she was saying. "While you have sex?"

Samantha nodded. *It's an agreement that we have with them. They get to watch one couple a year, one week a year, and they stay out of town and let us hunt and gather in the forest. It's a good arrangement,* she added, a little more vehemently than necessary.

That's what Samantha and I were doing when we were taken, Aaron added, flushing slightly. *We were thrilled to be chosen—it's an honor—and then those men came and surprised us, and next thing we knew we were trapped. The tree guardians tried to save us, but the Storm Quellers killed one of them, and then the rest left us alone.*

"Why would they kill one of them?" Darius mused. "They worshiped the one near Shaleton. If these are the same creatures, wouldn't that be like killing their god?"

"Who knows," Jasper replied with a shrug. "I don't think any of them were sane—this tree guardian included. We may never understand."

I don't want to, Tobias wrote, scowling as he showed the paper to Jasper. *I just want to forget it ever happened.*

Jasper felt the same way, though he didn't think he'd be able to for a long time. "So what did this tree guardian do to Tobias?" It seemed like Aaron and Samantha and even Tobias were all remarkably unconcerned with Tobias's inability to talk. There had to be a reason behind it.

I think it just gathered his psychic energy, only it didn't wait for him to give it off, it pulled it out of him, Samantha said with a sigh. *That's why it rejected me and Aaron, we didn't have enough left. It wasn't worth the effort.*

"But Tobias was still relatively strong because they hadn't had him long." Darius didn't make it a question.

Right. Aaron smiled wryly as everyone's gaze swiveled to him. *They didn't feed us much, or let us out, or put us anywhere we had any chance of getting away. They wanted us alive for the sacrifice, but they didn't want us to fight back.* He snorted, the sound mostly lost in the clacking of train wheels beneath them. *I think they'd hoped to sacrifice us last year, but they have this weird idea about the first full moon, and they didn't get us to Shaleton in time.*

"Thank the sun," Darius muttered, and Jasper silently agreed with him. He didn't want to imagine how Tobias would have reacted if they hadn't found Samantha.

"So what now?" he asked, still unsure why the three of them were so unconcerned about what the tree guardian had done to Tobias. "What do we need to do now?"

We wait, Tobias wrote, scribbling out the word before either Aaron or Samantha could answer.

That wasn't the answer Jasper wanted to hear. "But—"

We wait, Samantha repeated, squeezing Jasper's hand gently. *When the tree guardians take the psychic energy we give off naturally, it drains us a little. Not much, just enough to leave us a little tired, but it builds back up quickly. We think that this one just took a lot from Tobias, so it's affecting his psychic abilities too. He's just drained, and when he gets his strength back, he'll be fine. It's just going to take a while.*

"Are you sure?"

No. Samantha shook her head sadly. *But it's our best guess.*

Jasper nodded, reading into it what she wasn't saying. They didn't have anything else to try, either, so waiting and hoping was their only option. "Then we wait," he said, forcing a smile he didn't feel to his lips. "As long as it takes."

EIGHT days later, when they finally pulled the train into Brightam's Ford, Tobias still couldn't talk, and Jasper pulled Samantha aside as they disembarked. "We've waited," he said in a low voice, hoping that the others wouldn't overhear. "And nothing's happened."

I know. Samantha pushed her hair back and sighed. *I thought he'd have improved some by now, at least.* She was obviously as upset about it as Jasper was.

"So what do we do now?" he asked in a low voice, looking around to be sure Tobias wasn't near. He hated feeling like he was going behind Tobias's back, but when Jasper had tried to talk to him about it this morning, he'd pulled away, refusing to touch the notepad and pen Jasper had held out to him and never once meeting Jasper's gaze. "There has to be something."

There might be. Samantha glanced around too, then turned so she was looking Jasper directly in the eyes. *There was one other thing Aaron and I talked about, but I don't know if it'll work.*

"What?" Jasper didn't care how crazy she thought it sounded or how little chance she thought it had of working. He needed to do something to try to help Tobias, and if the thing Samantha and Aaron had talked about had even the slightest chance of working, he needed to know what it was.

We were thinking that maybe the tree guardian drained him so much that, well, his mind became like yours or Darius's or Carla's and he can't use his psychic powers anymore.

Jasper didn't see how that helped. "What does that mean?"

I'm getting there. Samantha flashed a strained smile. *This is hard to explain, but basically, Aaron says there's a way he can, um, unlock someone's mind and let them use psychic powers. So, in theory, if we can do that, we can do it to Tobias and he'd be able to talk again.*

It sounded reasonable, but Jasper could sense the hesitation in her voice and knew that there had to be a catch. "So why don't you try it?'

We don't know if it will work. Samantha held up a hand as Jasper opened his mouth to protest. *Aaron overheard his father talk about it one time, but he's never seen it done, or tried it. He knows what to do—we think—but not if it will work, and we don't want to get Tobias's hopes up until we do.*

Something heavy settled in the pit of Jasper's stomach. "How would you find out?"

Samantha ducked her head briefly. When she lifted it again, her bottom lip was caught between her teeth. *We want to try it on you first.*

CHAPTER
TWENTY-THREE

JASPER blinked, reviewing what he'd just heard and trying to make it come out as something different. No matter how many times he went over it, it always sounded the same, and he ended up tipping his head to the side and giving Samantha an incredulous look. "You want to what?"

Try it on you first, she repeated, amusement coloring her tone. *That way we'll know if it works or not before talking to Tobias.*

"But how? I've never had psychic powers. Hail, it hurts me when one of you talks to me without physical contact!"

Exactly. Samantha looked at him earnestly. *That makes you perfect. If we can unlock your psychic potential, then we'd know for sure that it would work on Tobias. We'll know we did it right.*

Understanding dawned, casting a gloomy light over the entire situation. "So if it doesn't work, we'll know that wasn't a viable solution for him."

Right. Samantha picked up a lock of hair and twirled it around her finger. *If we can unlock your potential, we'll know Aaron remembered right. If we can't, we won't even try on Tobias. If we can, and it doesn't work on him, we'll know we were wrong about why he can't talk.*

"Again." It came out harsher than Jasper intended, and Samantha hung her head.

Yeah, she said, her hair falling to block her face. *Again.*

"What does it involve?" Jasper asked, not quite sure he could believe he was doing this. "If you try to unlock my, uh, buried psychic powers or whatever it is?"

Latent powers, Samantha corrected. *Everyone has them, or they wouldn't give off psychic energy.*

"Okay," Jasper said, quirking his lips up into a small smile. "What does it involve if you try to unlock my latent psychic powers?"

Nothing on your part.

"That's not what I mean."

I know. Samantha flashed a small smile as she took him by the arm and started walking. *Did Tobias ever tell you about how we can make people think things? And some of us can make people feel things?*

"Yeah." Jasper left it at that, figuring that the arguments he and Tobias had about the issue weren't Samantha's business, particularly not since they'd been resolved long before he met her.

Okay, she said, glancing over at him as they stepped over more train tracks. Carla and Darius had maneuvered the train on to the most out of the way holding tracks in the train yard, which meant that they had to cross the entire yard to get to the garage where they'd left their SUV. *It's like that, sort of. We won't make you think or feel anything, but it's going into your head like that and then... flipping a switch, I guess. It's hard to describe.*

"Will it hurt?" Jasper lowered his voice a little as they approached the SUV. Tobias was already inside, sitting in the back with his knees pulled up to his chest, looking small and vulnerable, and Darius, Carla, and Aaron were packing the things they'd pulled off the train into the back. There wasn't much. Most of their stuff had been left in Shaleton and the furnishings and supplies from the train stayed with it.

I don't know. The pitch of Samantha's voice was lower as well, as though she were consciously speaking only to Jasper. *I hope not, but I can't promise anything. We've never done this before. We'll try not to hurt you and stop—if we can—if it does, but that's all I can promise.*

Jasper nodded. It wasn't the most comforting thing to be told, but at least he knew it was honest. And really, if it worked for both him and

Tobias, it would be worth some pain. Temporary pain would be far better than leaving Tobias like he was. "Okay."

Samantha tilted her head to the side. *Okay what?*

"I'll do it. Or let you and Aaron do it. Whatever." Jasper waved his hand to indicate the semantics really didn't matter. He'd do whatever Samantha and Aaron needed him to for a chance at helping Tobias. "When should we? And where?"

Tomorrow, Samantha said after exchanging a glance—and probably more—with Aaron. *Aaron and I will get ready tonight, and we can slip away somewhere in the morning. I don't want anyone else to know until we've tried it.*

Jasper wasn't sure how he felt about that, but he nodded in agreement anyway. "All right. Tomorrow. Early. If it works, can you try it on Tobias tomorrow too?" He didn't want to leave Tobias upset and unable to talk for a moment longer than he had to.

We'll try. She squeezed his arm, stopping his protest. *I don't know how much energy this is going to take. If it works, and we have enough energy, we'll try as soon as we find out. But I'm not going to try if we're too tired. That would be dangerous.*

Jasper nodded. He didn't want that, either. "As soon as possible after we know, then, right?"

Of course. I don't want him to wait any more than you do. Samantha grinned and let go of Jasper's arm, effectively ending the conversation.

Jasper scowled but decided it wasn't worth pursuing. He climbed into the SUV instead, taking the middle seat in the back so he could sit next to Tobias, and left the two center chairs and the front seat for Aaron, Samantha, and whichever one of Carla and Darius didn't drive. Tobias looked at him as he sat down, giving Jasper a little hope, but looked away again before Jasper could say anything. As Jasper buckled his seat belt, Tobias fixed his gaze out the window and pulled his knees in tighter as if he wanted to take up as little space as possible.

"Hey," Jasper said, putting his arm around Tobias's shoulder and doing his best to ignore the flinch. "We're going to figure this out."

Tobias shrugged, pulling away as best he could in the small space, and Jasper sighed as he let go. Tomorrow couldn't come soon enough.

THEY spent that night in Jasper's safe room as the storms raged outside, none of them getting much sleep. The room had been crowded with four adults. Six—as Darius and Carla hadn't had time to get home before the storms hit—was claustrophobic. Jasper was glad they hadn't had time to go over to his neighbor's house to retrieve Kyree before they'd had to hide. Six adults and a dog would have been unbearable.

When the radar finally indicated it was clear the next morning, Jasper pushed his way through the closet into his bedroom, wryly thinking that even with the window, it was safer than that night in the clearing or any of the nights he spent hiding in the woods outside Shaleton. Before, when he'd been the man who had almost been caught in a coastal storm in Crittendon, the precaution of the safe room had made perfect sense. Now, as the man who had survived standing in the storm and sleeping in trees, the safe room seemed overly cautious.

The others seemed to think so too. Darius and Carla grumbled under their breath and Tobias, Samantha, and Aaron scowled as they left the room. Tobias in particular had seemed exceedingly uncomfortable all night, and half the time Jasper should have been sleeping, he'd spent worrying about him. The other half he'd spent worrying about what Samantha and Aaron were about to try.

Breakfast seemed to take forever, yet when Samantha put her hand on Jasper's arm and tilted her head to the side, it seemed too soon. *You ready?*

Jasper felt anything but ready, but he couldn't back out now, though, not with how miserable Tobias was, so he nodded. "Yeah. Where do you want to do this?" Tobias had already disappeared and Darius and Carla had gone out to finish unpacking the car, so they could have done it right there, but it didn't feel right. Not when anyone could walk back in at any time.

Aaron and Samantha shared a glance. *The barn?* Samantha asked, shrugging. *Unless you think Tobias will be there.*

"There's only one way to find out." Jasper had no more idea than Samantha and Aaron where Tobias had gotten to, but the barn seemed their best bet. He would feel weird doing it in his bedroom or the guest room, the rest of the house was too exposed, and he didn't want to get too far away from his friends in case something went wrong. The barn, being close by, yet not someplace his friends were going to walk into without reason, was ideal. "If he's there, we can find somewhere else."

He wasn't. They trooped out to the barn and found it empty except for the horses. Jasper's neighbor had obviously been diligent in coming by to feed them—their stalls were clean and their feed tubs half-full—but Jasper doubted he'd be by for a few more hours. He had his own animals to take care of first.

After a quick glance to reassure himself that the barn was empty, Jasper sat down on one of the hay bales and looked expectantly at Aaron and Samantha. "What do you want me to do?"

You might want to lie down. Jasper shrugged at Aaron's suggestion and lay back so he was stretched across the hay bale, his feet resting flat on the barn floor. Aaron sat down on the floor next to him and gently touched one finger to Jasper's temple. *Just stay still.*

"Okay." Jasper closed his eyes, ready and waiting, but nothing happened. Seconds ticked by with no sign that Aaron was there except for the slight pressure on Jasper's temple, and he started to wonder when it was going to start. He was just about to open his eyes to ask when he felt pressure inside his skull, moving around like Aaron was literally poking into all the corners of his brain. It wasn't painful at first, just strange, but then Aaron pushed against something and Jasper gasped as pain shot all the way down to his toes.

Stay still. Aaron put a finger against Jasper's other temple. *This is probably going to be painful.*

Jasper braced for the pain, but it was like nothing he'd ever experienced before. The agony he'd felt after Durrysville and during the fight was stubbing his toe compared to this. He imagined Aaron ramming against a door inside his head, trying to break it down, and every time Aaron hit it, it felt like Jasper was being thrown to the ground from a great height or being crushed under the weight of a vehicle.

Just when Jasper thought he couldn't take it anymore, Aaron shoved harder than he had before. The pain was blinding, but when it faded, Jasper noticed a buzzing in the back of his skull. Gradually, it resolved itself into words, Samantha's voice echoing in his head even though she wasn't touching him.

... it work? He's not—

Give it a minute, Sam. The light pressure of Aaron's fingers left Jasper's temples, and he blinked his eyes open, turning his head to the side so he could see Samantha and Aaron.

"Sleet! That was...," he started, then decided to think it when he saw their amused expressions. *Horrible.*

But it worked. Aaron leaned back, bracing himself with his hands spread behind him. *Sorry it hurt so much but—*

Jasper cut him off, thinking loudly so that he would be sure to be heard. *You can try this on Tobias today, right?* He really wasn't interested in the how or why of how easy it had been. He just wanted to know if it was easy enough to help Tobias or if they'd have to wait another day.

Both Samantha and Aaron pinched the bridges of their noses, making pained expressions. *You don't have to scream. We're right here.* Samantha said, squeezing her eyes shut and rubbing along her nose like she was trying to get rid of a headache. Jasper supposed it was their equivalent of covering their ears.

Sorry. I'm not exactly good at this, yet. It felt odd just to think, and he had no idea if he was just letting Samantha and Aaron hear him, or if the surprise would be ruined should Tobias happen to stumble along. *I have no idea how this works.*

You'll learn. Samantha held out a hand and pulled Jasper into a sitting position. *Mostly, you'll just talk like this. There are ways to keep things private between two people, like when you, uh, talk really quietly in someone's ear?*

Whisper, Jasper told her, and she nodded.

Right. Like when you whisper. And you can yell too, like you just did, to make sure more people hear you or to force words into someone's head. She smiled softly. *You'll figure it out.*

I hope so, Jasper said wryly, shaking his head. *What about hearing things from other people?*

Only if you try, Aaron said, climbing to his feet and dusting his hands off on his pants. *Unless they're broadcasting like this, of course. You're not going to pick up stray thoughts.* He patted Jasper on the shoulder. *Try not to worry so much.*

I'll give that a shot. Jasper rolled his eyes as he stood. He wouldn't trade the past several weeks for anything, but sometimes it felt like worry was practically all he'd done since meeting Tobias, and he didn't see that changing any time soon. Even if this worked and gave Tobias his abilities back, Jasper still had to get used to his. By the time he managed that, the wet season would probably be over, and that meant Tobias would be leaving.

Do that, Aaron said, heading for the door of the barn and pulling it open. *Now, where do you think Tobias is?*

AS IT turned out, Tobias had taken advantage of the brief break in storms and retreated to the woods. He was sitting on a log, his hands in his lap and his eyes closed as he leaned against the tree behind it. He was so still that for a minute, Jasper thought he was asleep, but then Samantha stepped on a twig, snapping it, and his eyes shot open.

He started shaking his head as soon as he saw them and pulled one knee up to his chest as though he were trying to be inconspicuous. It was a futile effort as they'd already seen him, but it slowed Jasper's steps, and he watched Tobias carefully as Samantha and Aaron approached him.

Tobias was withdrawn—Jasper had known that—but it was just now he could see the full effect this was having on him. There were dark circles under his eyes, his hair hung limply around his face, and he looked too thin in the baggy jacket he'd pulled on. Even his body language was different, weary and slow like it hadn't been before he'd been captured, and though Jasper knew that some of it was from a year of stress and worry since Samantha and Aaron had been taken, he could see the difference between now and when he'd first woken up on the train.

His heart clenched as he closed the distance between them, taking a seat on the far end of the log and letting Samantha talk to her brother without his interference. Aaron hovered nearby as well, staying back behind Samantha so he wasn't crowding Tobias, and Samantha crouched down putting her hand on her brother's knee.

How are you feeling? she asked. It was weird for Jasper to hear the conversation that only a few hours earlier he would have been completely oblivious to, but weirder still not to hear Tobias answer. Instead, Tobias turned away, resting his chin on his knee and pulling it in closer to his chest.

You're not even going to try? Samantha asked, her voice soft, and that earned her a glare that she shrugged off in the manner of siblings everywhere. It was going to take more than that for Tobias to scare her off, a fact she made clear as she took Tobias's bent leg and physically pulled him back so he was looking at her. *Can Aaron try something?*

Tobias's eyes narrowed further, but he tilted his head to the side and quirked an eyebrow, which was apparently enough for Samantha. *We think we know something that might help. Aaron knows how to unlock psychic powers in people who don't have them. We were thinking that maybe the tree guardian drained you to the point that you don't have any unlocked power left, and that's why you haven't healed yet.*

But if that's the case, we should be able to unlock it and heal you, Aaron continued, stepping in to rest his hands on Samantha's shoulders. *Can I try?*

Tobias shook his head as he tried to pull his leg out of Samantha's grip. She didn't let go, so he twisted his upper body instead, gazing forlornly over his knee at Jasper.

We know it works, Aaron said, his fingers twitching on Samantha's shoulder. *I've done it before.*

He's unlocked someone else's mind, Samantha clarified as Tobias swiveled back to look at them with wide eyes. *But we think that it will work on you too. It's worth a shot, right?* She cast a gaze toward Jasper, and he knew that was his cue.

Please? he said, biting back a grin when Tobias almost fell off the log as he looked over at Jasper with an incredulous expression on his face. He flailed, his arms windmilling as his eyes widened further, and it was only Aaron and Samantha pushing him back up that kept Tobias from hitting the ground. When he was settled again, Jasper scooted forward on the log, took Tobias's hands between his, and looked him in the eyes. *It worked on me. Doesn't that at least make it worth a try?*

Tobias's mouth fell open and he stared incredulously at Jasper for a moment before he smiled, flung himself forward, and wrapped Jasper in a hug. Even without words, Jasper could tell how thrilled Tobias was. He gave himself a moment to hold Tobias close before he pushed the issue. When Tobias stopped trembling in his arms, Jasper kissed his temple. *Let him? Please?*

Tobias pulled back enough to look Jasper in the eyes, and stared at him as though he were searching for something. Jasper didn't know what and didn't want to push him, so he just held Tobias's gaze, doing his best to let everything he felt show in his eyes. Finally, just when Jasper was sure he'd failed, Tobias nodded, and relief flooded through Jasper.

Just try to relax, Aaron said once Tobias was settled with his back to Jasper's chest. He put his fingers against Tobias's temples just as he had with Jasper, squared his shoulders, and closed his eyes. *Hold still.*

The seconds ticked by, marked only by the leaves rustling in the wind. Jasper waited, counting each one, hoping Tobias's stillness meant he wasn't in pain and not that it wasn't working. Time seemed to slow, even the wind lessening as he waited, and Jasper's fingers began to twitch. Surely it had been long enough. Surely something should have happened by now. Surely they should know one way or the other by now, but Aaron wasn't pulling back and Tobias wasn't moving and—

Jasper.

He stilled, blinking when he realized Tobias was looking over his shoulder at him, his brown eyes warm now instead of wary, and Aaron had stepped away. "Did it work?" he asked, falling back on his voice as he completely forgot how to speak telepathically. "Can you talk again?"

Yeah. Tobias smiled, glancing appreciatively at Aaron before looking at Jasper again. *All better.* A surge of happiness, love, and desire swept over Jasper and he grinned, recognizing it as Tobias's telling him that he could share his emotions again as well.

The thought briefly crossed Jasper's mind to wonder if he could share his feelings as well, but then he caught the sexy undertone of what Tobias was sending to him and all thoughts of additional abilities were pushed from his mind. He could figure that out later. Right now, it had been far too long since he and Tobias had been alone.

Thank you, Jasper said to Aaron and Samantha as he pulled Tobias to his feet. He wanted to lean in and kiss him right now, to celebrate this the way it should be celebrated, but he knew that if he did that, he wouldn't be able to stop, so he laced their fingers together instead, and tugged Tobias back toward the house. They had lost time to make up for.

THE moment they reached Jasper's bedroom, Tobias pushed him against the wall, kissing him hungrily as he pressed his body against Jasper's. Jasper closed the door so none of their houseguests would interrupt them and returned the kiss, pushing off the wall and guiding Tobias to the bed. He'd dreamed about having Tobias in his big bed those nights they'd spent huddled in too-small beds along their trip, and he wasn't going to give up on that because they couldn't walk an extra five feet. He wanted this to be perfect.

They deserved it after what they'd been through.

Without breaking the kiss, he pushed Tobias onto the bed, climbed on after him, and straddled his hips. He rubbed their groins together, moaning at the friction through their clothes, and smiled as Tobias's arms came up to wrap around his neck.

You can talk while you kiss me, you know, Tobias said, smiling against Jasper's lips. *It's like whispering dirty words in my ear, except better, because we can still do this.* He slid his tongue forward, stroking it over Jasper's, and Jasper moaned.

Sleet, Tobias, he said, moaning again as Tobias thrust his hips up, rubbing their groins together again. Jasper felt like a teenager as Tobias slipped his hands under his shirt and pushed it up as far as it would go, and when Tobias's fingers dipped beneath the waistband of his pants, Jasper's breath hitched. *Not going to last if you keep doing that.*

Good. Tobias smirked and rolled, pinning Jasper to the bed. *I don't want you to.*

But—

No. No more waiting. Tobias ground his hips against Jasper's then pulled back just enough to shimmy out of his shirt. *We can go slow later.*

It was an impossible request to refuse, and Jasper nodded, pulling off his own shirt before fumbling with the buttons of Tobias's pants. *All right,* he agreed as he leaned in for another kiss. *Fast now. Slow later.*

Tobias grinned as he pushed Jasper's pants down to his knees and leaned in again, rubbing their bare cocks together. *Exactly.*

Jasper practically came just from the husky tone of Tobias's voice and he groaned as he wrapped his hands around Tobias's hips, holding him in place as he thrust up. Tobias slipped his hand between their bodies, wrapped it around both their cocks, and stroked once, twice before Jasper came, calling out Tobias's name both verbally and telepathically. Tobias came right after, falling forward and burying his head in Jasper's shoulder as he shuddered. His orgasm rocked Jasper too, leaving him gasping for breath and clenching at the sheets beneath him as Tobias carried him along the wave a second time.

When it was over, they lay tangled together on top of the sheets, breathing heavily as they slowly came down. Jasper pressed his hand against Tobias's back, feeling the rise and fall of his chest and the steady thump-thump of his heartbeat as it returned to normal. He rubbed his hand up Tobias's spine, smiling as he shivered, and turned his head to press a soft kiss to Tobias's temple. *Slow now or later?*

Jasper felt more than saw Tobias's smile, but his chuckle was unmistakable. *Now,* he said, stroking Jasper's chest and leaning in for a soft, sensual kiss. This was what Jasper had dreamed about, and he opened his mouth willingly, sucking Tobias's tongue in and curling his own around it. He could feel the emotions echoing back and forth between them even more now, but unlike the first time he'd felt Tobias's emotions, he liked it. It added to the experience, making it easy for him to get lost in Tobias's touches and overwhelmed by the sensation of their bodies moving together.

He didn't know how long they'd been kissing when Tobias pulled back, looking down at Jasper with a soft gaze. *Jasper?* he asked, his voice more tentative than Jasper had ever heard it before. *When the wet season is over and I go home, will you come with me?*

The question took Jasper by surprise, but he didn't have to think about the answer long. As much as he'd longed for this, here in his bed, being here didn't feel right anymore, and he knew that it would be even worse without Tobias by his side. Jasper could fit in with Tobias's people, but Tobias would never fit in here, and there would always be problems if they stayed. It made sense for them both to go.

"Yes," he said, echoing the word mentally a moment later. *Yes.*

EPILOGUE

THE last storm of the wet season struck in the early hours of the morning, a small thunderstorm that didn't wake any of them and merely left slightly wet ground as a sign of its passing. Three days after that, Jasper loaded up Darius's old SUV—a fair trade for the house, the barn, and the few animals Darius and Carla had wanted—and slipped his hands into his pockets as he leaned against it, waiting for Tobias.

"Having second thoughts?"

Jasper smiled. He should have known that Darius and Carla would show up today. He hadn't told them specifically when they were leaving, but he wasn't surprised they knew. *No. I don't belong here anymore.* Darius could hear him now without pain thanks to a trick Aaron had figured out not long after he'd healed Tobias, but the fact that Jasper automatically used telepathy instead of his voice spoke volumes about how out of place he'd felt since returning home. Even opening his mouth to speak to Darius was an effort, and the few times he'd ventured into town, he'd found himself wanting to shrink back the way Tobias had on their first trip.

Darius sighed. "Figured, but I had to ask."

Yeah. Darius had asked Jasper if he was sure every time they'd seen each other since the day he'd agreed to join Tobias. Even as Jasper started closing down his life in Brightam's Ford, selling and giving away the things he couldn't take with him and making sure the animals Darius and Carla wouldn't be able to care for had homes, Darius had kept asking if he was sure. He never pushed, but he never quite accepted Jasper leaving, either. There was always that question in his eyes, that tiny spark of hope that Jasper knew he had to crush now. *I'll keep in touch.*

"Over the mountains?" Darius raised an eyebrow. "How?"

"I don't know, but I'll figure out a way," Jasper said, using his voice for the first time since his last trip into town so that Darius would know he meant it. The one regret Jasper had about leaving was that Darius and Carla weren't coming with them and that there was a good chance he'd lose touch with his closest friends. He wasn't going to let that happen if there was any way he could prevent it. "Maybe you and Carla can bring supplies over once or twice a year. There's probably a good trade."

"Show me a good route and I'll think about it," Darius said, his smile letting Jasper know that he was forgiven for leaving. "I'm not taking anything over those mountains blind."

"I'll see what I can do." Jasper bumped his shoulder against Darius's and matched his grin. "Take care of my house, all right?"

"Take care of my car." Darius pushed off from the SUV and gave it a once over glance. "She's in good shape."

"So's the house."

"And it'll stay that way. The barn's getting turned into a warehouse, though."

Jasper had expected something like that. Darius and Carla couldn't keep the animals and travel out to the west coast for most of the dry season, so Jasper had sold them and decided not to ask if Darius was going to find a use for the barn or just tear it down. It was oddly reassuring to know that he was going to use it.

The front door opened then and Tobias and Aaron stepped out, followed by Samantha, Carla, and the dog. The two women had grown close over the two months they'd waited for the storms to stop, and Samantha slipped her arm around Carla's shoulder and hugged her before climbing into the car and calling the dog up with her. Aaron followed, getting into the middle set of seats with Samantha, and Tobias and Carla came around to stand next to Jasper and Darius.

"So I guess this is goodbye," Carla said, squeezing Jasper in an unexpectedly tight hug. "Try to let us know how you're doing."

"I will," Jasper said, trying to keep the surprise out of his voice as she turned to hug Tobias just as tightly. Darius followed suit, hugging Jasper like he never had before, and slapping him hard on the back before he turned to envelop Tobias in a similar embrace.

His hands shaking, Jasper held out the last set of house keys he'd kept, offering them to Darius. It was the final exchange that would make this permanent.

"No." Darius stepped back, holding his hands up and shaking his head. "Keep them. You never know if you might need them again. You're always welcome back, you know. Both of you."

"All of you," Carla added, glancing at Aaron and Samantha sitting patiently in the vehicle. "Don't forget that."

"I won't." Jasper managed a small smile before pulling Darius and Carla in for one last hug and climbing into the car. The slamming of his door felt awfully permanent, but he didn't let himself look back and instead focused on the road ahead. *Where to?*

North, Tobias said. *As soon as you find a road that takes us that way.*

There was one not far out of town and when Jasper pulled out on the road, he headed straight toward it. He looked back once, glancing in the rearview mirror to see Darius and Carla standing on the porch, their arms around each other's waists as they watched the SUV drive out of sight, and then looked ahead again to focus his eyes on the road.

Tobias reached across the center console and squeezed Jasper's hand. *You'll see them again.*

He had no more reason to think that than Jasper did, but somehow, when Tobias said it, it felt right, and Jasper knew that it was true. He would see his friends again, someday, and until then, he had everything he needed right here. *Thanks.*

Tobias smiled, his love and affection surging into Jasper, and as the house faded from sight and Brightam's Ford fell away into the distance, Jasper grinned, his heart feeling truly light.

He was going home.

NESSA L. WARIN lives in a fantasy world that's mostly inside her head, though her physical address is in southwestern Ohio. Her two cats kindly play along with her fantasies and graciously let her pay all the bills, but they do require her to provide pampering on a regular basis. Nessa enjoys exploring the wonders of this world through travel—something her cats strongly disapprove of as it cuts into their pampering time—and can find whimsy in the most mundane places. When the real world becomes too much, Nessa enjoys dressing in costume and going to Renaissance Festivals and fantasy conventions. A short trip to either does wonders for her state of mind, so she makes sure to attend at least one of each every year. These trips help Nessa add to her collection of faerie and dragon art, and she swears she will frame and hang all the prints she's collected sometime soon.

When she's not living in a fantasy world, Nessa enjoys tasting and learning about wine, particularly since it's one of the few things she and the rest of her family agree on. She's a regular at the wine tastings held by her local wine shop, and considers it a sin for her wine rack to have more empty spots than full ones. She'd prefer her wine rack to be filled with Pinot Noir, Malbec, and Syrah, but one of her favorite things about wine is the way it can always surprise her. More than once she's been taken aback by which wine she likes best at a tasting, and she loves the way her wine rack illustrates the joys of trying new things.

Follow Nessa on Twitter @nessalwarin and Facebook at NessaLWarin. She can also be reached at nessa.l.warin@gmail.com.

Also from NESSA L. WARIN

STAMP of FATE

NESSA L. WARIN

http://www.dreamspinnerpress.com

Also from NESSA L. WARIN

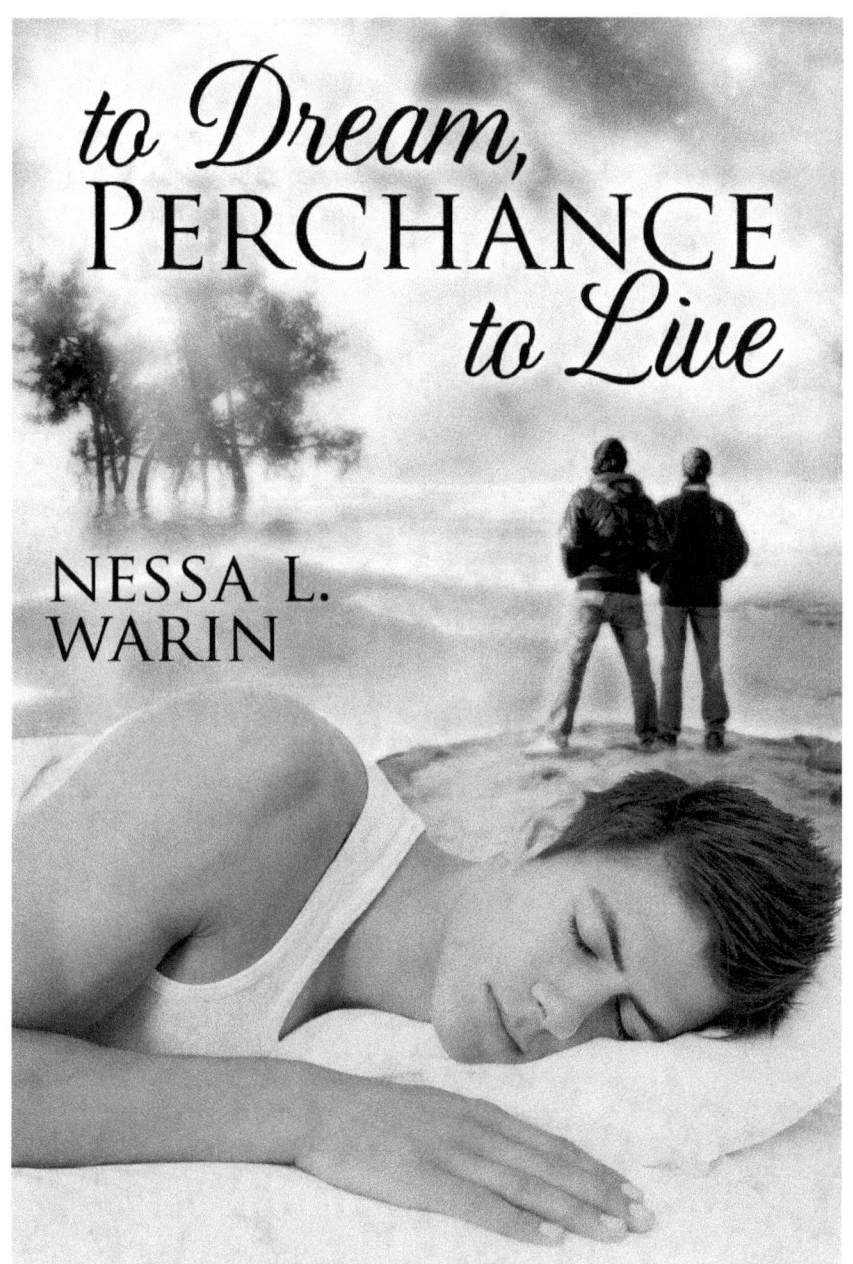

to Dream,
PERCHANCE
to Live

NESSA L.
WARIN

http://www.dreamspinnerpress.com

Also from NESSA L. WARIN

Sauntering
VAGUELY DOWNWARD

NESSA L. WARIN

http://www.dreamspinnerpress.com

Also from NESSA L. WARIN

the stars are brightly shining

nessa l. warin

http://www.dreamspinnerpress.com

Also from DREAMSPINNER PRESS

**desert
world**
A L E G I A N C E S

L Y N   G A L A

http://www.dreamspinnerpress.com

Also from DREAMSPINNER PRESS

AN ARGO
NOVEL

CATALYST

CLAIRE
RUSSETT

http://www.dreamspinnerpress.com

For more of the
best M/M romance,
visit

Dreamspinner Press

www.dreamspinnerpress.com

www.ingramcontent.com/pod-product-compliance
Lightning Source LLC
Chambersburg PA
CBHW051634260626
47170CB00004B/1174